PRAISE FOR THE NOVELS OF
#1 NEW YORK TIMES BESTSELLING AUTHOR
BARBARA FREETHY

"In the tradition of LaVyrle Spencer, gifted author Barbara Freethy creates an irresistible tale of family secrets, riveting adventure and heart- touching romance."
*-- NYT Bestselling Author **Susan Wiggs***
on Summer Secrets

"This book has it all: heart, community, and characters who will remain with you long after the book has ended. A wonderful story."
*-- NYT Bestselling Author **Debbie Macomber***
on Suddenly One Summer

"Freethy has a gift for creating complex characters."
*-- **Library Journal***

"Barbara Freethy is a master storyteller with a gift for spinning tales about ordinary people in extraordinary situations and drawing readers into their lives."
*-- **Romance Reviews Today***

"Freethy's skillful plotting and gift for creating sympathetic characters will ensure that few dry eyes will be left at the end of the story."
*-- **Publishers Weekly** on The Way Back Home*

"Freethy skillfully keeps the reader on the hook, and her tantalizing and believable tale has it all-- romance, adventure, and mystery."
*-- **Booklist** on Summer Secrets*

"Freethy's story-telling ability is top-notch."
*-- **Romantic Times** on Don't Say A Word*

Also By Barbara Freethy

CLOSER TO YOU

The Callaways #11

BARBARA FREETHY

HYDE
STREET
—PRESS—

HYDE STREET PRESS
Published by Hyde Street Press
1325 Howard Avenue, #321, Burlingame, California 94010

© Copyright 2016 by Hyde Street Press

Printed in the United States of America

Cover design by Damonza.com

ISBN: 978-1-944417-06-2

Prologue

Waterford Institute of Technology, Ireland

Seamus Donelan rubbed his tired eyes as he looked up from his computer. It was almost ten, well past time to call it a night and go home. The university's janitorial staff would be in to clean his office soon. He needed to leave and let them do their work, but returning to his empty apartment would only remind him of how alone he was and how long he'd been alone.

When he'd been younger, caught up in his ambitions, inventions, and patents, home had been the last place he'd wanted to be. To change the world, he had to live in that world—*all over that world*. He'd traveled for weeks, sometimes months, at a time. He'd told himself he'd had a higher purpose, one that would benefit millions of people. But his family hadn't seen it that way.

One day he'd come home and his wife and two daughters were gone. Tricia had taken his girls back to the States, to her parents' home in San Francisco, to the city she'd grown up in. Yes, they'd had a bitter fight the night before, but he'd never imagined she'd leave him in such an abrupt and brutal way. She hadn't even called him on the phone. Instead, she'd left him a letter reminding him of how many times she'd warned him and pleaded with him to put their family first; he didn't remember hearing one damn word.

The truth was that he hadn't been listening. He'd been caught up in his passions and his ego, his belief that he deserved everything that he desired. He'd been living in a cloud, confident that he could have it all, that he could walk above and over everyone else, and that no one would ever get hurt.

A lot of people had gotten hurt—especially his daughters—and that was a pain he would never be able to let go.

With a sigh, he got up from his chair and stretched his arms above his head. He felt more tired than he had in a long time. He'd thought teaching would rejuvenate him, but the young minds he saw every day in his classroom only reminded him that his youth had passed. He had done more than most men in science. His legacies would live beyond him—all but one of his inventions. That one had to be hidden away—forever.

He walked across the room. On the coffee table in front of the brown leather couch was a large box he'd started packing earlier in the day. Three months ago, he'd promised the young and brilliant scientist Ian Callaway that he'd send him his great-grandfather's earliest science journals, and tomorrow he would do that.

He hadn't meant to take so long, but things had come up, and he'd hesitated over asking Ian for a favor in return. Finally, he'd written Ian a long note. He hoped Ian would come through for him. But only time would tell.

A creaking door and a footfall down the hall suddenly got his heart pounding. His office door was locked, but he was very aware of how alone he was in the building.

It was probably just the cleaning service, he told himself, but he wasn't convinced. Too many odd things had happened lately. He thought he'd covered his tracks, but now he had the terrible feeling that his old life was catching up with his new one.

A shadow appeared outside the frosted glass of his office door. He could see nothing more than the silhouette of a man, a man working on the door lock. He didn't have much time.

He ran over to his desk and opened the locked drawer with shaky hands.

He grabbed what he needed and then moved back across the room. He placed the item carefully inside the box he was sending to Ian, hidden away under the journals, and the small package addressed to Grace. Then he closed the box, quickly wound the packing tape around it and dumped it through the postal service drop slot in the wall behind his couch. Hopefully, it would go out in the morning no matter what happened tonight.

The door burst open behind him. Before he could turn around, something hard came down on his head. An explosion of pain ran through him, as well as a feeling of terror.

He'd tried to stay away from evil, but sometimes science led to the dark as well as the light.

He fought to stay awake; he had a feeling if he didn't, he'd never see the light of day again...

One

San Francisco, California

"If you don't come to Thanksgiving, Ian, we're bringing Thanksgiving to you," Kate Callaway said, the fierce light in her blue eyes matched by the same gleam in her twin sister Mia's eyes.

Ian frowned as he ran a hand through his hair and stared at his younger sisters, who'd unexpectedly appeared at his apartment. He'd pulled an all-nighter at the lab and had gotten home and to bed a little before five a.m. "What time is it?"

"It's three o'clock in the afternoon," Kate replied, pushing her way past him. A confident, athletic, blue-eyed blonde, Kate never waited to be invited into a room. "You were supposed to be at Mom's an hour ago."

"You look exhausted," Mia commented, as she followed her twin sister inside.

Mia was also blonde with blue eyes, but she was softer than Kate, more artistic, more nurturing, and usually less of a pain in the ass. But the two of them together had always spelled trouble for him.

"What have you been doing?" Mia continued, giving him a thoughtful look.

"Or should we say *who* have you been doing?" Kate asked with a wicked sparkle in her eyes. "Is there someone here? Is that why you look like you just got out of bed?"

"No. I'm alone, and I've been working. I had to get a project done before the holiday weekend."

"Did you make it?" Mia asked.

"Barely. What are you two doing here?"

"Mom sent us to get you," Kate replied. "She wasn't sure you'd make it over there on your own."

"I'm coming, but I need to take a shower and change first."

"That does seem like a good idea," Kate said, wrinkling her nose at him.

"Then why don't you let me get to it?" He waved them back toward the door. "We'll catch up later."

"Promise you'll come, Ian," Mia said, worry in her eyes. "We hardly ever get to talk to you anymore now that I'm living in Angel's Bay and Kate is in DC. I barely heard anything about your trip to Ireland. I know you met with some famous scientist, but what else happened?"

"It was all good."

Mia sighed.

Kate rolled her eyes and said, "Surely you can do better than that."

"I'll fill you both in tonight," he promised. "Just give me a chance to pull myself together."

"We can wait for you and give you a ride to the house," Kate offered.

His gaze narrowed. "Hang on a second. Did you two come here to get me or to avoid having to help Mom make dinner for thirty-seven people?"

"It's forty-one this year, with all the new spouses and babies," Mia corrected.

"And Mom is acting like a drill sergeant," Kate put in. "I already set all the tables."

"And I made three pies," Mia put in.

"We needed a break," Kate added.

He smiled. "No wonder you volunteered to come and get me."

"We also wanted to make sure you were coming," Mia said. "That part was true."

"What about the men in your lives? Where are they?"

"Jeremy took Ashlyn and some of the other kids to the beach," Mia said, referring to her new husband and stepdaughter. "So they are safely out of Mom's crossfire."

"And Devin is visiting an old friend in the city," Kate said, mentioning her boyfriend. "He'll meet us at the house in a while."

"So you and Devin are still going strong?"

"We are," Kate said with a sparkling smile. "Devin moved his investigative services to DC so I could continue to work out of the FBI field office there. We're both busy doing our own thing, but when we come home, we're together. I wasn't sure I could have a career and love, but it turns out I can."

"Of course you can," Mia said. "You just had to find the right person to share your life, and you did. I can't wait to stand up for you at your wedding. Trust me, marriage is amazing."

"Did you set a date?" he asked Kate, running a hand through his hair. "Did I miss that?"

"No, right now we're happy to just be together. A wedding is down the road."

He was happy for both of his younger sisters but also reminded that he hadn't thought about love in a very long time. Work had quite simply taken over his life. He knew that had to change. His grandmother had sent him all the way to Ireland to talk to Seamus Donelan, a former scientist turned professor, who should have served as a cautionary tale, because the brilliant Seamus had lost his entire family after putting all of his focus on work.

He had thought about making some changes in his life after that trip, but then he had gotten unexpected funding for a research project he was involved in, which had led to a whirlwind three months of work. He couldn't believe it was already Thanksgiving, with Christmas not too far off. He would take the break he'd promised himself starting on Monday, but for now he needed to shower off his week-long work binge and get ready for a Callaway Thanksgiving.

"Look, as much as I'd like to be your escape hatch," he said dryly, "I'd prefer it if you two left now. If you're committed to staying out of the house, you could always go chase down Dylan or Hunter," he added, referring to his two brothers.

"They're already at the house. And Annie is on her way," Kate replied, referencing their other sister.

"We'll go," Mia said, dragging Kate toward the door. "But be there by four, Ian, or we'll send more Callaways to strong-arm you."

"Don't worry. I'll be there. I'm starving."

Kate laughed. "There will be four perfectly roasted turkeys, so you should be able to satisfy that appetite."

As he opened the door, he was surprised to see a delivery man walking down the hall with a large box in his hands. He hadn't rung anyone in, and he lived in a very secure building—at least most days.

"Ian Callaway?" the man said.

He nodded.

"Sign here."

He scrawled his name on the electronic device, then said, "I didn't know you delivered on the holidays."

"Every day this time of year."

"How did you get into the building?"

"One of your neighbors let me in. Have a good day."

"A delivery on Thanksgiving?" Kate queried, a thoughtful gleam in her eyes. "What is it?"

"No idea."

"Do you want us to wait while you open it? You seem a little bothered at the delivery man's presence," Kate noted.

"I don't need an FBI agent to help me open a box. I just don't appreciate it when my neighbors ring people in."

"What kind of work are you doing these days?" Kate asked.

He could see the beginning of a long line of questions in her gaze. "We'll catch up at dinner."

"You never want to talk about what you do."

"It's boring science stuff. At least, that's what the two of you used to say about my projects."

Mia laughed. "He's got us there, Kate."

"See you at the house."

After his sisters left, he locked the door and set the box down on his dining room table. When he saw the address from Ireland, his worry eased.

The package was from Seamus Donelan. Seamus had told him that he had journals from Ian's great-grandfather, who'd been Seamus's high school teacher and one of his first science mentors. He'd promised to send them along when they'd met in Ireland in the summer.

He ripped open the box. Sure enough, there were at least a dozen old leather journals, as well as a thick envelope labeled miscellaneous. There was also a sealed smaller box with the name Grace O'Malley scrawled across the brown packaging and an address. Lastly, he pulled out a folded piece of paper with his name on it.

Ian, I hope this note finds you healthy and happy and that you've taken some time to slow down. As we talked about during your visit, there is so much more to life than work. Don't make the same mistake I did. Don't lose everything in your quest for the biggest breakthrough the science world has yet to see. Many have come before you; many will come after you. Live your life, find love, be at peace.

I have sent you your great-grandfather's journals. I hope they inspire you as they did me. I also have a favor to ask you. I saw that you are attending the Science Summit in South Lake Tahoe next week. My youngest daughter Grace lives there. I have tried to send her things before, but she always returns them unopened. I think if you delivered the enclosed box to her personally, she might accept it.

I'm sure this is the last thing you want to do, but I hope you will consider granting me this wish. If not, I have put her address on the box. At the very least, perhaps you could drop it off at the mailbox. You'll note that Grace's last name is O'Malley. She took her mother's name after the divorce. It broke my heart, but what could I say? I'd made my choice, and she'd made hers.

Thank you so much for your consideration.

Seamus

Ian set the letter down with a frown. The last thing he wanted to do was track down Seamus's angry and estranged daughter in Tahoe, but he was going there on Monday, and Seamus had been nice enough to send the journals, so how could he say no? He didn't like to owe people. Someone did a favor for him; he returned it.

He'd do the drop-off in person, and if Grace didn't want whatever her father had sent her, she could ship it back to him.

In the meantime, he had Thanksgiving to get to.

———◆◆———

An hour later, Ian arrived at his mother's house in San Francisco. He'd grown up in the large two-story house that sat on a street parallel to the Great Highway, directly across from the beach, and visiting always brought back good memories. At thirty-two, he was the second oldest of six kids. His brother Dylan had beat him by a year. Then came Hunter, Annie, and the twins Kate and Mia.

His mom had taken time off from her nursing career when they were small, but even when she'd gone back to work, she'd always been there for whatever they needed. His dad was a retired firefighter, who now worked some construction jobs for his Uncle Kevin when his workload got busy. Both his brothers were firefighters, having followed in his father's footsteps. Firefighting was a Callaway tradition for generations, but he had never had any interest in pursuing that career. It had always been science for him.

His sisters had also chosen different career options. Annie was a graphic designer and artist, while Mia's penchant for art history had led her into running an art gallery in the small coastal town of Angel's Bay, where she'd found the love of her life and an adorable stepdaughter. Kate had become an FBI agent two years ago and loved being in the center of the action.

It had been awhile since he'd seen all of his family in one place. And, of course, it wouldn't be just his immediate family, but all the Callaway relatives who were in town. His Uncle Jack and Aunt Lynda and their tribe of eight would be there, all of whom were now married or involved with someone, many with kids or babies on the way. His Uncle Kevin and Aunt Monica would also be present with more of his cousins, and there might possibly be some relatives from his Aunt Elaine's family who were Coulters, not Callaways, but just as loved.

"Ian," Emma said, giving him a hug. A sparkling, attractive blonde fire investigator, Emma had recently become one of his favorite cousins after their trip to Ireland, where he'd gotten a chance to get to know her better.

"How are you?" he asked.

"I'm good. I'm so glad you came. I wanted to tell you something. It's about the little girl we met in Kenmare."

"Shannon?" he queried, remembering the freckle-faced, redhead with the toothy smile who'd taken an instant liking to Emma and Max.

"Yes," she said with a happy nod. "It's taken us three months, but Max and I finally located her biological father. It took some doing, because he went under a different last name than the one Maeve gave us. Anyway, he lives in a small town in Texas. He's married and has a couple of children. I've spoken to him on the phone, and he said he was stunned to hear that he even had a child. Apparently, Shannon's mother never told him about the child, who was a product of a one-night stand. Max and I are going to fly to Texas to see him tomorrow."

"Really?" he asked in surprise. "Why?"

"Because Shannon's great-grandmother's health is worsening by the minute, and Maeve is extremely worried about Shannon being put into foster care."

"Isn't there anyone closer who can help out?"

"There's really not. And our grandmother is worried about Maeve and Shannon, and you know I can't say no to helping Grandma."

He had to admit he had trouble with that himself. "I get it."

"It will be a quick trip. I'm hoping that Shannon's father will turn out to be a good guy who wants to raise her. Maeve hates the thought of Shannon going to strangers, and so do I."

"That's quite a hope." He wasn't at all convinced anyone was going to get the miracle they were looking for. "But can I just say there was probably a reason why Shannon's mother never told him she was pregnant?"

Emma's smile dimmed. "I've thought that as well, especially when there was a name change, but Max has run a preliminary check on him, and nothing came up. He's not a criminal but that doesn't necessarily make him a good guy."

"If he is her father, doesn't he have a legal obligation to take her? What if you find out he isn't a good guy, but he wants her? Does he get her?"

Emma sighed. "I don't know. I don't want to get into all the legal stuff yet. I just want her dad to be great and to want to raise her. Every child should feel that love from their parent. Anyway, I guess I'll find out this weekend, and we'll take it from there. How's your work going? Have you put your plan of slowing down your life into motion?"

"Not yet, but I'm about to. I'm heading up to the mountains on Monday."

"For skiing?"

"Yes, and also for a science and technology conference."

Emma gave him a frown. "Ian, that is not a vacation; that's work."

"It's a little of both."

"I hope so. You know what that Irish professor told you about letting ambition overwhelm your personal life."

"I do, and I agree in principle. I actually just got the journals Professor Donelan had promised to send me when we spoke this summer. I'm excited to see what kind of science our great-grandfather was interested in when he was alive."

"Grandma will be happy about that. You should tell her."

"I will. Is she here?"

"In the den. She's having an okay day; she's a little tired. To be honest, I think she's depressed about Maeve's condition. They grew up like sisters and being back in Ireland with her a few months ago made her feel closer to her again. Now, she's feeling the sadness and pain of Maeve's illness."

"I'll go say hello."

"I'll catch up with you later."

As Emma disappeared into the other room, his older brother Dylan approached and gave him a slap on the back. Like most of the Callaway men, Dylan had dark hair and blue eyes, same as Ian. Dylan was stockier in build, however, and while Ian prided himself on being fit, Dylan probably had a few notches on him in that department, too. But then Dylan spent his days as an active firefighter, while he had to get to a gym and an elliptical to get his heart rate up.

"Glad you made it," Dylan said. "It's been awhile."

He nodded, noting the weariness in his brother's eyes. "You look tired."

"Just got off a shift," Dylan replied, running a hand through his hair.

"Busy night?"

"Extremely. I'll catch up on my sleep during my upcoming turkey coma," he joked. "And don't give me some scientific reason why turkey doesn't cause sleepiness. I don't want to hear it. You already ruined Santa Claus and the Easter Bunny for me."

He was very aware that he'd ruined a lot of his siblings' beliefs with unwanted scientific evidence. It had taken him a long time to learn how to shut up and let them believe what they wanted to. "You were at least seven before I told you the truth about Santa," he said. "Well past the age where you needed to believe in an old man with a belly full of jelly and a sack full of presents."

Dylan grinned. "So are you killing any woman's dreams these days?"

"Not in some time," he said dryly. "Too busy to date."

"Too busy for sex? Seriously?"

"I didn't say sex; I said dating."

"If those two aren't the same, you're doing it wrong. By the way, I'm heading down to Newport Beach on Saturday. I'm meeting up with Jeff. Any chance you want to come along?"

Jeff had been Dylan's best friend growing up and had spent a lot of time at their house. "That sounds fun, but I'm going to Tahoe on Monday for a conference."

"Now, that doesn't sound fun," Dylan teased. "Don't you ever relax, Ian?"

The question was becoming a popular refrain among his family members. "I'm going to hit the slopes while I'm there."

"I would hope so. You know what you should do?"

"What?" he asked warily.

"You should take the Mustang up to Tahoe."

"The car you've spent the past year restoring? You're volunteering to lend it to me?"

"When is the last time you drove something other than a slow sedan? Take it up to the mountains, have some fun."

"There's snow in the forecast."

"She can handle the snow. There's nothing better for relaxing than a long drive in a fast car."

He wasn't surprised that was Dylan's viewpoint. His brother had been obsessed with cars since he was five.

"Seriously," Dylan added. "I won't take no for an answer. Come by tomorrow and get the keys."

"All right," he said with a shrug. He actually wouldn't mind leaving his car behind. It was due for some maintenance, and he hadn't had time to get it done. He could drop it off at the shop before he headed to Tahoe.

"Good. Finally, you're willing to take my advice."

He laughed as his younger brother Hunter came up to join them. Hunter's hair was a lighter shade of brown, and his eyes a lighter blue. As usual, he hadn't considered Thanksgiving an opportunity to wear anything other than faded jeans and a T-shirt.

"What advice are we talking about?" Hunter asked. "Women? Did Dylan tell you about the groupie who's stalking him?"

"No," he said, now wondering if there was more behind the shadows in his brother's eyes than work weariness.

"She's not stalking me," Dylan said with annoyance. "She just brought me cookies as a thank-you for saving her life."

"And she gave you her phone number." Hunter turned to Ian. "And she's totally hot. Blonde hair, nice rack, legs for days—"

"Okay, that's enough," Dylan said, giving Hunter a sharp look. "She was the victim of a fire. I don't take advantage of vulnerable women."

"I was joking. Why are you so touchy?" Hunter asked, giving Dylan a speculative look. "Wait a second, you don't *like* her, do you?"

"I'm not touchy; I'm tired. I'm going to get a drink."

"What's wrong with him?" Ian asked as Dylan took off down the hall.

"Don't know," Hunter said with a shrug. "But he's been off his game a week now. What's new with you? Did you win a Nobel Prize yet?"

"Not yet. You break any bones lately?" Hunter currently held the record in the family, having broken his left arm twice, his right leg, a wrist, some bones in his foot, and a couple of fingers. While one of those injuries had come on the job as a firefighter, the rest had come from his physically adventurous off-duty activities like helicopter skiing and rock climbing.

"Not one. I'm in a dry spell," Hunter joked. "Too much work, not enough play."

"Ian," his mother Sharon said, interrupting them with a happy smile. A short redhead with a warm and sparkling smile, his mom had always lit up a room. She gave him a hug and a kiss on the cheek. "Now I'm happy. All my kids are home."

"I haven't seen Annie yet," he said.

"She just got here. She's outside, I think. I want to talk to you, Ian. It's been some time since we've had a one-on-one chat."

By the determined gleam in her eye, he had a feeling that chat was going to include some strong words about taking a day off and calling home more often.

"I think you're in trouble," Hunter joked. "She's looking at you like she did when you used her crystal wine glasses to run a science experiment."

"He's not in trouble," Sharon said, her gaze narrowing on his face. "At least I hope not, but we do need to catch up."

"I'd love to do that."

"Good. But it will have to wait," his mother continued. "It's time for dinner. The dining room is for the older generation. You can both grab seats at the tables in the den or on the back patio."

"We're still at the kids' table?" Hunter complained. "It's not so bad for me, Mom, but Ian is an old man."

"I'm one year older than you."

"Feels like a lot more." Hunter grinned back at him. "Let's go find seats closest to the buffet table."

"You got it."

As they entered the den, he saw his cousins picking seats at various tables. There were a lot of couples now and kids, too. It felt strange to still be very single even though he had Dylan and Hunter to hang with, and Annie, too. But seeing the former rebel of the family, Aiden, with a wife and two kids made him realize how quickly time was passing. He'd put his work before everything else and it was going well, but one of these days he might want to have a personal life. He might not want to end up like Seamus Donelan who'd lost his wife and two daughters to ambition. It was just hard to stop doing what he knew how to do to explore a personal relationship. He'd always been better with facts than feelings. But his IQ was off the charts. He could figure out how to do both, couldn't he?

Two

⟶⟩✠⟨⟵

The kids were tired and cranky. As Grace O'Malley surveyed her second grade class a little before three on Monday afternoon, she was thrilled to see the minutes ticking away toward the three o'clock bell. While theoretically the children should have been recharged after the Thanksgiving holiday, most of them had eaten too much sugar and not gotten enough sleep, thereby making for a rough Monday. The fact that the weather outside was also dark and gloomy with a big snowstorm in the forecast didn't help.

"So, tomorrow," she said, holding up a kid's book in her hand, "we're going to be reading *Madeline's Christmas Miracle* together and talking about our holiday plans. I also want you to come in with a couple of ideas for projects you might like to do for the school-wide science fair next week. It's going to be a lot of fun." She gave them all a smile. "Everyone get some good sleep tonight and come back tomorrow rested and ready to work. Okay?"

Some of the kids nodded; a few yawned. She took that as a win.

The bell rang, and with a sudden burst of renewed energy, the children jumped up and bolted from the room. Only one lingered behind, seven-year-old Tyler Stark. Tyler's mother, Carrie, was a fifth-grade teacher at the school and one of Grace's best friends. Tyler often stayed after school to help her straighten up the classroom until his mom was ready to go home, which was usually closer to half-past three.

Grace liked Tyler a lot. He was an eager, intelligent, curious child with blond hair and hazel eyes. He loved to read and often begged her for one of the books from the classroom to take home with him.

"Can I read *Madeline's Christmas Miracle* tonight and bring it in tomorrow?" he asked eagerly. "I promise I won't forget. I really want to read it."

"We'll all read it together tomorrow."

"But it's good practice," he reminded her.

"You can take one of the other books home if you want."

"I want that one," he said, a stubborn glint in his eyes. "I *need* to read *that* one."

She was a little surprised by his vehemence. He was such a good-natured kid; she didn't understand his unexpected tone of desperation. "Is something wrong?"

He stared back at her, then slowly shook his head, which wasn't at all convincing.

"Tyler?" she prodded.

Before he could answer, the door opened and Tyler's mom Carrie walked in. A tall, willowy blonde, Carrie looked unusually pale and stressed. Now, she was worried about Carrie, too.

"Everything okay?" she asked quietly.

"Sure," Carrie said, a stressed note in her voice. "Tyler, honey, I need to talk to Grace alone for a minute. We'll be right outside, okay?"

"Okay," Tyler said.

Grace followed Carrie into the hall, feeling very uneasy. "What's going on?"

Carrie drew in a breath. "I just got a call from Kevin's commanding officer. His unit was ambushed."

"Oh, no," she said, horrified at the news. Carrie's husband Kevin was in the Army.

"Kevin was injured. He's alive, but his condition is serious. He's being flown to the base in Germany. I don't know any more details than that. I have to get to him as soon as I can."

"Of course you do."

"I checked on flights. I can get on a plane leaving from Reno at seven tonight. I should be able to beat the storm. But I can't take Tyler with me, and my parents are in Florida until Christmas. I don't have anyone to watch Tyler."

"I'll watch him," she said immediately.

"Are you sure? I don't know how long I'll be gone."

"It doesn't matter. I'm happy to do it. You need to be with your husband."

Relief flooded her eyes. "Thank you. I have to tell Tyler I'm leaving, but I don't know what to say. He's been worrying all weekend about whether his dad will make it home for Christmas. It's been a long year, Grace. Now this..." She battled against tears. "I have to hold it together."

"You will." She gave Carrie a hug. "And don't worry about Tyler. We are best buds. We'll be fine."

"He does love you a lot."

"I'm crazy about him, too." She opened the classroom door, and they walked back inside.

"I have to go away for a few days," Carrie told her son, putting on a happy face for him.

"Can I come?" Tyler asked quickly.

Carrie shook her head. "No, I'm sorry, honey, not on this trip."

"Why do you have to leave?" Tyler whined. "Are you going to be gone as long as Daddy?"

"No, just a few days, and then I'll be back. While I'm away, you're going to stay with Grace, okay?"

"Okay. But will you and Daddy be back before Christmas?"

Grace's heart broke at the plea in his voice. She could see Carrie trying hard not to cry.

"I will definitely be here for Christmas," Carrie said,

giving him a hug.

"What about Daddy?"

"We'll have to see. I know he wants to be," Carrie said, avoiding a promise she might not be able to keep. "You'll be good for Grace, won't you?"

Tyler nodded, but there was more worry in his eyes now.

"Good." Carrie looked at Grace. "I'll take him home, pack a bag and then drop him off at your house. It will be easier for you to be in your own place."

"I could come over to your house," she offered.

"No, it's fine. I'll bring him by in about an hour, okay?"

"That's perfect. I'll make dinner for us." She looked at Tyler's unhappy face and could see the storm clouds gathering in his eyes. "So, Ty, maybe you and I can read *Madeline's Christmas Miracle* tonight."

He perked up at her words. "We don't have to wait until tomorrow?"

"Don't tell anyone, but we'll get a head start."

His smile made her feel better. She didn't know how long she could keep a smile on his face, but she would try as hard as she could to make it last as long as possible.

After Carrie and Tyler left, she quickly straightened her classroom and then headed into the parking lot.

Whitmore Elementary School was located in South Lake Tahoe on the California side of the lake. Surrounded by tall, towering ponderosa pines, with the magnificent Sierra Nevada Mountains behind the building and a view of the lake from the front, the school was one of the prettiest she'd taught at. She'd been there for three years, having moved to the mountains from San Francisco. She'd never been a city girl, and Tahoe suited her far better than the busy streets of San Francisco.

On her way to the small one-story house on a hill she rented off Pioneer Trail, she stopped at the supermarket and picked up extra food and snacks for her and Tyler. She'd just set her grocery bags on the kitchen counter when the doorbell rang.

She opened the door, expecting to see Carrie and Tyler on her doorstep, but it was a man, a very attractive man with dark-brown hair and striking blue eyes. He wore black jeans that hugged his lean legs and a black wool coat over a dark-blue sweater. There was a package in his hands and a question in his eyes.

"Are you Grace O'Malley?" he asked in a husky male voice that for some reason sent a shiver down her spine.

She didn't know why she was tempted to say no, but some instinct of self-preservation told her the question was more important than she knew. Still, she found it difficult to lie. "I am. Who are you?"

"Ian Callaway. I have something for you from your father."

Now she knew why she'd suddenly felt uneasy. Even from here, she could see the return address for Waterford, Ireland. She hadn't been back to Ireland in over a decade, and she hadn't seen or talked to her father since then.

"I don't want anything from my dad," she said firmly.

"He thought you might say that. That's why he sent me. He wanted me to deliver a more personal message. Would it be possible for me to come inside? It's starting to snow."

She'd been so caught up in the package in his hands that she hadn't realized how quickly the weather had worsened. But was she really going to invite this stranger into her home?

"I promise you I'm not dangerous," Ian said, as if sensing her reservations. "I'm a scientist. Your father and I are— friends."

Her gaze narrowed. "That hesitation doesn't sound like you are *good* friends."

"More like recent friends. I met him this summer when I visited my family's home in Ireland. My great-grandfather, Donald Rafferty, was one of your father's early teachers."

She remembered her father talking about his mentor Donald Rafferty, which made her feel marginally better about the stranger on her porch.

A gust of wind blew snow into her face, and she waved

him inside. "You've got three minutes."

"Then I better talk fast," he said, as he stepped into her house.

She closed the door behind him to keep the freezing air out of her living room, but she had to admit to feeling a bit more shivery and tingly with Ian inside her house. He didn't look threatening; he was too handsome for that. He had an air of intelligence that backed up his claim to be a scientist, but she still sensed that the reason he was here was going to turn her life upside down.

He walked into the living room, where he set the box down on a table next to her couch.

"When is the last time you spoke to your father?" he asked.

"Ten years ago. What did he want you to tell me?" She crossed her arms in front of her chest.

"That he was sorry he'd been a lousy father."

"Well, that's great. Being sorry doesn't make everything all right."

"I'm sure it doesn't. Can I sit down?"

"You're not going to be here that long."

"Got it. Look, I don't know what went down between you and your father, but Seamus expressed tremendous regret about losing you, your sister, and your mother. When I visited him at his office in Ireland, he told me that he'd put his professional life ahead of his family for years, that he had chosen ambition over love, and if he could do anything over, he would change that."

"Unfortunately, you don't get do-overs in life," she said harshly, trying not to be moved in any way by his words.

"Sometimes you do," he countered.

"You think I should forgive him?"

He gave her a long look and then shrugged. "Honestly? I don't know. I know more about your father's work than I do about the man who raised you."

"He didn't raise me; my mother did. So, how you think you can come into my house and tell me to forgive my father—"

"Hold on," he interrupted, putting up a hand. "You're right. I have no business telling you anything."

"I'm glad we got that straight."

"To be frank, I didn't even want to deliver the package, but he sent it to me along with my great-grandfather's journals, and he asked me to do him a favor. He knew I was going to be attending a science conference here in Tahoe, so dropping this off would be on my way. He suggested that a personal plea to you might make you open the package. Apparently, you've sent several back unopened."

"Apparently, my father doesn't take a hint."

"You hate him so much you don't want to know what he sent you?"

"It's none of your business."

"I'm just surprised you're not curious."

His words rang an old bell in her head. Her father had always told her that curiosity was what had driven him to his greatest successes. "Intellectual curiosity was my father's most notable trait, but it's not mine, especially not when it comes to him. I learned the hard way that what I don't know about him hurts less than what I do know."

Ian Callaway stared back at her, his gaze sharpening at her words. "It sounds like he hurt you deeply, Grace."

"He hurt all of us, my mother most of all. He might be a hero to the scientific world, but he's not to me."

"He said that he regretted his failure as a family man."

"That's what he told you? That he had regrets? That he failed at being a husband?" Anger ran through her. "Did he also tell you that he had a long-term affair? Did he mention that he had another child, a son, who is only ten years younger than me?" She blew out a breath at the stabbing pain that ran through her.

Surprise ran through Ian's eyes. "No, he didn't tell me any of that. I'm sorry."

"You're not the one who needs to apologize."

"True. I know better than to get in the middle of

someone's family problems, so I should have followed my first instinct and dropped the package in the mail and let you send it back."

She was somewhat mollified by the compassion in his eyes. "That probably would have been best. You can leave the package here. I can take it to the post office tomorrow."

"All right."

"So you're here for the science summit?"

"I am, yes."

"I've heard it's going to bring in a lot of cash for local businesses in the quiet time before Christmas, so I guess that's a good thing. But, as you might imagine, I'm not a big fan of scientists."

He gave her a small smile. "We're not all the same."

He certainly didn't look anything like her father, but that didn't mean he didn't suffer from the same traits. She'd seen firsthand that with great intellect sometimes came a great ego. "What kind of science do you do?"

Before he could answer, the doorbell rang. "Excuse me." She walked back to the door and opened it. Tyler was on the steps.

"Mom says it's snowing so hard she wants to get on the road," Tyler told her.

She nodded and waved at Carrie, who quickly drove down the snowy street. She hoped Carrie would be able to make it to Reno before the storm got worse; it was pretty bad already. She took the booster car seat out of Tyler's arms and motioned him inside.

"Hi," Tyler said to Ian, as he dropped his backpack on the ground. "I'm Tyler."

"I'm Ian."

"Are you Grace's boyfriend?" Tyler asked.

"No, he's not," Grace said quickly. Tyler had been in such a bummed-out mood all day, she'd almost forgotten how curious and welcoming he normally was.

"That's too bad. My mom says you should get a boyfriend," Tyler told her. "She said you're too pretty not to have one."

"Thanks," she said, brushing some snow out of his hair. "Why don't you take your bag into the guest room? You know where it is."

"Can I watch TV?"

"Sure. I'll start dinner in a few minutes."

"We're going to read the book later, right?" he asked worriedly.

"We are," she promised. "I brought it home with me."

"And we have to pick out my science project, too," he told her. "Mom was going to help me, but now she's gone. She doesn't know when she's coming back."

"I can help you. It's all going to be good, Tyler. I promise."

"Okay," he said with relief.

He picked up his bag and went down the hall.

"Cute kid," Ian said. "I take it you're babysitting."

"I am, and he is cute. I just hope he can stay as happy and innocent as he is right now," she murmured, thinking about the long trip Carrie had in front of her and all the things that could go wrong.

"What does that mean?"

"I'm watching him while his mother flies to Germany. His dad is in the Army, and he was injured today. He's being flown to the hospital there, and my friend Carrie is on her way to see him. She didn't tell Tyler where she was going. She didn't want him to worry. She doesn't know what kind of condition her husband is in or whether..." She didn't even want to finish the horrifying thought.

"That's rough. I hope he'll be all right."

"Me, too. He's been deployed for over a year. He was supposed to be home for Christmas. Now this..." She paused, realizing the depth of conversation she was having with a total stranger. "So that was definitely more than three minutes."

"Yes, it was," he said with a small smile. "Did you know that your father still has your picture on his desk at the university—you, your mom and sister? You were about seventeen, I think. He showed it to me when I was there."

Her gut tightened at his words. "I don't care."

"He said you changed your last name after you left."

"To my mom's maiden name, yes."

"That seems like a big decision."

"It was something my mother wanted." She didn't add that she'd been a little conflicted, but she'd been so hurt by her dad's betrayal and her mother's pain that she'd gone along with it. "Anyway, you should go. I'm sure you have things to do. Where are you staying?"

"The Silverstone Hotel and Casino. I haven't checked in yet. I decided to stop here first."

"Silverstone's is beautiful. It was just finished six months ago. It's very modern and luxurious."

"That's good to hear."

She moved across the entry and opened the front door again. She was shocked by the blizzard of snow that flew into the room. It had only been ten minutes or so since Tyler had arrived, but now the wind was blowing hard, the snow coming down so thick she could no longer see the front lawn or the road. She really hoped Carrie would make it over the mountains to Reno. The storm was coming in from the west, and she was headed east, so hopefully she was in front of it.

"Whoa, it's gotten bad," Ian said, looking over her shoulder.

Too bad for him to leave, she realized. Not only were there near white-out conditions, her partially-paved, steep driveway turned into a slippery slide on days like this, and he was parked in front of her garage, at the top of the hill.

"Dammit," she muttered, as she closed the door. "You better stay here until it lets up."

"Are you sure? The hotel is only a few miles away. I can probably make it."

Sure that she wanted to let this far-too-attractive man with the most compelling pair of blue eyes that she'd ever seen stay in her house for the next few hours? Not for one second. But she didn't appear to have another choice. "You'll never get down my driveway in this. The last time I tried, I ended up in the ditch by the side of the road. My landlord has been promising to redo the pavers with a heat sensor, but that hasn't happened yet."

He didn't look too happy at the sudden turn of events, which made two of them.

"All right, if you're okay with it."

"It's fine. I was going to make dinner for Tyler and myself. You might as well join us. Hopefully, the storm will pass quickly." She couldn't believe she'd just invited him to dinner.

Damn her father for sending one more problem into her life...

—➤➤◀◀—

"I can cook," Ian told her, as she led the way into her small kitchen.

"Well?" she questioned, a little surprised at the offer.

"I don't have any Michelin stars," he said dryly. "But no one has complained. Why don't you let me make dinner? As a thank-you for saving me from crashing my way down your driveway."

"I can't ask you to do that, Mr. Callaway."

"You're not asking; I'm offering. And I think you can call me Ian."

"All right. Then you better call me Grace." She paused, as he peeked into the grocery bags she had yet to unload. "I was just going to make spaghetti, salad, and garlic bread. It's Tyler's favorite meal, so you really don't need to help."

He pulled out the pasta and the ground meat. "Do you have fresh tomatoes?"

"I got some for the salad."

"Looks like you have plenty. We can put a few in the sauce. And you got fresh garlic—good. Why don't you go relax or spend some time with Tyler? I've got this."

She frowned. "It seems a little weird that you came to deliver a package and now you're cooking me dinner."

"I completely agree. It is weird, but here we are," he said with a shrug. "To be honest, I feel a little guilty for bringing you the package and asking you to open it. I didn't know the circumstances of your relationship with your father. I knew you were estranged but not some of the reasons why. When he asked me for a favor, I didn't feel I could say no. Your dad had gone to some trouble to send my great-grandfather's journals. I owed him. I don't like to be in anyone's debt."

Despite his suggestion that she check on Tyler, at the moment she was far more interested in him. Ian had shed his heavy coat and pushed up the sleeves on his sweater as he got the meat into the pan and filled a pot with water for cooking the pasta.

He was really an attractive man, she thought, her senses stirring with emotions that went far beyond irritation and annoyance now. She'd met a few scientists over the years, and Ian looked nothing like any of those men. He was tall and fit, and moved with athletic grace. He had a face that could be on a magazine cover and penetrating blue eyes that told her he had the determination and the intellect to get to the heart of anything. She'd already told him far more about her relationship with her father than she'd told anyone else in her life, and she had no idea why.

"Cutting board?" Ian asked.

She started, realizing she was staring at him, then said, "Corner cabinet."

He pulled out the board and started dicing tomatoes as skillfully as any TV chef she'd ever watched, which was pretty much her experience with cooking in the past decade. Her mom had not liked to spend time in the kitchen, and neither she nor her sister Jillian had ever mastered anything but the basics.

Watching Ian cook reminded her of her early childhood when her grandmother had lived with them for a few years and had cooked a hearty meal every evening. But she really couldn't compare Ian to her short, plump grandmother.

She smiled to herself. Ian caught that smile, giving her an inquiring look. "Something funny?"

"Not funny, just surreal. You're a scientist, yet you also like to cook. The two don't seem to go together. My father never set foot in the kitchen."

"At its core, cooking is science, so to me it's natural."

"I suppose you could make that claim. I asked you before, but you didn't answer. What kind of science do you do?"

"I started with a PhD in physics."

"Like my father," she said with a bit of a sigh.

He shot her a look. "And hundreds of thousands of other people."

"Wait. You said you started with that degree?"

"Yes. Three years ago, I became very interested in hydrology, so I got a master's degree in that."

"What is hydrology?"

"Simply put, it's the study of water, which is one of our most important natural resources. Without it, there is no life on earth. But the quality and supply of water has become a complex and difficult problem, especially in other poorer parts of the world. Clean water is becoming one of the biggest challenges of this century."

"So you're solving that problem, taking on that challenge?"

"Trying," he said, giving her a smile. "I started a company called Access Water last year. My very small team has been focused on building a mobile water filtration system that will allow ordinary people in third world countries to filter and clean their own water with something that looks like a very big straw. It's transportable and easy to use. It could be a game changer."

She was struck by the passion in his voice when he spoke. He wasn't talking about something in terms of it making him money but in terms of it changing the world. She was impressed. She was also once again reminded of her father: his extensive education, his big, ambitious dreams.

"Sorry, that was probably more than you wanted to know," Ian said. "My brothers and sisters usually tell me to shut up after a few sentences when I start talking about science."

"What you're doing sounds amazing."

"It will be if we can get the device to the people who need it the most." He took a moment to stir the meat and add garlic to it, then continued. "Unfortunately, global politics keeps getting in the way of science. I'm hopeful that the summit this week will be a step forward. We need our government representatives to stop thinking of science in partisan terms. We all live on the same planet."

"I didn't realize the summit was about clean water."

"It's not limited to that. The conference will be bringing together many different disciplines, everything from bioengineering to environmental science, global health and stealth technology."

"You mean, like drones?"

"And things you couldn't even imagine. Technology is driving innovation in ways we haven't seen in decades. It's an exciting time." He paused. "If you like science."

She had the strangest feeling that he could make her like science, and that seemed crazy. She'd hated the world that had taken her father away. She'd known Ian for under an hour. Despite his beautiful blue eyes and sexy smile, this man was not going to change her life. He was only here until the snow stopped. Then she'd never see him again.

Three

⟶➤⟿⟫⟪⟸⟵

Grace did not like scientists; that was clear. As soon as he'd told her about his job, she'd taken off to check on Tyler. Obviously, he reminded her of her father.

From any other person in the world, that comparison would have been a compliment, because while Seamus Donelan might have been a horrible husband and father, he was a brilliant scientist and inventor. He held a dozen patents. He'd created numerous devices that had quite literally changed the lives of millions of people. It was a shame that Grace couldn't see or couldn't acknowledge that side of her father.

It wasn't his business, though. He didn't need to get any more involved. He'd done what Seamus had asked him to do. He'd brought the package to Grace. What she did with it now was her choice. And he was fairly certain that choice would be to take it to the post office as soon as possible.

Grace was beautifully stubborn, with her snapping green eyes, gorgeous cloud of dark-red wavy hair that fell around her shoulders, her pale, creamy complexion with a few freckles to add interest, and then there was her tantalizing mouth…soft lips contrasted by a sharp edge to her voice. She was a mix of soft and hard. She was kind and generous when it came to Tyler, to helping out Tyler's mom, to letting him stay for dinner because of a snowstorm, but she was tough and unforgiving when it came to her father, to a backstory that still pained her.

Maybe she had every right to be unforgiving. He didn't know Seamus well enough to defend him. Certainly, what Grace had told him about an affair—another woman, another child—had not been part of his conversations with Seamus. He couldn't imagine how he would feel if his father had done that to his mother. Perhaps he would be just as unforgiving. *No perhaps about it, really.* He had a strong sense of what was right and what was wrong. He had much more trouble with grayed-out middle ground. He didn't like it when things didn't make sense, and to counter that, he usually tried to make them make sense. But this wasn't his problem to solve or figure out.

Grace Donelan O'Malley could make her own decision when it came to her father.

He just wished she didn't paint all scientists with the same brush.

Didn't matter, he reminded himself. He was here for the conference and for a few days of relaxation. As soon as the snow stopped, he'd go to the hotel and move on with his life. Hopefully, he'd finally be able to forget about Grace, because the real reason he'd brought her the package was because he hadn't been able to stop thinking about her since he'd seen her photo in Seamus's office several months ago. At the time, he'd had the sense that Grace was looking right at him, asking him for something. It had been the strangest sensation he'd ever felt.

Now that he'd met her in person, hopefully he could move past the ridiculous feeling that they were somehow connected, that they shared some destiny. He didn't even believe in fate. But the trip to Ireland, the time spent with his relatives there, and even the Irish lilt in Grace's voice had connected him to the Emerald Isle, to the feeling that impossible magic just might be possible.

He smiled to himself at that random thought. He didn't believe that at all. What he was feeling wasn't magic; it was just attraction, sexual chemistry, a biologic need. Everything could be explained with science if you looked hard enough for the answer.

He poured the spaghetti noodles through a strainer, then took them to the table along with the sauce, the salad, and the garlic bread.

Grace and Tyler appeared in the doorway just as he was about to call for them.

"We smelled food," she said with a sparkle in her eyes, looking more relaxed than she'd been earlier.

"Spaghetti is my favorite," Tyler said, sliding into a chair and grabbing a piece of garlic bread.

"Mine, too," he said, taking the seat across from Tyler.

As Grace joined them at the table, another odd feeling ran through him. Aside from Thanksgiving, he hadn't sat down for a dinner at a family table in a very long time, and it felt good. *Maybe too good.* This wasn't his life. He might be willing to slow down, but he wasn't going to stop doing what he did, which was trying to make the world a better place. And Seamus had already proven how difficult that was to do and keep a family happy, too.

But he didn't want Seamus's life; he wanted his own.

He filled his plate and decided to change the subject running around in his head. "I heard you two laughing," he said. "What were you doing?"

"Tyler was helping me make up tomorrow's lesson plan," Grace answered, as she scooped salad onto her plate.

"You're a teacher?"

"Yes, second grade. I'm Tyler's teacher, in fact. His mom, my friend Carrie, teaches fifth grade."

"I see. How is Grace as a teacher?" he asked Tyler.

"She's good," Tyler said, as he sucked in the spaghetti noodles dangling from his mouth.

"I should probably say something about that," Grace said to Ian with a helpless smile. "Shouldn't I?"

He grinned. "I don't know. My brother Hunter still eats spaghetti that way, and he's thirty-one."

"You have a brother?"

"I have two brothers and three sisters."

"That's a big family."

"And it's only the tip of the Callaway iceberg. My father is one of six, and most of his siblings have large families, so it's a big group when we all get together. Thanksgiving got up to forty-one people this year."

Her eyes widened. "Seriously? How many turkeys was that?"

"Four, plus a roast beef and a ham. My mom was the host, but everyone pitched in and somehow we managed to clear out the buffet table by the end of the day."

"That sounds crazy and chaotic."

"It always is, but also fun."

"I met some Callaways in Ireland; they were from Wexford. Two guys who would be in their early twenties now—they might be your cousins."

"No doubt. I haven't explored the Irish Callaway side of the family. When I was in Kenmare and Waterford, it was to get to know my grandmother's relatives, and she was a Rafferty."

"Well, you can always go back."

He gave her a thoughtful look. "I know you don't miss your father, but do you miss Ireland?"

"All the time," she said, her tone turning nostalgic. "I loved growing up there. It was so beautiful: the lush green hills, the turquoise blue of the water, the small towns, the music, the laughter, and the stories. Everyone in Ireland is a storyteller. I think I missed that the most." Wistfulness filled her eyes. "I hated leaving Ireland, but my mother was from San Francisco, and she wanted to come home."

"You still have a hint of Ireland in your voice, but you said you haven't been back in a long time."

"Not for over a decade."

"Is that because you don't want to run into your father?"

"It was in the beginning, but now it's because my life has moved on. I moved up here three years ago, and I really like Tahoe. It's not Ireland, but I love the mountains, the seasons, the small-town feeling. It's become home."

"It doesn't get boring?"

"Not at all. There is a lot to do here with boating and hiking in the summer and skiing in the winter. The winter holidays are beautiful. The trees are dusted with snow. Fires are burning in every fireplace, sparkly lights on all the trees. It's quite pretty—almost magical."

He found himself completely captivated by the picture she'd painted, the joy in her voice. It almost made him want to stay until Christmas just to see what she was talking about.

"Santa comes, too," Tyler popped in. "Do you think Mommy will be back in time to take me to see him?" he asked Grace, a worried look in his eyes.

"I'm sure she will be," Grace replied. "We have lots of time until then. Why don't you eat some of your salad?"

"I don't like tomatoes."

"Well, you can pick those out." Grace turned back to him with a smile. "So, tell me more about you, Ian. Where do you live?"

"San Francisco. I have an apartment near the Marina."

"That's a lovely area. My mom lives in Noe Valley, in a house not far from where she grew up."

"And your sister?"

"Jillian moved to Sonoma last year. She's the assistant manager of a boutique hotel in the wine country."

"Did your mother ever remarry?" he asked carefully, knowing he was probably treading back into painful territory.

"She did—three years ago. Jerry is a good man. He owns a construction business, although he's semi-retired now. He's home by five every night. They have dinner at six. They have couple friends and travel together at least three or four times a year."

Jerry definitely did not sound anything like Grace's father Seamus. "I'm happy for her."

"So am I. It took awhile, but she finally got over my dad's betrayal. Or at least, she moved on. I don't think she'll ever forget the pain she went through. She really loved my father, but he obviously didn't love her."

"Maybe it wasn't that simple."

She raised an eyebrow. "What does that mean?"

At her challenging tone, he realized he should have kept his mouth shut.

"You really want to defend him, don't you?" she continued.

"Not at all. I just don't think that relationships are ever simple. Only the two people involved really know what's going on, what's at stake, who's at fault."

"My dad cheated on my mom. He's at fault."

"That is inexcusable."

"Do you believe that, or are you just saying that because you've suddenly found yourself in quicksand?"

He smiled at her sharp question. She might hate her father and everything he stood for, but Grace had inherited Seamus's intelligence. However, he was smart enough not to point that out. "I am quickly realizing that everything involving your father is quicksand," he said. "But to your question, I do believe cheating is inexcusable. If someone wants out of a relationship, they should just get out."

"Exactly. Have some guts. Cheating is spineless and cowardly."

"Is there dessert?" Tyler asked, interrupting what had become a rather tense conversation.

Grace's attitude immediately changed as she realized she'd been neglecting Tyler. "There's ice cream, but you should do your homework first. Once that's done, we'll get dessert and read *Madeline's Christmas Miracle* together."

"We have to figure out what I'm going to make for the science fair, too," Tyler reminded her. "Mom was going to help me. We were going to make something really good to show Dad when he comes home for Christmas."

"We'll talk about that after you finish your homework,"

she said. "Why don't you take your plate to the counter and then get started?"

As Tyler left the room, Ian couldn't help saying, "You really hate science so much you don't want to help a second grader with his project?"

She shot him an irritated look. "I don't hate science, and, of course, I'll help Tyler."

"Good, because you're a teacher, and science should be one of your top priorities."

"Second grade is more about reading and math."

"But it should also be about science. In fact, every grade should be about science."

"Just because you love it—"

"No," he interrupted, feeling an intense desire to make her understand. "It's not because I love it; it's because science is how we improve the world. And we need scientists. Those are the people who are curing diseases, inventing technology that helps paralysis patients walk again, creating computer systems that enable people to do business over the world, developing software that makes all of our lives easier." He could hear the passion in his voice and knew he was overstating, but it bothered him that she would let her feelings about her father color her thinking about science, especially since she was a teacher.

"I told you; I'm not against science," she defended. "I understand the need to educate the next generation and to stimulate them enough to strive for new breakthroughs in every discipline."

"Well, I'm happy to hear that."

"I just don't care much for ambitious, self-absorbed scientists, Ian, and most of the ones I've met are exactly like that. I'm not just talking about my dad. His friend and partner, Harry Ferguson, was just as bad. The man's ego was enormous; I don't know how he got his head through the door. He talked to his wife and my mother like they were idiots."

"That's two men."

"Oh, it's not just men," she said hotly. "There was also

Paulette Ramone. She ran through four husbands before she was forty, and she treated my mom like she was the hired help when she came for dinner. She loved to be the center of attention at the table. She'd hold everyone captive with monologues on her latest chemical experiment. I grew up in a world of self-absorbed, brilliant people, Ian, and maybe what they did was awesome, but who they were and how they treated people—not so great."

He frowned, hating to agree with her, but he did know both Harry Ferguson and Paulette Ramone and they were not his favorite people. "There are still hundreds of thousands of other people working hard and quietly in labs around the world, Grace. I could counter those three people with three more who are dedicated, altruistic, determined to do good. Shall I go down the list?" He didn't normally need to defend his field, but he could, and he would.

She let out a sigh. "No. I'm sorry, Ian."

"Really?" He was surprised by her sudden cave-in. "You're changing your attitude just like that?"

"No. But I realize that I'm insulting you with my gross generalizations, and that's not right. You were nice enough to cook me dinner, and you don't deserve to be battered by my old resentments."

Now he liked her even more. Smart, honest, and self-aware.

"I think it's the package from my dad that rattled me," she continued. "Believe me, I don't spend every waking minute hating on him. He's in the past, and I've successfully left him there most of the time. But you showing up with that package sort of made that impossible, which is probably why he sent you. He wanted to give me a more forcible reminder, and it worked."

"Does that mean you're going to open the package?"

"No. I think it's better if I just send it back. I might share DNA with my dad, but that's it. I'm grown up. I'm twenty-seven years old. I don't need him in my life, and he certainly never needed me in his."

Ian wasn't so sure about that, but she'd already made one big concession; he wasn't going to push for more. "I understand."

"Do you? It sounds like you grew up in a happy family."

"That's true, but I know that not all families are like mine."

"What are your parents like? What do they do?"

"My mom Sharon is a nurse. My dad Tim is a retired firefighter. He followed in a long family tradition of firefighters. My grandfather always told us that the Callaways were born to serve and protect, and many of them became firefighters to do that."

"Were you tempted to be a firefighter?"

"Not even for one second," he said with a shake of his head. "I was always about school. I loved to learn. My brothers Dylan and Hunter, however, answered the call. They're both firefighters in San Francisco."

"And your sisters?"

"Annie is a graphic designer, Kate is an FBI agent in DC, and Mia runs a small art gallery in Angel's Bay."

"That's quite a group," she said, sipping her water.

He laughed at her description. "You don't know the half of it; lots of big personalities."

"Where do you fall? Are you the oldest?"

"No, that's Dylan. I'm second from the top, then comes Hunter, Annie, and the twins, Kate and Mia. We're all fairly close in age, which made for a lot of noise and chaos."

"You have an affectionate tone in your voice when you talk about your family," she observed.

"They're family. Are you and your sister close?"

"We talk quite often, but we don't see each other as much as we used to." She put her napkin on the table. "Thanks for dinner, Ian. It was very good."

"Hard to screw up spaghetti."

"I doubt you would screw up anything you set your mind to making—the scientist in you."

"I'm going to take that as a compliment," he said with a

smile.

"You should."

He picked up his plate and stood up. "I'll clean up."

"No, you will not do that," she said, also getting to her feet. "You cooked. I'll do the dishes." She glanced out the window where a gusty wind was splattering snow against the pane. "I don't think you'll be able to leave any time soon. So feel free to relax in the living room, watch television, or you can borrow my computer. It's on the desk if you want to go on the Internet."

"My computer is in the car."

"And that's probably where it's going to stay for a while," she told him. "Are you going to have withdrawal?"

She was joking, but there was some truth to her words.

"I can unplug—when I have to."

"That's good. A lot of people can't." As her gaze moved to the window again, her expression grew worried. "I hope Carrie made it to Reno. She's going to go nuts if she can't get on a plane tonight."

"You haven't heard from her, so that's a good sign."

"I hope it is."

As Grace cleared the table, he went into the living room. Tyler was kneeling on the floor in front of the coffee table, writing something on a piece of binder paper.

"I'm done," Tyler told him, holding up a page of ten words. "Can you check them to see if they're right?"

He looked through the spelling words as he sat down on the couch. "They look good to me."

"Where's Grace?"

"She's cleaning up. She'll be out in a minute."

"I have to think of a science project."

"What kind of a project?"

"I don't know. My mom said we could do something with the solar system. We could make planets and stuff."

"That's a cool idea."

"But Amy said she might do that, and I want to be different. What else could I do?"

"Lots of things."

"Like what?"

He considered the question. It had been a very long time since he'd thought about a science experiment appropriate for a child. He actually probably hadn't thought about it since he was a little kid. "Let's see. You could build a volcano and make it erupt."

"Really? How would I do that?" Tyler asked, wide-eyed.

"It's all about mixing the right substances together." He thought about what Grace might have in the house. "It's possible I could show you now. Let's go into the kitchen and see if we have the right ingredients."

"Okay." Tyler got up and ran into the kitchen ahead of him. "We're going to make a volcano for my science project," he told Grace as he barreled into the room.

"That sounds messy," she said, giving Ian a questioning look.

"It's not too bad," he replied. "It's an easy experiment. All we need is baking soda and vinegar. Do you have those two items?"

"I think so." She opened a nearby cabinet and pulled out the items he'd requested.

"And a glass," he added. He grabbed a dishtowel and spread it out on the counter. Then he picked Tyler up and sat him on the counter next to him. "Tell me what you know about volcanoes."

"They're big mountains and sometimes hot lava comes out of them," Tyler replied.

"Very good. The word volcano comes from the name of the Roman god of fire, Vulcan."

"I didn't know that," Tyler said, awe in his voice.

"Underneath the mountainous volcano is a pool of molten rock. When the pressure from the pool builds up, the volcano erupts. During the eruption, gases and rock shoot up through the opening and cause a flow of fiery lava." He paused. "Now, if you were doing this for the science fair, you would actually make a volcano. You could build it out of an egg carton or clay or anything else you wanted."

"Can we do that tonight?"

"No, that part takes much longer. What I'm going to show you now is how we can make an eruption."

"Okay," Tyler said, completely caught up in the experiment.

He picked up the box of baking soda and handed it to Tyler. "Pour that into the glass."

"How much?" Tyler asked.

"About this much," he said, holding his fingers an inch apart.

Tyler did as he was told. "Is that good?"

"Yes. Now the vinegar." He opened the bottle and handed it to Tyler. "Pour it in slowly."

As the vinegar hit the baking soda, the liquid started to pop and within a few seconds, a swirling volcano of liquid grew and rushed over the edges of the glass.

Ian watched Tyler's face with appreciation. He'd forgotten that feeling of amazement and wonder. It had happened so often when he was a kid. It still happened now occasionally, but not as frequently as he would like.

"That's so cool," Tyler said.

"And messy," Grace observed.

Despite her words, he saw the smile in her eyes. She might not like science, but she was a teacher, and she could clearly see that Tyler had learned something in a fun way.

"When can we make the volcano?" Tyler asked.

"I'm sure your mom will want to help you with that."

"What if she doesn't come back in time?"

"Let's talk about that tomorrow," Grace interjected. "Did you finish your math homework?"

"Almost," he answered.

"You do that while Ian cleans up his experiment," she said. "Then I will scoop up some ice cream and meet you in the living room. We can read the story before you go to bed."

Tyler jumped off the counter. "If my mom doesn't come back tomorrow, do you think you could help me build the volcano, Ian?"

"Uh...maybe," he said haltingly, seeing the plea in Tyler's eyes.

"Ian has to work," Grace said.

He saw the disappointment on Tyler's face, and he wanted to erase it. Tyler's dad had been gone a long time, and now his mom had mysteriously left. Tyler was probably smart enough to put those two facts together somewhere in his brain. "I can help you tomorrow if your mom isn't back," he said.

"Okay," Tyler said happily, then left the room.

"Breaking a promise is worse than making one you know you won't keep," Grace said with a frown.

"If I make a promise, I keep it."

"So you're going to blow off your conference to make a volcano with a second grader you met two hours ago?"

"The conference doesn't start until Wednesday. I have some time. Did you see the look on his face when the vinegar met the baking soda?"

"Yes, he was very impressed."

"Because science is impressive," he reminded her.

"You're not going to win me over, Ian."

"We'll see. I don't quit easily."

"I can see that."

Grace's phone began to ring. She pulled it out of her handbag and said, "Hello? Carrie? Did you make it to Reno?" She paused for a few moments and he could hear Carrie's agitated voice on the line. "That's a drag," Grace said finally. "But the storm should pass soon. Don't worry about anything here. I will take great care of Tyler. Have a safe trip and say hi to Kevin for me."

As she set her phone down, she said, "Carrie's flight is delayed until ten, but she's hoping to still get out tonight. She's going out of her mind not being able to get to Kevin and not having any real information about his condition. She spoke to the hospital and all they could tell her was that he was in surgery." She drew in a deep breath. "He just has to be all right."

"Keep the positive thoughts."

"I'm trying." She cocked her head to the right, giving him a thoughtful look. "I'm surprised you believe in positive thinking. That sounds a little too unscientific for you."

He smiled. "You can blame my mom for that. She's always been a big believer in positive thinking. Now, isn't it time for ice cream?"

"It's always time for ice cream. But nice dodge."

"You're not the first non-science lover I've met, Grace. I grew up with five of them. I know when it's time to quit while I'm ahead."

"I don't think you're ahead, Ian."

He grinned. "You haven't kicked me out into the blizzard yet, so I must be breaking even at least."

"I'm just a very kind person. To repay me, you can scoop," she said, handing him a gallon of ice cream and a scooper. "I have to warn you my freezer works a little too well. It might be rock solid."

"No problem. I worked at Hobey's Ice Cream in San Francisco when I was in high school."

"Seriously? You worked in an ice cream parlor? I would have thought you'd be tutoring in a science lab."

"I did that, too, but my brother Hunter talked me into taking his shift at Hobey's for him. It was supposed to be for a week but it ended up being a month. Then I figured out Hunter wasn't actually going to come back."

"It took you a month? I thought you were brilliant."

He laughed. "Not where my younger brother is concerned. He's very good at getting people to help him out."

"Well, it was nice of you to do that, and now I'm prepared to be impressed with your scooping skills."

"I'll see what I can do." As their gazes met, he realized how much he wanted to impress her with skills that had nothing to do with scooping ice cream.

Her green eyes flickered with gold, and he thought the same idea might be running through her brain, too. They'd met only hours ago, but he felt like he'd known her much longer, wanted her...forever...

He sucked in a breath at that disturbing thought and focused on the ice cream, doling out some extra big scoops for himself. It wasn't a cold shower, but it was the next best thing.

Four

G race practically ran out of the kitchen after Ian handed her two bowls of ice cream.

For a second there, Ian had looked at her like he wanted to kiss her. Heat had swept through her at that realization, along with the shocking thought that she wanted to kiss him, too. She was incredibly attracted to him and thoughts of his hands on her body and his lips on her mouth were suddenly running around in her head.

No! No! No! She could not fall for this guy.

She paused in the dining room and drew in a few deep breaths.

So what if Ian had the most incredible eyes of any man she'd ever met—a gaze that seemed to see into her soul, a smile that made her insides melt, a voice that made her palms sweat. He was wrong, all wrong, so wrong.

She wasn't going to make her mother's mistakes. She wasn't going to choose someone like Ian, someone who wanted to change the world the way her father had.

She wanted a man who would put her at the center of his world, who would always be there, someone she could count on, someone she could love with the fierceness of her heart and who would love her the same way.

She might have left Ireland behind, but she had never forgotten her heritage, her desire for a love that would sweep her away, the kind of love that poets wrote about. How many times had she listened to her Irish grandmother talk about her husband, about the love that had brought them together, the destiny of their souls?

Too many times to count.

Maybe it was romantic foolishness to believe that kind of love existed; she certainly hadn't seen much sign of it, not even with men who weren't scientists, but that didn't stop her from thinking it was still out there.

She didn't want to settle. She wanted all...or nothing.

"Grace?"

Tyler's voice brought her back to reality. She made her way into the living room. He was kneeling on the floor in front of the table, and she set his ice cream down in front of him. "Are you done with your math?"

"Yes. Do you want to check it?"

"I'll do that in a minute. Why don't you eat first?"

"Okay." He scooped up a big spoonful of ice cream and put it in his mouth, smearing his lips with chocolate. "It's good."

She laughed. "See if you can get more of that inside your mouth."

"Daddy and me like chocolate the best of all. Mommy likes vanilla. Daddy makes fun of her for that."

"There's nothing wrong with vanilla."

"When is my mom coming back?"

"I don't know, Ty, but we're having fun, right?"

He nodded. "I like Ian. He's cool."

"I like him, too."

"Maybe he should be your boyfriend."

"And maybe you should finish your ice cream," she said. "Then we can read together."

As she finished eating, she couldn't stop her gaze from darting toward the kitchen door. She wondered what was keeping Ian. Maybe he'd decided to put a little more space between them, too, because she knew the sparks between them had not been one-sided.

—➤◄—

Ian ate his ice cream standing at the kitchen counter. He needed a minute to get his head together. Since the storm showed no sign of abating, he was going to be at Grace's house for a while, and he really did not need to do anything stupid—like kiss her. That would be a mistake and he didn't like to make mistakes. He was too intelligent to ignore the warning signs, the predictable outcome. He was very good at anticipating cause and effect. And with most women, a kiss led to what they both wanted. But in this case...well, he actually had no idea what either of them really wanted beyond seeing just how hot the heat could get.

His phone buzzed, and he was more than happy about the interruption. He pulled it out of his pocket and said, "Hello?"

"Hey, Ian, it's Emma. I promised you an update so here it is."

"You spoke to Shannon's biological father?"

"Yes, but it didn't turn out quite the way I hoped. He met us at a bar because he didn't want his wife to hear our conversation. She doesn't know anything about his one-night stand, which apparently happened the first year of their marriage."

"He sounds like a winner."

"He's not a great guy," she said, disappointment in her voice. "He doesn't want to mess up his marriage by bringing a child he doesn't even know into his life."

"But he does have legal obligations as the biological father."

"Yes, but what kind of life would that be for Shannon?"

He could hear the strain in her voice and having spent time with her on their trip to Ireland, he knew how much the little girl had gotten under her skin, especially since Emma had confessed to him that she'd had trouble carrying two pregnancies to term and wasn't sure she'd ever be able to have a child. "So what are you going to do?" he asked.

Silence met his question. Then she said, "I have kind of a crazy idea..."

He had a feeling he knew exactly where she was headed. "You want to adopt her."

"I do. You really are intuitive, Ian."

"What does Max think?"

"I haven't said the words out loud yet. I wanted to hear myself say it to someone else, and I thought you might be a good choice. You met Maeve and Shannon when we were in Ireland."

"So did Burke," he reminded her, referencing her oldest brother.

"Burke would tell me not to do it. He'd say it was too complicated. That I'm not thinking it through, that raising someone else's child is a huge commitment."

Which were all the things he wanted to tell her, but all he said was, "What do you think?"

"That all that is true, but I fell in love with that little girl. If her dad was a great guy, and if he wanted her, I'd let her go. I'd take her there myself. I'd make sure she was happy, but that's not going to happen."

"Can you adopt her that easily? Aren't there legal hoops to jump through?"

"Her father said he'd sign away his parental rights so that she could be adopted. She's not a baby; she's not going to find a home that easily. I know Maeve would love for us to take her, and I can't help thinking it's why Grandma sent me to Ireland."

"It sounds like you've considered all the options. You're a smart woman, Emma. You've always known what you want, and you've never been afraid to go after it."

Emma had been one of only a few female firefighters in San Francisco, and then she had broken down more gender barriers by becoming a fire investigator. Her husband Max was just as strong as she was. He couldn't imagine two people better suited to be parents.

"This is different," Emma said. "It's not about what I want, or it shouldn't be. It should only be about what's best for Shannon."

"A woman who wants to love her and be her mother seems like a good option to me. But you already know that, Emma."

"I think I would be a good mom."

"I know it. And I suspect Max has already figured out where you're headed."

"He does know me pretty well," Emma admitted. "So it's not completely crazy?"

"Oh, it's definitely crazy, but it's you. You said in Ireland that you'd always felt like you had to work harder to be a Callaway, because your mom married into the family. You know what it feels like to be adopted by someone who really loves you."

"I do know. And I want Shannon to have a family. But I'd be taking her away from Ireland."

"She's young; she'll adapt."

"Thanks, Ian."

"I didn't do anything."

"You heard me out. And you didn't judge. My siblings love to offer their opinions."

"Siblings are good for that."

"I hope I didn't take you away from work."

"Actually, I'm in Tahoe."

"That's right—the conference. How's that going?"

"It hasn't started yet, which is a good thing, because there's a blizzard going on right now. In fact, I didn't even make it to my hotel. I promised Seamus Donelan that I'd take a package to his daughter. I got stranded at her house."

"That sounds interesting."

"You could call it that."

"So our Ireland trip hasn't let you go, either."

"No, it hasn't. But when it stops snowing, that will be the

end of it."

"We'll see. What's Donelan's daughter like?"

"Nothing like him," he said.

"Is she single?"

"Yes, but that doesn't matter."

"Maybe it should. When's the last time you had a girlfriend?"

"Good-bye, Emma."

"Fine. I won't meddle, but I will give you some advice. Have fun, Ian."

"I wouldn't call this fun."

"Then you're not trying hard enough," she said with a laugh.

He smiled as the call disconnected. His body was all about fun with Grace but his brain had more than a few reservations. He'd always gone with his brain. Maybe it was time to change that.

—⟫⟪—

When he entered the living room, he found Tyler snuggled up next to Grace on the couch.

"You're just in time," Tyler told him.

"For..." he asked.

"*Madeline's Christmas Miracle*," Tyler said with a happy smile.

"You do not have to listen to this," Grace said. "In fact, Tyler and I can go in the other room."

"It's fine. I'm already intrigued."

She gave him a doubtful smile. "Sure you are."

"Please, go ahead." He settled into the armchair next to the couch as Grace encouraged Tyler to read the story, helping him as he stumbled over a few words. As Tyler got tired, she took over.

He liked the sound of her voice, the silky Irish lilt that seemed to bring the story alive. He could imagine her whispering in his ear as he kissed her, touched her, made love to her. She'd be passionate, he had no doubt about that. Her green eyes would sparkle with desire. He'd already seen a hint of that back in the kitchen. And the memory made his body harden.

How on earth was she still single?

Maybe there was a man in her life, but if there was a boyfriend, where was he? She'd mentioned no one, and she appeared to live alone. The guy could be working or out of town. Or maybe there was no one in her life, no one serious, no one to care that he was probably going to be spending the night with her.

He smiled to himself. Maybe not with her exactly, but he couldn't see how he was getting his car out of the snow before morning.

He shouldn't be remotely happy about that fact. He should be pissed and irritated that he wasn't in the nice hotel room he'd booked, that he didn't have his computer to look at, or the journals to read, or any other work to do, because it was all in his car and blocked by a few feet of snow.

But he couldn't summon up anger or annoyance. He was actually quite comfortable in Grace's warm and cozy living room. As he looked around, he saw touches of her everywhere, from the photographs of Ireland on the walls, to the floral upholstered chair he was sitting in, the homemade quilt on the back of the sofa, and a collection of teacups in a corner display case. It reminded him of the inn he'd stayed at in Kenmare. It was inviting and individual, much like Grace. She'd disliked him as soon as he'd spoken her father's name, but that hadn't stopped her from opening up her home to him, from being kind and generous.

He really hadn't met anyone like her before, and he was just as mesmerized by her now as he'd been the first time he'd seen her photograph.

He felt like he could sit here forever. Grace's voice was like a soothing musical instrument with just the right high notes to keep his interest. Tyler was as enthralled as he was, although Tyler was much more caught up in the actual story than in the storyteller.

Madeline's Christmas Miracle was a schmaltzy holiday story about a six-year-old girl whose grandmother told her that Santa didn't just show up on Christmas Eve but that he actually flew back and forth across the sky throughout the month of December. If Madeline watched the sky and caught a glimpse of Santa's reindeer, any wish she made would come true. In Madeline's case, she wanted a puppy for Christmas, but her single mother didn't have enough money to buy her one.

In the end, Madeline saw Santa streaking across the sky the week before Christmas. She closed her eyes and made a wish. On Christmas morning, she ran to the tree, but she was disappointed. There was no puppy, just a stuffed animal, all her mother could afford. She tried to be brave and not cry, but she was sad.

Later that day, she went into the backyard. She was sitting alone when a little dog came squirming under a fence and ran over to her. She thought her Christmas wish had come true. But her mom said they had to put up signs and find the dog's owner.

To make the incredulous story even more unbelievable, it turned out that the puppy belonged to a couple who had to move away to a place where they couldn't have a dog. Madeline got to keep the puppy, and she named it Rudolph after the reindeer she'd seen the week before Christmas.

"Read it again," Tyler said as Grace closed the book.

"We'll do that tomorrow," Grace told him. "It's time for bed."

"I want to look outside first," Tyler said. "Maybe I can see Santa's sleigh. Then my Christmas wish will come true."

"Santa wouldn't be flying in a snowstorm," Grace said.

Ian was impressed with how quickly she'd come up with that rationalization.

Tyler looked disappointed, but even he couldn't fight the logic of that argument. Instead, he said, "Can we look tomorrow night, Grace?"

"Sure. Now it's time for you to go to bed. Why don't you brush your teeth, and then I'll be in to say good-night?"

"Okay." Tyler got up from the couch. "Night, Ian."

"Good-night, Tyler."

As the little boy left the room, Ian immediately started shaking his head. "Seriously, Grace? How can you read that book to your students? They're going to be standing outside every night for a month looking for Santa."

"It's just a story, Ian. And kids this age are always looking for Santa."

"Really? Tyler is about seven, right? That's getting a little old to believe in Santa Claus."

"I don't think there's an age where you have to stop believing in anything," she countered.

He knew the skepticism clearly showed on his face, but he couldn't hide it. "I know you hate science, but you can't tell me you believe in Santa Claus."

"I believe that some things in this world are unexplainable and that miracles happen. How they happen is obviously impossible for any of us to know. But, yes, I can believe in things I can't see or fully understand. I have hope and faith. I'm Irish."

"I'm Irish, too, at least a part of me is, but you're setting Tyler up for a fall. He's not going to see Santa. He's not going to get his wish, which I'm guessing has something to do with his dad coming home."

Her smile faded at his words. "Maybe Kevin will come home for Christmas."

"What if he doesn't?"

"I don't want to think that way." She met his gaze. "There's enough bad stuff in the world. Is it really that wrong to want children to keep their innocence as long as possible? There's something so joyful and beautiful about a child who still believes in impossible things. I want them to keep that faith as long as they can. Reality will be there when they're ready. I don't have to be the one who crushes their dreams."

He frowned, remembering someone else telling him

something very similar not so long ago.

"What?" she asked, tilting her head to the side as she gave him a thoughtful look. "What did I say that got you thinking?"

"Nothing."

A knowing smile spread across her face. "Wait, I know. You killed someone's innocence, didn't you? Was it one of your siblings? Did you tell them Santa didn't exist?"

He didn't like how easily she'd read him. "Possibly," he admitted. "They were old enough to know better."

"Like how old?"

"Six or seven, I don't remember—about Tyler's age, I think. My mom was really upset with me."

"I'll bet."

He smiled. "I didn't just take down Santa. I included the Easter Bunny and the Tooth Fairy. Hunter told me I destroyed his life, but he always exaggerates."

"Is he your younger brother?"

"Yes, he is. I didn't tell my sisters, though. I played along with their silly trips to see Santa at the mall."

"Was it that difficult?"

"In my head...yes."

"I bet you have an extremely high IQ."

He shrugged. "High enough to know Santa is just a character in a story."

"You don't really know that."

"I do," he argued. "The old guy in the mall is just working for minimum wage."

"I'm not talking about the Santa in the mall, Ian. I know you like things to add up. Two plus two always equals four, right?"

"It does equal four, Grace."

"I know that. But I'm just saying that not everything in life adds up."

"You'd be surprised how much does...if you do the math."

"And you always do the math."

"It makes the world make sense."

She settled back against the couch, considering his words. "For the first time tonight, you actually do *not* remind me of my father."

He didn't know if he should be happy about that or not.

"My dad might have been a man of science," she continued. "But he wasn't averse to kissing the Blarney Stone to receive the gift of eloquence or putting out a mince pie and a glass of Guinness for Santa or Father Christmas, as we sometimes referred to him."

Ian was surprised by the softness of her tone. "That's the first thing you've said about him that doesn't hold disappointment or anger."

"To be honest, that's the first thing I've remembered about him in a long time that didn't upset me." She shook her head, as if she couldn't quite believe it. "I had my first taste of Guinness out of the glass he put out for Santa. I think I was about nine. I didn't really believe in Father Christmas anymore, but it was one of the few traditions we did together. And that Guinness was our little secret." She cleared her throat and got to her feet. "I'm going to check on Tyler. I'll bring you a pillow and some blankets for the couch. That's the best I can do. Even if the snow lets up, you'll have to dig your car out tomorrow morning."

"The couch will be fine," he said, as he stood up. "I appreciate your generosity, Grace, considering that I didn't bring you something you actually wanted."

"I'm not going to hold you responsible for that. You were doing a favor."

"Last time I make that mistake," he said lightly. "I usually make it a rule not to get involved with anyone's personal problems. It never works out well. I should have followed my gut."

"It hasn't been so terrible having you around. You did make us dinner and you came up with a science project for Tyler. Since I know you don't like debt of any kind, we'll call it even."

"That sounds fair."

Their gazes met again, and he felt the same intense pull toward her that he'd felt in the kitchen. He couldn't help the impulsive question that slid from his mouth. "Do you have a boyfriend, Grace?"

She started, a wary expression entering her eyes. "No, not at the moment."

"Interesting."

"I can't imagine why you'd think so."

"I think you can."

Her eyes glittered. "You're flirting with me?"

A smile curved his lips at her question. "Apparently not that well, if you have to ask."

"I'm flattered, but..." Her voice fell away.

"But you're not interested?"

Conflict warred in her eyes. "I'd be a liar to say that."

Heat ran through him at her honest words. "Good."

"Not good," she said, shaking her head. "We just met, and Tyler is here, and you're only in town a few days. So...I'm going to call it a night."

He knew she was right for all the reasons she'd just said and a dozen more, but he couldn't say he wasn't disappointed.

"If you don't want to wait for me to finish up with Tyler," she added, "you can grab some pillows and blankets out of the hall closet. And there's probably a new toothbrush in the bathroom cabinet. Good night, Ian."

"Good night," he said, watching her leave the room with mixed feelings. If it wasn't snowing, he would definitely be out the door, because Grace was stirring up some long-buried emotions. He hadn't been involved seriously with anyone in a long time, and he only dated women who didn't want more than he did. He knew Grace would want a lot from a man, and he was not that man.

But as he walked down the hall to grab a blanket out of the closet, he was shocked at the idea that he might want to be.

Five

Grace didn't sleep well. Her restless dreams were filled with memories of her father, the package he'd sent her, and Ian's talk about her father's regrets. Was she being unreasonably stubborn to want nothing to do with the man who had given her life? Was it a mistake to send the package back unopened?

On the other hand, did she really owe her father anything? He was the one who had betrayed her mother and the family. He was the one who'd abandoned them long before they'd left Ireland.

And why had her father sent Ian to deliver the package? If he wanted to see her, to make amends, to start a conversation, why hadn't he come himself? Obviously he knew where she lived. Was he just afraid to be rejected in person? Wasn't that just more evidence of his cowardice?

She hated that she was even thinking about him again. She'd chosen her mother's side years ago. It was too late to change back, and why should she? What had really changed?

Flopping on to her back as the morning light crept through the window, she was relieved that the long night was over.

She couldn't keep going around in circles in her head.

The best thing to do was to send the package back. She didn't need a father now, and she didn't need to bring her mother more unhappiness by reconnecting with her dad. She just needed to let things be.

As her mind moved away from her father, it went straight to Ian.

She'd had a few disturbing dreams about him, too, remembering how he'd looked at her in the kitchen, the way he'd flirted with her before she went to bed, and the fact that she'd acknowledged she was attracted to him.

But they'd only just met. She shouldn't want a man—a stranger—that fast. It had never happened before. She always took time to get to know someone, and whatever spark was there simmered for a while, then got stronger, and then there was a little more heat.

She heaved a sigh as she finished the rest of that thought...*and then the heat usually fizzled out.*

She ended up back where she started, wondering where was the *great love* her grandmother had spoken about and why was it taking her so long to find it?

But that great love could not be with a man of science, even if he did make her want to throw herself into his arms. She needed a man like her mother's second husband, someone who would always be there, who cared about her more than his work or the rest of the world.

Besides, Ian wasn't going to be in her life past the next hour probably. As soon as he could dig his car out of the snow, he'd be gone, so this whole rumination about whether or not she should get involved with him was completely pointless.

Getting up from bed, she walked over to the window and looked outside. Several feet of snow had crept up to her windowsill from the ground, and the trees were completely white. It was cloudy but not snowing anymore. Hopefully, the storm had passed.

She took a quick shower and got dressed. Then she woke up a sleepy Tyler and told him to get up while she headed to the kitchen, where she could already smell coffee brewing.

When she walked into the room, she discovered that Ian hadn't just made coffee; he'd also made breakfast.

"Morning," he said cheerfully, looking as sexy as he had the night before. There was a new growth of beard on his face, and his hair was a bit tousled, but that only added to his appeal.

She'd really hoped that her dreams had made him more attractive than he really was, but that wasn't the case. Her stomach churned, and little tingles ran down her spine when their gazes met. She was immensely relieved when he looked away.

"Scrambled eggs are ready," he told her, sliding the eggs onto three plates. "Is Tyler up?"

"He's dressing." She moved over to the coffeemaker and took a mug out of the cabinet. "I said we were even last night, Ian, but now you've pulled ahead again with this generous effort to make us breakfast."

"I was hungry. You had eggs, bacon, and bread. I just put it together."

She liked that he didn't expect to be praised for just being helpful. She sighed, thinking she really needed to start finding things she didn't like about him. She took a sip of coffee, then set down her mug and buttered the toast popping out of the toaster. She put the toast on the plates while Ian got the bacon, and a few minutes later, they sat down at the table together. Tyler came into the room with a sleepy face and slid into the chair across from her.

One bite of Ian's eggs made her wonder why she'd been settling for yogurt and oatmeal the past few months. He definitely had a magic touch in the kitchen. Not that he'd admit it was magic, she thought, smiling to herself. Ian was all about science. Add one ingredient to another and voila— breakfast.

"Something amusing?" he asked her, a quizzical gleam in his eyes.

"No," she said, deciding not to share. Thankfully, the

buzzing of her phone precluded another question from him. She got up and grabbed her phone to read the text, thinking it might be from Carrie, but it was from the principal of her school.

"Is that my mom?" Tyler asked.

"No, it's the school," she replied. "Two large trees are blocking the entrance and part of the playground, so they've decided to call it a snow day."

"No school?" Tyler asked with a surprised and wide-eyed grin.

"That's right. But I thought you loved school."

"I do, but there's tons of snow outside. Maybe we could go sledding." He gave her a hopeful look.

"That's a thought."

"And we could make my volcano later," Tyler added, turning his pleading smile on Ian. "Right? You said we could do it after school. How about after sledding? You could come with us if you want."

"Ian has to go to work," she interjected. "He's in Tahoe for a conference, Tyler."

"Maybe he has a snow day, too," Tyler suggested.

Ian laughed. "You know, Tyler, I've never had a snow day. Growing up in San Francisco, the worst weather we got was rain or fog."

"Then you should go sledding with us. Do you know how to sled?"

"I do, but I haven't done it in a while."

"Your conference isn't beginning today?" she asked, quite sure that spending more time with Ian would be a mistake.

"It doesn't officially begin until tomorrow. There's a cocktail party tonight, but that isn't until six, so I have some free time."

"Then we can go to the snow park," Tyler said, deciding for all of them.

"Works for me," Ian said.

She hesitated as two pairs of male eyes turned on her.

She found it impossible to say no to either one of them. "All right. I'm in."

"Yay!" Tyler said, clapping his hands together.

She laughed at his over-the-top happy grin, and wondered why she'd even considered refusing. She'd promised to do everything she could to keep a smile on Tyler's face so he wouldn't miss his mom or his dad, and if sledding was going to make him happy, she'd cheerfully take him down as many runs as he wanted. "But," she said, suddenly remembering *why* there was a snow day. "We're going to have to shovel some snow so we can get a car down the driveway."

"I can help you with that," Ian offered.

"You're going to have to, if you ever want to leave here."

"I'm not really in a hurry," he said, giving her a warm smile that made her insides melt.

And she really wasn't in a hurry for him to leave, although she knew she should be.

"I'm in a hurry," Tyler interrupted. "Can we start shoveling snow now?"

"After breakfast," she told him. "Eat your eggs, buddy. You're going to need your strength."

She was going to need some strength, too—not just to shovel snow, but to not let Ian Callaway get any further under her skin.

———※※———

Thirty minutes later, she had set up Tyler and Ian with shovels and a snow blower that she'd retrieved from the garage. She had to take the items through the house since the garage door was blocked with snow. Once the guys got started, she returned to the house to put on warmer clothes. She'd just put on her coat and boots when her phone rang, and Carrie's number flashed across the screen. Her heart leapt into her throat as she threw up a silent prayer for good news.

"Hello?"

"It's me," Carrie said, a shaky note in her voice. "How's Tyler?"

"He's fine. How are you? How's Kevin?"

"He's back in surgery. I got to see him an hour ago, and he woke up for like a minute. He said he loves me and Tyler. He said to make sure Tyler knows that, as if—as if he's afraid he won't make it." Her voice broke. "God, Grace, it's so hard to see him like that. I want to make him better, but I can't."

"Oh, Carrie," she said, her heart twisting at the pain in her friend's voice. "You just have to keep the faith. They have good doctors there. They're going to do everything they can to save his life."

"I'm trying to be strong, but they said he has a pulmonary embolism, a blood clot in his lung, or something like that. They have to go back in even though he's very weak. He's got a broken leg, a broken wrist, cracked ribs, and internal injuries. He looked really bad and yet really good, too. I hadn't seen him in so long. I didn't want to cry in front of him, but it was difficult to be positive. I hope he knows that I have faith in his recovery. I hope I didn't blow that."

"You didn't. You couldn't. How long will he be in surgery?"

"I'm not sure." She took a breath. "I just need him to be okay, Grace. I need him to live. He's my best friend. He's the love of my life. He's Tyler's father. He has more to do. He has to make it."

"He will be there for you and Tyler," she said fiercely. "Kevin is a tough guy. He's a fighter."

"If he dies, I don't know what I'll tell Tyler."

"Don't even think about that now."

"I'm trying not to. Wait, why did you answer your phone? I was just going to leave a message. I thought you'd be in class. It's not recess, is it? I'm all screwed up on the time difference."

"It's a snow day. Some trees fell down, so they called off school. But the storm has passed and as soon as I can clear my driveway, Tyler and I are going to go sledding."

"Oh, he'll love that."

"He seems pretty excited. He's a great kid, Carrie."

"He is pretty special," Carrie agreed. "He's got a lot of his father in him."

Grace took a breath, thinking she should probably mention Ian. "I need to tell you something, Carrie. It's not a big deal, but last night right before Tyler arrived, a friend of my father's dropped off a package for me from my dad."

"What? Now he has someone making personal deliveries? He doesn't quit."

"No, he doesn't. I told Ian, that's his friend, that I wasn't going to open it, and I would send it back. He didn't really care. He was doing my dad a favor, but while we were having this discussion, the snow was coming down, and to make a long story short, Ian's car got stuck in my driveway, and he wound up spending the night on my couch. He had dinner with Tyler and me. In fact, he made dinner."

"Oh, okay. Well, that's all right. He knows your dad, so he's probably a good guy. Is he your dad's age?"

"No, he's my age, and in the interest of full disclosure, he is gorgeous—dark hair, blue eyes, sexy smile, the whole package."

"Well…maybe your dad sent you something good after all," Carrie said, her voice losing a lot of its earlier tension.

"He's something all right, but he's a scientist, so nothing is going to happen."

"You can't judge every guy with a science degree by your father's standards."

"I know, but I can't overlook the similarities between them, either. He's here for a science conference, and he seems to be involved in some pretty important work. I know what that means—the world comes first, family comes second. Anyway, I don't need to be bothering you with this."

"Actually, it's a nice distraction. You sound like you like him despite the fact that he shares something in common with your dad."

"He's…interesting and really attractive. It's been awhile

since I felt butterflies in my stomach."

"Butterflies are good. You don't have to marry him, Grace; just give yourself a chance to get to know him."

"He's only in town for a few days."

"A lot can happen in a short period of time."

"He also has great admiration for my father."

"Many people do, Grace."

"I know. But how can I like someone who admires my father? That seems crazy."

"Or maybe you can separate how someone who knows your father on a professional level feels about him and how you feel about him?"

"I'm trying to do that, but when it comes to my dad, I tend to see red. Anyway, as for spending more time with him, Tyler invited him to go sledding with us, and Ian accepted."

"Sounds like he might be interested in you, too, Grace."

"I don't really know why he said yes. Oh, and he also showed Tyler how to combine vinegar and baking soda to make a volcano erupt. They have plans to build a volcano for the science fair later today."

"That's great and a real relief. I promised Tyler I'd help him, and I was feeling guilty about being gone."

"Don't feel guilty. I promise to take extra special care of your son."

"I trust you completely, Grace."

"Thank you. You need to take care of yourself, Carrie. Don't forget to eat something once in a while."

"I'm not at all hungry, but I will try to force something down."

"Good. Do you want to talk to Tyler?"

"I do, but..." Her voice cracked again. "I don't want to cry, and I'm afraid I will, and that will upset him. Tell him I love him, and I'm blowing him kisses; I'll talk to him later."

"I will." She set down her phone and let out a breath. She couldn't imagine the terror Carrie was going through, and she sent up another prayer for Kevin to pull through.

She slipped on her coat and headed to the front door. On

her way, the package her father had sent her caught her eye. She needed to get rid of it; she didn't even like it sitting on her table, a reminder of a life she didn't want to think about, a man she'd said good-bye to a long time ago.

She grabbed the package and took it with her. She'd put it in the car and they could drop it off at the post office on their way to the snow park.

Today was not a day for thinking about the past or the future, just the present. She couldn't help Carrie or Kevin, but she could make the day as fun as possible for their son, and she intended to do just that.

Having Ian along wouldn't be bad, either. It was just some harmless fun; then he'd go back to his life, and she'd go back to hers.

***

It actually felt good to shovel snow. Ian hadn't done any physical labor or had a workout in a couple of weeks. Normally, he made it his mission to get to the gym before he went to the lab, but he'd been working long hours to get the prototype done. A couple of big companies were interested in buying the device, and hopefully, they'd be able to sell it and move on to manufacturing and shipping in the first quarter of next year. But that part of the business was more in his business partner's hands, which meant he could start thinking about what was next. He had a few ideas, but he was still pondering the pros and cons of each.

He wanted to be inspired. He wanted to push the envelope on everything he did, but he felt a little burned out. Hopefully, the conference would give him back some creative mojo. There was nothing more invigorating than talking to people who saw a world with no barriers, no limits, no walls or obstacles that they couldn't go over.

Confidence sometimes turned into a gigantic ego, but not in everyone. There were a lot of good people in science who had more idealism than ambition. Unfortunately, it was usually the big egos that took the stage, that were the face of his world. He didn't usually care. In the past ten years, he'd only been concerned with what he needed to get done. But lately he'd started to reevaluate his rather detached stance when it came to the bad apples in his field, and it wasn't just because of Grace's opinion. In the past year, he'd begun to see how partisan policy makers could set back a much-needed project purely for political reasons, and that needed to be kept in check. He might not be able to change the world, but he could make sure that the projects he was involved in were not colored by greed and a thirst for power.

"Are we done yet?" Tyler asked, interrupting his thoughts.

The little boy's face was red from exertion, and the shovel in his hands was as tall as he was.

"I think we are," he said, taking a look around. They'd cleared the snow around the car and he'd cleared the driveway with the blower. The sun had come out, and the ice was starting to melt, sending a river of water down the hill. The area in front of the garage was still piled three feet high with snow, but they could clear that later and take his car to the snow park.

Grace came out of the house with the package from her father in her hand. "I thought I'd drop this at the post office. It's near the snow park."

"Sure," he said, masking the disappointment he felt. It was none of his business, but he thought she might be missing out on something by not at least opening the box. "Let's take my car. Tyler and I are tired of shoveling, and the garage is going to take more work."

"I'm sorry I didn't help more," she said, giving him an apologetic smile. "I got a few calls."

"It's no problem." He put his arm around Tyler's shoulders. "Us men took care of it for you, didn't we, Ty?"

The little boy gave a vigorous nod. "I helped a lot."

"I appreciate that so much," Grace told Tyler. "Do you want to use the bathroom before we go?"

"Okay," Tyler said, dropping the shovel, then running into the house.

He picked up the shovel and set it next to the garage.

"Thanks for doing all this," Grace said.

"No problem. It was a good workout."

Her gaze ran down his body as he made the statement, and then she blushed when she realized he'd caught her. "See anything you like?" he drawled.

"You look like you work out a lot; that seems unusual for a scientist."

"Physical health is an important component to brain health." At her smile, he added, "And, yes, I realize I sometimes give more intellectual information than is required. It's a bad habit."

"It's probably more annoying that you're always right."

He liked the teasing light in her eyes. "You've already figured that out?"

"I should have said that you *think* you're always right."

"Too late to take it back. And I am *mostly* right; I wouldn't say always. The minute you think you've conquered it all is when you stop trying, stop searching for innovation. I wouldn't want to fall into that trap."

"That's an interesting way to look at it," she said thoughtfully.

"Still comparing me to your father with every statement I make?"

"Not my father, in this instance."

"Then what kind of men have you been hanging out with?"

"Let's just say their intellect hasn't necessarily been their strength."

"So pretty boys with big muscles."

She laughed. "Nothing wrong with that. But you do know you just described yourself, right?"

"No way."

"Would you feel better if I said you were ruggedly handsome with big muscles and left off the pretty?"

"I would," he admitted, having more fun talking to Grace than he had in a long time. She didn't take herself too seriously, which made him not take himself too seriously, and that felt freeing. "So, who was your last boyfriend?"

"Boyfriend? I don't know. What constitutes a boyfriend anymore? I dated a sound engineer at Harvey's last summer. I got to see some great concerts for free, but it didn't last past September."

"Your call or his?"

"Mutual—well, maybe more me than him. There just wasn't enough there. What about you? Who was your last girlfriend?"

He actually had to think for a moment. "It's been awhile. I've been busy. I guess Vanessa was the last woman I dated for more than a few weeks. But like you, there just wasn't enough there to keep things going."

"And you don't have time for dating anyway, right?"

Since he'd told every single person in his family that exact thing on Thanksgiving, he could hardly deny it now. "There hasn't been a lot of extra time of late, but that's going to change."

"Why would it change? What would make you lose your drive to work?"

"I'm not saying I'd lose it, but I could balance it out."

"I suppose you could—if you really wanted to."

Now he knew she was talking about her father again. "You know what's ironic, Grace?"

"I have a feeling you're going to tell me."

"Your dad told me three months ago that when you and your mom and sister left that nothing was worth that loss. He warned me about getting into the same position, becoming too obsessed with discoveries and potential miracle-making devices. He said ambition had been his downfall."

Her frown told him she really didn't want to believe anything he was saying.

"I know that doesn't play into the story that plays through your head," he added, "but it is what he told me. He said that I should use him as a cautionary tale."

She stared back at him for a long moment. "Well, I don't know what to say to that—good? So he finally learned a hard lesson? But it was way too late."

"He understood that. He said he deserved what he got. I think your father went back into teaching as some sort of penance for his ambition."

"Maybe he just wanted to mold the next generation."

"That might have been part of it, I suppose." He paused, knowing she wouldn't like his next statement, but he couldn't stop himself from saying it. "You know, you're a little like him, Grace."

"That's not a compliment," she said sharply.

"But it's a fact. You're a teacher. He's a professor. Seems like you both want to influence young minds."

"Okay, I think we're done talking about my dad." She turned toward his car, then paused, frowning. "This is your car?"

"Who else's would it be?"

"It doesn't look like you."

"You don't think a red '76 Ford Mustang looks like me?" he said with a small smile.

"It seems a little out of character for what I know about you."

"What would you have expected me to drive?"

"A conservative sedan."

"So a boring car."

She gave him an awkward shrug. "Sorry, but yes."

He grinned. "My car needed some repairs. This is one of Dylan's cars. He has a passion for restoring muscle cars from the 60s and 70s."

She smiled back at him. "I was right. What do you normally drive?"

"An electric car."

"Of course you do. That makes more sense." She pulled on the door handle. "Can you unlock it?"

He took out his keys and flipped the locks. She tossed the

package into the backseat and shut the door as Tyler came out of the house.

"I'm ready," Tyler said.

"We need your car seat," Grace said.

"I'll get it." Tyler ran back to the house.

"I'm going to grab my bag," she told Ian. "I'll be back in a minute."

"No problem. I would like to stop at Silverstone's before we go to the snow park, if you don't mind. I'd like to change clothes and check into the hotel. Does that work for you?"

"Of course."

"Great." As Grace went into the house, he couldn't help but watch her walk away, and the sway of her hips sent another jolt of desire through him. This snow day was probably a bad idea, but there was no way he was backing out. He might only have a little more time with Grace before she found a way to get him out of her life, and he was going to enjoy every second.

Six

When had smart become so sexy? Grace cast a sidelong look at Ian as he drove toward his hotel.

Maybe it was because he looked nothing like an intellectual right now but more like a super attractive guy who was ready to play.

She shivered at the thought of playing with Ian—and she wasn't thinking about the snow park, but something a little warmer, a little softer, and a lot more private.

As Tyler broke into her thoughts with a question about where they were going, she was reminded that she had a chaperone in one energetic seven-year-old so she needed to get her head together and focus more on being a great babysitter and less on being Ian's play partner.

She couldn't stop the heat that spread through her cheeks at that reckless thought, and she deliberately looked out the window, hoping Ian wouldn't notice, because he seemed to spend as much time staring at her as she did at him.

"Everything okay?" he asked her.

"It's great," she said, as he turned in to the hotel parking lot.

"You seem a little…nervous."

She wasn't about to admit to that, so she found another

excuse. "Well, we are about to walk into a lion's den of scientists."

"I think you'll be safe in the lobby."

"We could wait in the car."

"It's too cold," he said, as he parked the car. "I promise I'll be quick."

"It's fine. Tyler and I will look around the gift shop."

"Maybe I can get Mommy a present," Tyler said.

"That's a good idea," she replied. "We'll find something perfect for her."

They entered Silverstone's through the casino entrance, and Tyler was immediately entranced by the flashing lights, bells, and whistles of the slot machines. She kept a tight grip on his hand as they made their way to the lobby.

While Ian got in line to check in, she and Tyler went into the large gift shop. Expensive dresses and jewelry took up one side of the shop; Tahoe tourist items, toys, and stuffed animals filled out the other side. And in the back was a market filled with snacks and drinks.

Tyler found a large display of stuffed bears completely fascinating.

"Do you think we could get one of these for Mommy?" he asked. "She says it's okay to sleep with bears, cuz they protect you at night."

She had a feeling Tyler wanted the bear for himself. "That seems like a good present. You can give it to her when she comes home."

"I thought she was going to call today."

"She did call. She really wanted to talk to you, but she had to go, so she said she'd call later."

"Where did she go?" Tyler asked curiously.

"Uh, she went to talk to some other teachers," she said, making up the lie and hoping it wouldn't contradict whatever Carrie had told Tyler.

"At a school far away?"

"It's a little far away," she said, not wanting to scare him. "I told her we were going sledding and that we would make a volcano later. She really liked your idea for the science fair."

Tyler beamed. "She did?"

Grace nodded. "Yes, she did. Now, why don't you pick out your bear?"

"I can't decide if I want a white one or a brown one," he said, looking at the large display.

"Take your time." She wandered a few feet away to look at some earrings when she suddenly heard her name.

Turning her head, she was shocked to see her father's former partner and friend, Harry Ferguson. He'd aged in the ten plus years since she'd seen him, his jet-black hair a pepper-gray now, a dozen or more lines around his eyes. His slacks and sports coat hung loosely on his thin frame, and there was a tension to his mouth despite his smile.

"Grace Donelan. It is you, isn't it?" he asked.

"Yes," she said, not bothering to correct him on her change of name. "You must be here for the conference."

"I'm one of the keynote speakers," he said proudly.

"Congratulations." She looked toward Tyler, who was still debating between bears, then turned her attention back to Harry.

"How's your father?" Harry asked. "Have you spoken to him lately?"

"No, not in years. You would probably know how he is better than me."

"Ah, so you're still estranged," he said with a small nod. "I thought things might have changed since he went into academia."

"Nothing has changed," she said shortly.

Harry gave her a speculative look. "What are you doing in Tahoe?"

"I live here. I'm a teacher—elementary school."

"Science?"

"Mostly reading and math in second grade."

"That's a shame. Science should start early."

She sighed, deciding she didn't want to get into that debate again.

"Your mother—how is she?" Harry continued.

"Fine. She remarried a few years ago."

"I knew it wouldn't take her long to find another man—a *better* man. I'm not as big a fan of your father as I once was, Grace. He pulled the wool over my eyes as well as your mother's."

She really didn't want to ask why. She just wanted to get out of the conversation.

"It wasn't just his affair with Catalina Moriarty and the child he tried to hide," Harry added. "He had a lot of other shady things going on. I never thought my good friend would betray me the way he did."

"Apparently, my father's betrayals sneak up on you," she said, unable to keep the bitter edge out of her voice.

As she finished speaking, a younger, more attractive version of Harry joined them. It had been a long time since she'd seen Harry's son Westley as well. He'd definitely improved with age, although he hadn't been bad at fifteen, when his brown eyes and sandy-brown hair had inspired a huge crush for her twelve-year-old self. They'd spent a summer holiday together, and she'd spent most of that time mooning after him. Of course, he'd barely noticed her. He'd been far more interested in her older sister Jillian.

"Look who I found, Westley," Harry said. "It's Grace Donelan."

Recognition dawned in his eyes. "Grace? Well, you really grew up." Appreciation ran through his gaze. "Last time I saw you, you were skinny, sunburned, and had a long red braid down your back."

"Thanks for the flashback," she said dryly.

"What are you doing here? Are you here with your father? I didn't think he was coming." Westley said.

"No, I live here in Tahoe."

"Seriously? That's quite a change from Ireland," Westley said.

"Yes, it is."

"Is your sister here, too?"

"No, she lives in Sonoma."

"Westley recently joined my company," Harry interjected, a proud gleam in his eyes.

"I must say I'm a little surprised," she said. "I thought you were more into blondes than books, Westley."

He smiled. "At fifteen I certainly was. But I found I could do well at both."

She almost laughed at his smug reply. She should have figured he'd be as cocky as his father.

"I'm on the business side of the company," Wesley added. "I leave the brilliant science to my dad. I make sure we're profitable."

"Grace," Tyler said, drawing her attention to him, as he came over with the bear he wanted.

"Did you pick one, Ty?" she asked.

"This one," he said, holding out the brown bear. "He'll protect us."

"Great." She took the bear, then looked back at the Fergusons. "It was nice to see both of you again."

"Is this your son?" Westley asked.

"No, he belongs to a friend. Have a good conference."

"We should get together," Westley said. "For old time's sake. I think you still owe me an ice cream."

"I'm fairly sure that's your debt. You're the one who knocked my cone out of my hand."

"Funny, I remember it the other way." He gave her a charming smile. "Either way, maybe it's a little cold for ice cream; we could get a drink."

"I'm sorry. I'm really busy this week. I hope you both enjoy Tahoe."

"Seriously, you're just going to blow me off?" Westley asked, walking with them to the cash register.

"I'm watching Tyler all week. I really don't have time for a drink."

"Can't you leave him with a babysitter?"

"I'm the babysitter, and I'm sure you have more important people to hang out with than me."

"I hope you're not saying no because of what went down with our fathers. Their fight doesn't have to be ours."

"I have no idea what you're talking about," she said, handing her credit card to the cashier. "I haven't spoken to my father in a very long time."

He gave her a thoughtful look, but before he could comment further, his father called to him.

"Looks like you're needed," she said, glancing at the older, sophisticated blonde woman who had joined Harry. "Who's that?"

"Senator Connie Barrows. She chairs the Senate Committee on Commerce, Science, and Transportation. I do need to say hello."

"Of course."

"Can I have your number, Grace? I'd like to find some time to catch up."

She really didn't want to give Westley her number, but he was being persistent, and it was easier just to say yes. She had nothing against him; she just didn't want to be part of his world.

After getting her number, Westley joined his father and the senator while she finished her transaction. She handed the bag with the bear to Tyler. "Do you want to hang on to this guy?"

"Okay," Tyler said.

"Do you know what you're going to name him?"

"I think Mommy should decide. When do you think she'll be back?"

"I'm sure it won't be too long," she said vaguely. "Let's go see if we can find Ian."

"There he is," Tyler said, pointing to the front of the store where Ian had joined the Fergusons and Senator Barrows in conversation.

"Maybe we should give him a second."

"I want to show him my bear." Tyler pulled her along with his hand. "Ian," he said loudly. "I got a bear."

Ian looked away from his conversation to give Tyler a

smile.

She was happy to see there was no annoyance on Ian's face. She could remember many times when her father had looked at her with irritation when she'd had the nerve to interrupt him. But Ian's expression was nothing but warm interest. As Tyler pulled his hand away from hers and ran to Ian, she could see that the little boy was clearly infatuated. She had to admit she felt a similar happy and giddy tingle when Ian's gaze moved from Tyler to her.

There were three other people in their space, but she barely saw them. She just saw Ian. And that was a little terrifying.

"That's a great bear," Ian told Tyler.

"It's for my mom. He'll protect her when my dad's away."

"He looks fit for the job," Ian said.

"You know Ian?" Westley asked.

"We met recently," she returned. "I'm sorry that we interrupted your conversation. Ian, we can wait for you by the door. Take your time."

"I'm done." Ian glanced back at the group. "Senator Barrows, Mr. Ferguson—I look forward to hearing your speeches. Westley, I'm sure we'll see each other again."

Westley tipped his head in acknowledgment.

"I would like some one-on-one time, Ian," Senator Barrows said. "If you have some time?"

"I'll make time," he replied.

"Good. I think we might find some mutual interests."

"Can I second that?" Harry asked. "I've been following your work the past year, Ian; I'm very impressed. You have a brilliant future ahead of you, and I'd like to be a part of it."

As both the senator and Harry regarded Ian with genuine admiration, Grace had a feeling that Ian had downplayed some of his accomplishments to her. It took a lot to impress Harry, and she suspected the senator would be a tough sell as well. Westley didn't look nearly as happy with the praise being heaped on Ian. Maybe there was some jealousy there. Westley had always been super competitive, and she had a feeling that Ian was the kind of guy who won without even appearing to try.

"I'll be around all week and I'm happy to meet up," Ian said, "but right now I have some sledding to do." He put a hand on Tyler's shoulder and gave her a smile. "Let's go."

"Of course," she said, murmuring good-bye to the Fergusons.

"Don't forget about that drink, Grace," Westley said. "You'll be hearing from me."

She simply smiled, but she could feel Westley's curiosity following them down the hall. She didn't really care what he thought about why she and Ian were together. She wouldn't see any of these people in a few days. Once they left Lake Tahoe, her world and their world would never intersect.

As they walked toward the parking lot, Ian gave her a speculative look. "You didn't seem that surprised to see your father's old friend and partner."

"I spoke to Harry for a few moments before you got there."

"How was that?"

"Fine. He seems the same. He did make a point of telling me that he was sorry about my parents' divorce and that my father had betrayed him, too."

"By doing what?"

"No idea. I didn't want to ask."

"So you and Westley are going out for a drink?"

Was there a note of jealousy in his voice or was she imagining it? "He said he wanted to catch up, but I don't think he'll call. Once the conference gets started, he'll be busy."

"Do you want him to call? Is there some history between you?"

"He knocked my ice cream cone out of my hand when I was twelve, and he broke my preteen heart by only being interested in my sister," she said candidly.

Ian smiled. "I forgot you knew each other as kids."

"Yes, but he wasn't at all nice to me when we were kids. Although, he just reminded me that I used to be super skinny, with braces and a long red braid down my back. No wonder he wasn't interested."

"He seems interested now."

"Oh, I doubt that."

"Maybe you'll get a second chance," he suggested.

"I don't want one. Westley was always cocky, but he seems even worse now." She paused, looking at Ian. "He didn't like it that the senator was giving you so much attention."

Ian shrugged. "I don't know why. He's on the business end of his father's company from what I understand."

They got into the car and for the next few minutes Ian focused on getting out of the parking lot.

"I do kind of wonder what my father did to Harry," she murmured. "They were best friends for a long time."

"You should ask your dad."

"You know that's not going to happen. And what purpose would it serve? I'm sure my father would spin it in his favor."

"Or he might tell you the truth. He seems very self-aware at this point in his life." Ian paused. "So where are we going?"

"There's a snow park about fifteen minutes from here. They have sleds and tubes to rent. I feel a little guilty taking you away from your conference. Are you sure you wouldn't rather be at the hotel, rubbing elbows with your peers and the leaders in your industry?"

"Plenty of time for that. Right now, I'm happy to rub elbows with you," he said, a sparkle in his eye that told her he wasn't exactly interested in her elbows. "And Tyler, of course."

"Of course," she said, her nerves tingling. Good thing she had a seven-year-old chaperone to stop her from doing something reckless and stupid.

Seven

G od, Grace was pretty, especially with her cheeks red from the cold and her green eyes sparkling with happiness after their recent tube run down a moderately steep hill at Haywood Sno-Park.

They'd been at the park for several hours, taking only a short break to grab lunch in the café before heading back out to the groomed sled and tube runs. They'd taken turns going solo and in doubles with Tyler, who was having a ball. The kid was a bundle of energy; he never seemed to run out of steam. Even now, he was practicing making snow angels.

Ian turned his gaze from Tyler back to Grace and felt a punch in the gut when she smiled at him and dusted the snow off her jacket and out of her hair. She'd had a crash landing on her last run, ending up in the thick snow instead of on the tube.

"That was fun," she told him. "I haven't been tubing in two years."

"I could tell you were rusty."

"You weren't exactly an expert."

"I, at least, know how to stay on the tube," he teased.

"I was distracted by someone yelling *watch out*. Wait, wasn't that you?"

"I was catching up to you a little faster than I thought."

"So you're to blame for my crash."

"I would never admit to that."

She grinned. "Fine. You think what you want—I'll think what I want."

As long as she was thinking of him at all, he felt good. In fact, he didn't just feel good, he felt great. "I can't remember the last time I took a day off to do something like this," he said.

"You mean live life?" she asked with a pointed gaze.

"I guess you could say that," he admitted.

"Fresh air and fun looks good on you, Ian. You should try it more often."

"I might have to do that, Grace." Their gazes clung together and the mood went from light and teasing to something far more serious. "Thanks for inviting me along," he added quietly.

"I think it was Tyler who invited you," she said. "But I'm glad you came. It was fun. You're very good with kids."

"Probably comes from growing up in a big family. There are always a lot of children around."

"Are any of your siblings married with kids?"

"Mia, my youngest sister, was the first to tie the knot last year. Her husband Jeremy has an eight-year-old daughter, Ashlyn, so she's the first grandchild. My parents already love her to death. The rest of us are hoping that dampens my mother's craving to be a grandmother."

"She gives you a hard time about that?"

"If I let her corner me. But it's not so much about me having kids as it is about me slowing down, taking a breath, living life—as you just said."

"She sounds like a wise woman."

"She is."

"Look what I made," Tyler said, jumping to his feet and waving his hand toward the impression he'd left in the snow.

"That's great," he said. "I can definitely see the angel's wings."

"Do you want to make one with me?" Tyler asked hopefully.

Lay down in the cold snow and wave his arms? He suddenly wanted to do nothing else. "Sure. As long as Grace joins us."

She gave a helpless shrug. "Why not? I'm already pretty wet."

"Don't worry; we'll get you out of those wet clothes very soon," he promised, his mind immediately bringing up a tantalizing image of Grace in total naked beauty. He'd love to see if those freckles on her nose ran down the rest of her body.

Grace gave him a warning look. "Do not go there, Ian."

"Are you reading my mind?" he muttered.

"You're not as complex as you think you are," she said, flopping down in the snow. "Let's make some angels."

He lay down on Tyler's other side, and the three of them spent the next few minutes trying to make the best angels they could.

"Yours is the best," Tyler told him as they got to their feet and surveyed their efforts.

"Yours is good, too," he said.

"My dad used to make good angels," Tyler added, shadows taking over his eyes. "Do you think he'll make some with me at Christmas?"

Seeing the kid's desperate eyes, Ian really wished Tyler had directed his question at Grace instead of him. She might think he was good with kids, but that was more with fun activities, not deeply serious questions that he didn't know how to answer. "I know he wants to," he said.

"Do you think he remembers how? It's been a long time," Tyler said.

"Absolutely." His gut twisted at the pain in Tyler's eyes. It was bad enough that Tyler's father wasn't here but knowing that the man was fighting for his life made Tyler's innocent inquiries so much more difficult to hear. "You know what we should do now?" he asked.

Tyler still seemed a little bummed and just shook his head and kicked at the snow.

"We should make the volcano."

Tyler's head picked up at that. "Can we?"

"I have time." He looked at Grace. "What do you think?"

"That's a great idea," she said, giving him a look of gratitude.

"We'll need to pick up some supplies," he said.

"There's an art supply store I use for classroom projects; they should have everything we need."

"Let's go." Tyler ran across the meadow of snow toward the parking lot.

"Thank you," Grace said, falling into step with him.

"I don't know what you're thanking me for; I had no idea what to say. I mean, what if his dad doesn't come back?" he whispered.

Her brows drew together in concern. "I'm trying not to think about that. But the more time that passes between Carrie's calls, the more I worry. I just hope no news is good news."

They were only a few feet from the car when her phone rang. "It's Carrie," she said. "I need to take this."

"Go ahead. I'll get Tyler in the car."

As promised, he got Tyler fastened in his booster seat, then slid behind the wheel. He could see Grace talking, but she'd turned her back to them, and he couldn't tell by her stance what was going on. He hoped it wasn't the bad news any of them feared.

"Who's Grace talking to?" Tyler asked curiously.

"I'm not sure." He turned sideways in his seat so he could face Tyler. "What color do you think we should paint your volcano?"

"Purple," Tyler said immediately.

He laughed. He should have figured Ty wouldn't pick the more accurate browns or greens. But then, he was seven. If there was ever a time to have a purple volcano, it was probably now.

He smiled to himself, thinking Grace had already rubbed off on him a little, with her talk of protecting innocence as long as possible. In theory, he thought kids were better off with truth and education, but looking into Tyler's angelic little face, he found that a lot more difficult to put into practice. It had been much easier crushing his little brother's dreams when he was seven. He hadn't known any better then, but now—now he was more in the mood to make a purple volcano.

Grace got into the car a moment later. He could see the strain in her eyes, and he wanted to ask her what was going on, but he couldn't do that in front of Tyler. So he started the car and pulled out of the lot. "Which way to the art supply store?"

"Take a left at the next street and head down to Highway 50. It's a few miles from here."

As she finished speaking, she drummed her fingers restlessly against her thighs, and he impulsively put out his hand and covered hers. She started, and for a moment, he thought she might pull away, but then her fingers curled around his as she drew in a deep breath.

He held onto her hand until he had to let go so he could turn in to the parking lot of the store.

Once they got inside, he put Tyler in front of a display of fifty different paint colors and told him to take his time picking one out. Then he motioned Grace toward the end of the aisle so he could talk to her.

"What's going on?" he asked. "Was that Carrie on the phone?"

She darted a quick look at Tyler, who was a safe distance away. "No, it was Carrie's mother. Kevin has had another setback. Carrie doesn't want to leave his side."

"I'm sorry to hear that." He'd never met Kevin, but he felt like he was getting to know him through Tyler, and the man really deserved a chance to be a father to his incredible kid.

"Carrie's parents are in Florida, but they've decided to come back to Tahoe so that they can be with Tyler. They should be here tomorrow night. They asked me not to say anything to Tyler until then just in case their flights change."

"That sounds like a good idea. He'd have a million questions."

"None of which I can answer. I'm glad they're coming. He loves them, and he needs family around. Plus, I'm sure he'll be thrilled to go back to his house and sleep in his own bed." She drew in another breath. "I need to pull myself together."

"He hasn't noticed a thing."

She met his gaze. "But you did."

"Well, I've been trained to be observant."

"You are very intuitive, Ian, and I suspect that comes naturally. Anyway, we should get what we need for the volcano. I want to keep Tyler busy, and I really appreciate your help. But if at any point you want to call it a day, feel free. You've gone above and beyond."

"I'm happy to help. Science projects are always fun." He laughed as she rolled her eyes. She might not agree with him, but his words had successfully eased the tension in her face and shoulders. "I have to warn you—Tyler is very much in favor of a purple volcano."

"And you haven't tried to talk him out of it?"

"Surprisingly, no," he admitted.

"Maybe we could label the project: sunset at the volcano," she suggested. "We could even make a sky, surround the volcano with a landscape. If we put it in the center of a box, that might work."

"It sounds like you're starting to like this idea, Grace."

"I am a teacher, Ian. I like kids to push the envelope whenever they can."

"Finally, we're on the same page," he teased.

"Don't get too comfortable; I don't think we'll be on that page for long."

—⟫⟪—

Grace found herself smiling as they picked out art supplies and then headed back to Ian's car. Ian was great with Tyler, and while he'd tried to steer Tyler toward a more accurate depiction of a volcano, he'd been easygoing about the paint choices.

He also wasn't bad to look at, she thought, as he slid into the seat next to her and gave her an intimate look that made her heart skip a beat. If Tyler wasn't talking up a storm about all the things he was going to put on his volcano, she might have been tempted to bridge the distance between her and Ian and see if the kiss she was imagining could possibly be as good as she was thinking.

She shook that crazy thought out of her head as she deliberately looked away from him to fasten her seat belt.

It was just that she hadn't dated in a while, she told herself, trying to rationalize her feelings. But, no, that wasn't exactly it. She'd been on dates; she just hadn't met anyone who made her pulse pound or her palms sweat or who could send those little nervous tingles through her body. She couldn't remember when she'd felt this attracted to a man. It had been a few years at least.

But why this man? She silently groaned. Wrong man, wrong time, wrong place…she never seemed to get it right.

Ian was just killing time before his conference. That's all this flirtation was about, and she couldn't let herself forget that. Although, she might just let herself enjoy it. Because he was leaving. Nothing could happen. She didn't have to worry about next week or next month or next year, and there was something appealing about that.

To distract herself even more, she turned on the car radio.

Ian groaned as a Christmas song rang through the speakers. "Maybe keep going," he suggested.

"Really? You don't like 'Rudolph the Red-Nosed Reindeer'?"

"We're barely past Thanksgiving. And I prefer my music without reindeers."

"Good luck turning on the radio between now and Christmas then. Personally, I think it's fun. It gets everyone in the Christmas mood early."

"I like it, too," Tyler declared from the back seat. "Rudolph is my favorite reindeer. He leads Santa's sleigh. Maybe I'll see him tonight when I look out the window for Santa."

"See what you started?" Ian said.

She grinned. "And I'm not done." She looked back at Tyler. "Should we sing?"

Tyler instantly burst into song, remembering most of the words in the chorus, and she added her voice to his, just because it was fun, and because it would probably annoy Ian. Christmas was her favorite time of the year, and she wasn't going to let a cynical scientist ruin it.

Ian just shook his head and concentrated on the road, but she could have sworn she saw a smile playing through his eyes.

When they got back to her house, she was happy to see the snow in front of the garage had melted. In fact, it had turned into a sunny day, last night's storm only a distant memory. How different it would have been if Ian had come by today instead of yesterday. He never would have gotten stuck in her house. They never would have spent today together. Funny how timing could change anything and everything.

Ian parked in her driveway, and they walked up to the front door together. Grace pulled out her key, but as she looked at the door, her heart skipped a beat. It was slightly ajar. That was weird. She always locked the house when she left.

She looked back at Ian.

His gaze narrowed. "What's up?"

She tipped her head to the open door, not wanting to scare Tyler.

He picked up on her clue immediately. "You know what—I think I left my phone in the car," he said, making up a story on the fly. "Could you and Tyler get it for me?"

"Sure," she said. "Tyler, will you come with me?"

"Can't you do it?" the little boy asked, the exhaustion from the day making him cranky.

"But you're so good at finding things," she told him. "Come on."

"Fine." He set down the bag of art supplies he was carrying and followed her to the car.

She pretended to look for Ian's phone as Ian vanished into the house. She really hoped there wasn't someone inside. She couldn't imagine why anyone would break into her home. She lived in a modest neighborhood, and there had never been any crime. Perhaps she'd just left the door open, or Tyler had. She couldn't remember who'd gone out of the house last. It was probably nothing.

Ian appeared on the porch and waved her forward.

"Looks like Ian found his phone," she told Tyler, helping him out of the backseat where he'd been looking between the seat cushions.

She closed the car door, and they walked up to the house.

"Everything looks good," he told her. "I checked all the rooms. There's no one here."

She blew out a breath of relief. "I must not have pulled the door shut or locked it."

She walked into the house. As Ian had said, everything appeared perfectly normal. "Why don't you go take off your jacket, Tyler? Maybe change into some drier clothes."

Tyler nodded and went down the hall to the guest room. She followed close behind, making sure there was no one in his room before moving into her bedroom.

Everything looked fine, but the hairs on the back of her neck prickled. Something felt—off.

Her gaze caught on the dresser. Her bottom drawer was open a few inches. She hadn't gone into that drawer in months; it held her bathing suits and summer shorts.

She pulled open the drawer. Her clothes seemed messier than usual.

"What's wrong?" Ian asked from the doorway.

"Someone was in here. This drawer was open. It has my summer stuff. I wouldn't have opened it."

"Maybe Tyler did."

"I don't think so. He hasn't even come into this room as far as I know."

"Is anything missing?"

At his question, her gaze moved to her jewelry box that sat on top of the dresser. She opened the lid and saw her mother's emerald ring in its pillowed place. It was the most valuable piece of jewelry she owned. There was also a hundred-dollar bill under a pile of necklaces that was her emergency stash of cash.

"It looks like everything is here," she muttered. "But I still feel like someone was in this room." She wrapped her arms around her waist, feeling a chill that had nothing to do with the weather. "Why? Who would come through my house? And why wouldn't they take anything?"

"Maybe they were looking for something in particular."

Her gaze ran around the room, settling back on Ian. "I can't imagine what that would be. I'm a teacher. I don't have much of value, and what I do have, they didn't take. It doesn't make sense. Maybe I am imagining it. I just left the door open, and that's thrown me off, because I never do that. But today has not been a usual kind of day. The snow day, you, Tyler..."

As she met Ian's gaze, she saw him frown.

"What?" she asked. "What are you thinking?"

"Nothing. Just considering the possibilities."

"Like what?"

"You mentioned what's different about your life: snow cancelling school, Tyler being here, and me showing up with a package from your father."

"That package is still in your car. We never went to the post office. But someone wouldn't break in here because I got a box from my father."

"Maybe you should open it before you send it back. It

could be completely unrelated, but it's worth looking at. If someone broke in to this house and didn't take anything, then they were looking for something specific."

He had a point, but she wasn't entirely convinced.

"I'll get the package out of the car while you think about it," he said.

As he left, she drew in a deep breath and thought she smelled the faint hint of perfume or cologne. *Was she just imagining things? Or had someone really been inside her house?*

Eight

⟶⟶⟩⟨⟨⟵

Ian grabbed Grace's package out of the backseat of his car, his mind quickly computing all the facts he had so far, which weren't many. While there was nothing overtly disturbed in Grace's house, her front door had been open, and her gut told her that someone had gone through her room. The only factors that had changed in her life were this package and his arrival.

Actually, that wasn't completely true. She was watching Tyler, and that was different, but he doubted Tyler's presence would lure someone to break into her house.

Not that he could imagine why this package from Seamus could do that, either. But he was curious about what was inside.

When he returned to the house, he found Tyler and Grace in the kitchen, laying out the supplies they would need for Tyler's science project. He was impressed with her ability to focus on Tyler instead of on the fact that some stranger might have been in her bedroom.

"Do you want me to get started with Tyler while you open this?" he asked, holding up the package.

"What's that?" Tyler asked.

"It's from my father," Grace replied.

"Is it a present? I wish my dad would send me a present."

Ian felt a kick in his gut at the sadness that swept across Tyler's face, and he could see that Tyler's words had given Grace a new perspective on her package.

"Can I help you open it?" Tyler asked as Ian set the box on the table between Tyler and Grace.

"Sure," she said. "In fact, I think it's better if you open it."

"Chicken," Ian murmured, as he sat down next to Grace. "What if it's a snake?"

"Hey, you're the one who likes my father, remember? Do you really think he'd send me something dangerous?"

"No, I don't." Which was why he couldn't imagine the package had anything to do with a possible intruder.

"It's a cool box," Tyler said, as he pulled apart the brown wrapping paper to reveal a carved wooden box with a Celtic knot pattern on the top. "But I don't know how to open it." He turned the box over to look for a latch or an opening.

"You have to solve the puzzle before it will snap open," Grace said, staring at the box as if it were the snake she'd just suggested. Her skin had turned pale, and a tight line drew her lips together.

"How do we solve the puzzle?" Tyler asked.

"I—I don't remember," she whispered. "My dad used to bring me home puzzle boxes from everywhere he went, but he loved these Irish ones the best. You have to move the knots in a certain order along the tracks, or it will never open."

"What's inside?" Tyler asked.

"It could be anything." She dragged her gaze away from the box to look at Ian.

There was a plea in her eyes that tugged at his heart, but he didn't know what she wanted him to do. "Do you want me to try to solve it?" he asked.

"Would you?" she returned.

He could solve it in probably two minutes, maybe less, but that wasn't really the point. He could almost hear

Seamus's voice in his head telling him that Grace needed the journey, not just the end. "I don't think so," he said slowly.

"Why not? Don't you supposedly have a super brain?"

"You do?" Tyler asked in awe. "Like Superman?"

He grinned, Tyler's question breaking through the tension in the room. "Not quite, Ty. And Grace is exaggerating." He looked back at her. "I didn't say I couldn't do it; I said I wouldn't. This is your present, your puzzle to solve, not mine."

"Well, I don't remember how to do it," she said with a stubborn set to her jaw.

"I think you could remember if you wanted to."

She shot him an irritated look. "I don't want to. I want to wrap it up and send it back."

"Why?" Tyler asked curiously. "Are you mad at your dad?"

"It's complicated," she told him.

"Where does your dad live?" Tyler asked, obviously caught up in the idea of Grace having a father who wasn't around.

"He's in Ireland."

"Is he coming to see you at Christmas?"

"No, he's not. We don't see each other anymore."

"Why not? Did you do something bad?"

Grace let out a frustrated sigh, and Ian felt both amusement and compassion for her. Nothing like being peppered with questions by a seven-year-old on a subject she didn't want to talk about.

"I didn't do anything bad," Grace said. "But I'm a grown-up, and grown-ups don't always see their fathers at holidays. It's all good. You don't need to worry about it."

"When I'm a grown-up, I'll still want to see my dad and my mom."

"That's good, because they will want to see you, too." She paused. "Let's get started on the volcano. The puzzle box can wait." She pushed it across the table and looked at Ian.

"I'm going to let you start running this part of the project. I'll be back in a minute."

"Do you want to call anyone?" he asked, as she pushed back her chair and stood up. "About what you saw in your bedroom?" He chose his words carefully, not wanting to alarm Tyler.

She gave a helpless shrug. "What on earth would I say? That I have a feeling..."

"It's a little more than that."

"I need to think about it, Ian."

"Sounds like you need to think about a few things." He tipped his head toward the puzzle box.

She frowned. "Well, all you need to think about is building a purple volcano. I'm going to change my clothes."

As Grace left the room, he smiled at Tyler. "Let's get to work."

For the next hour, he kept his focus on the task at hand, pleased that Tyler had the same degree of commitment. The child was a little impatient at times, but Tyler followed directions well, and he had a great deal of enthusiasm for seeing his volcano come to life.

Tyler actually reminded him a little of himself at that age. Like Ty, he'd been inquisitive, asked a ton of questions, and had high standards for what he wanted to achieve. He was actually still like that, and he wanted this project to be as good as it could be.

As Grace had suggested, they built the volcano inside of a box so that they could add geographic features. Using egg cartons, cardboard, and some clay, the volcano soon began to take shape.

"This looks good," he murmured. "But I'm thinking we should add some more dimensions to the ground around the volcano, some rocks and trees, so that when the lava flows, it will have things to run over and around."

"We could get some rocks from outside," Tyler said eagerly.

"They might be buried under the snow."

Tyler frowned. "There's probably some by the back door, under the roof."

"That's a good thought. We can also look for some pine needles to use for our trees. But why don't we put on a base coat of paint first? While that's drying, we can look for our other materials." He undid the jar of white paint. "Let's start with this. Then we'll work our way up to purple."

"Can I do it?" Tyler asked.

"Of course. It's your project." He handed Tyler the brush and watched as he painstakingly painted the volcano. "Very good."

Tyler put down his brush. "Can we do purple now?"

"We need to let this dry first. We should probably save the purple for tomorrow."

"Tomorrow?" Tyler protested as he rested his head in his hands and let out a dramatic sigh. "That's forever from now."

He smiled. "It's not that long, and we want to make this really good, right? Sometimes that takes time. You have to be patient."

Tyler lifted his head and stared back at him. "My mom always tells me to be patient when I ask about when my dad is coming home. But I really miss him."

"I'm sure you do." His gut twisted at Tyler's words, but he tried not to let the stress show on his face.

"My dad is going to teach me how to throw a baseball when he gets back. He was a pitcher in high school. I want to be a pitcher, too."

"That will be fun. I liked playing baseball."

"Were you a pitcher?"

"No, I played outfield. You have to be quick to chase down fly balls."

"I'm fast. I could be an outfielder, too."

"You can be whatever you want to be." He paused as Grace came back into the room.

"You guys made some good progress," she said approvingly. "I'm impressed."

"We're only halfway done," he told her. "It's going to be

a lot more impressive than this."

"So what did I just hear you tell Tyler—you can be whatever you want to be?" she asked. "Are you encouraging him to be a scientist?"

"Actually, we were talking about baseball." He saw the surprise on her face. "I did occasionally close the books and throw a ball when I was a kid."

She gave him a skeptical look. "How often was that?"

"Usually when my mom forced me to go outside, or my brothers and cousins needed one more guy to play," he conceded. "I liked the game, but it often seemed like a distraction from what I really wanted to do, and that was to learn. As a teacher, you should appreciate that."

"I do. I love being able to show a child something they never imagined for the very first time. It's why I teach."

"Can I go look for pine needles and rocks now?" Tyler interrupted.

"That's a good idea. We're going to build some terrain," he told Grace.

"You can look in the backyard," Grace told Tyler. "Put your coat on first."

"Okay." Tyler slid into his coat and then ran out the kitchen door to the backyard.

"Thanks for taking the lead on this," she said, as she took the seat next to him. "I needed a minute to catch my breath."

"Did you decide what you want to do?"

"Still pondering. I looked through the rest of the house. Absolutely nothing is missing. Maybe I did just leave the door open. I was busy grabbing things when we were leaving. It's possible I didn't pull it shut. And the drawer in my room—I could have randomly opened it without thinking about it."

He could see that she was working hard to believe in her theory, but her instincts and her brain weren't on the same page.

"But," she added, "I think I'll take Tyler to his house tonight. I have a key. Carrie just wanted to make things easier for me by having Tyler stay here, but I'm sure he would be happy to go home and sleep in his own bed. And he has all his things there. Plus, his grandparents will be coming tomorrow night, so he's going to be back there soon anyway."

"That sounds like a solid plan. You have a very analytical and logical brain."

"And you think I got that from my father?" she asked with a dry smile. "You're fighting a losing battle, Ian, and, frankly, I don't know why you're bothering. You don't know my father that well. You met him once."

"You're right. I only met him the one time, but I have admired his work for years. Seamus is a brilliant man, and he has made some amazing contributions to science and the world. That doesn't excuse his behavior as a husband and a father, but maybe you just need to realize that he's not all good or all evil. He's a flawed human, like most of us."

"I do realize that—in my head. But my heart still hurts."

"I understand," he said, seeing the conflict in her eyes.

"I also have a lot of loyalty to my mother, Ian, so changing my mind about my dad feels like I'm betraying her."

"She really wants you to hate your father?"

"Yes, she does. That doesn't sound good, I know, but I think she needs me to back up her hate. That's why she asked Jillian and me to change our last name, and that's why we agreed. It felt like it was us against him. My mother was the person who'd always been there for me and my sister. How could we go against her?"

"I can't imagine having to make that choice," he said honestly. "I think she put you in an impossible position."

"I think she did, too, but she was so hurt and angry, I'm sure she didn't see it that way." As she finished speaking, her gaze moved to the puzzle box.

"You should open that," he said.

"I honestly don't know if I remember how."

"It will come back to you once you start playing around with it. Aren't you a little curious as to what is inside?"

"Maybe."

"I think it's more than *maybe*."

"I'm only going that far for now." She glanced at the clock. "It's almost five. You have a party tonight, don't you?"

"Oh, right." He'd completely forgotten about the opening night cocktail gathering. "That starts at six."

"You should probably go."

"I should," he agreed, but he made no move to get to his feet. A few days ago, he'd been eager to catch up with some of the brightest minds in his field; now he found himself reluctant to leave Grace. He wanted to keep talking to her. He wanted to see her open that puzzle box. And most of all, he wanted to kiss her.

It wouldn't be that difficult. She was only sitting a foot away from him. He could lean over and steal a kiss with only the smallest effort. He could taste the lips he'd spent the night dreaming about. He could run his fingers through her silky red waves. He could pull her up against his chest, feel those soft curves—but all that spelled danger. Grace wasn't a one-taste, one-kiss, one-touch, one-night kind of a woman. And she still had her seven-year-old chaperone who would come barreling through the door any second. He needed to put the brakes on his racing thoughts.

"You definitely should go," Grace said, getting to her feet. "And stop looking at me like that."

"Like what?"

"Like you're starving, and I'm a big juicy steak."

He smiled as he stood up. "Believe me, I'm not seeing a steak when I look at you."

"Ian," she said, her voice a bit breathy, her eyes shining bright. "We can't."

"Kiss?" he challenged. "Why not? I want to. I think you do, too." He could see her glistening lips, as he inched closer to her.

"Because..." She put a hand against his chest, stopping his forward movement. "You know why. You're leaving in a few days. I'm staying. Our paths will never cross again."

"I know that you're right," he admitted. "It is a bad idea. I spent most of last night calculating the odds of wanting more than one kiss from you, and the possibility of stopping at one seemed an unlikely outcome."

"Then we agree, although..." She tilted her head, giving him a quizzical look. "Do you always approach kissing a woman in such a scientific way?"

"Only the important ones."

His honest answer seemed to suck the breath right out of her. "Oh."

"Oh," he echoed, putting his hand over hers where it rested on his chest. The heat of her skin did nothing to dampen the growing need in his body. "But I don't always play the odds."

"You don't? That seems very unscientific and way too risky."

"Some risks are worth taking."

"Even if they open you up to emotional turmoil?"

"You can kiss without emotional turmoil. Kissing is part of a biological drive to mate. It doesn't have to have anything to do with the heart."

"Now you're just talking crazy. Kissing always has to do with the heart."

"Sounds like we need an experiment to test out your theory." He removed her hand from his chest and lowered his head.

She didn't pull away, but her tongue did make a nervous swipe across her lips, which only made him want to kiss her more. He took his time going in for the kiss, enjoying the quick intake of her breath as he got closer.

When his mouth finally touched hers, an explosion of heat swept through his body, and all his scientific analysis went out the door. There was no blood left in his brain for thinking; it was rushing to all the other parts of his body, taking him away on a river of desire and need.

And Grace didn't just let him kiss her. No, she kissed him back with her own fiery heat, opening her lips to his, inviting his tongue inside, taking him deeper, making him want so much more. All of his senses were completely engaged as he wrapped his arms around her and brought her breasts against his chest, her hips against his.

Her arms came around his neck, and even if he'd had a thought of ending the kiss, there was no way she was going along with it. Each short breath in between just sent them back in for another taste, another touch. They couldn't get enough.

He'd told her he could kiss without emotion. Desire and sex were basic human needs, but this felt like more, like the beginning of something...or maybe the end...the end of who he'd once been. He'd always been someone who could walk away and not look back, whose sole purpose in life was to create, invent, develop something new and then move on.

But this kiss, this need for Grace, was as old as time. He wasn't the smartest guy in the room right now; he was just a man who wanted a woman in the worst kind of way.

When Grace finally stepped back and out of his embrace, he felt an immediate icy chill, an almost desperate need to reach for her again. He was still starving, still thirsty, still wanting...

But Grace had taken a few steps away, adding more distance with each step until she was halfway across the room. He could see the sparkle in her green eyes, the pink swell of her lips, the red in her cheeks, the motion of her breasts as she drank in deep breaths of air.

He felt hard and tight and a little pissed off. He wasn't just frustrated; he was angry at himself. He didn't need this. He never should have started it. *What the hell was he thinking?*

"I thought you said you could kiss without caring," Grace said, her gaze raking his. "There's a lot of emotion in your eyes right now, Ian."

"Yours, too."

"I never said I wasn't emotional. That's actually my problem. I usually care too much. This was your experiment, not mine."

"Well, I never make conclusions based on one experiment."

"So you want to kiss me again? If you do, I think you'll like me even more," she said with a cockiness that already made him like her more.

Grace might not care for scientists, but he could see that she enjoyed a challenge. That was something they had in common. They both liked to win.

"And then what will you do?" she continued. "You'll be distracted by thoughts of me when you should be working on your next invention. You won't like that at all."

He probably wouldn't. "You have it all figured out," he said. "But what about you, Grace? Are you willing to risk kissing me again, liking me more—me, a man who stands for everything you hate?"

She frowned at that reminder, as if she'd almost forgotten who he was. And then he was a little sorry he'd brought it up.

Before she could answer, the kitchen door opened, and Tyler came in with his arms and hands overflowing with rocks and pine cones and small tree needles. He dropped some of his load on his way to the kitchen table.

"I got a lot," he said proudly.

"You did," he said, as he realized he'd completely forgotten about Tyler. He saw a flash of guilt in Grace's eyes as well. "We can make some excellent land features with that."

"Can we do it now?"

"Ian has to go," Grace answered for him. When his gaze swung to hers, she added, "Don't forget about your cocktail party."

He had forgotten, and that was because she was a huge distraction.

"And we should think about dinner," Grace told Tyler. "We can work on the science project tomorrow. It doesn't have to all be done tonight."

"But Ian has to help me. Will you come by tomorrow after school?" Tyler asked. "We still need to paint the volcano and you know how to do it the right way."

"I'm sure I could help you," Grace said.

"No, it's our project," Tyler said stubbornly.

The last thing Ian wanted to be was another man disappointing Tyler by not showing up. "I can help you tomorrow," he said.

"Are you sure?" Grace asked. "What about your conference?"

"I'll make it work. I told you before I like to finish what I start."

Her eyes gleamed at the double entendre in his words, but she didn't answer back.

"I'll meet you after school tomorrow, Ty." He pulled out his phone, then turned to Grace. "Why don't you give me your phone number? We'll touch base." He punched in the number she gave him, then gave her his.

"Why don't you wash your hands, Ty? Then we'll get pizza," Grace said.

"Okay. See you tomorrow, Ian," Tyler said happily. as he ran out of the room.

"I'll walk you out," Grace told him.

He grabbed his coat off the back of the kitchen chair and followed her to the front door.

She paused, her hand on the knob. "If you change your mind, we can finish the volcano without you."

"I won't change my mind. I won't let Tyler down."

"He's not your problem."

"I don't see him as a problem, just as a kid who has asked me to help him."

"You're being very generous."

He shrugged. "It's just how it is. When are his grandparents coming?"

"I'm not sure. They said they would call me when they figure out their flights. It will probably be evening, so after school would be the best time for Tyler. I just don't want to take you away from your conference, Ian."

He suspected that she wanted him to say no, wanted him

to let Tyler down, wanted him to prove to her again that scientists couldn't be trusted.

"It won't be too much. I'll have plenty of time earlier in the day to get to panels and speeches that I want to hear. Why don't I meet you at the school and follow you to Tyler's house? You're still planning to spend the night there?"

"I think it's the best plan. I've convinced myself that nothing happened here, but I don't want to take any chances."

"It's probably better if you stay at Tyler's," he said, feeling the same niggling doubt as she did. "What's the name of your school?"

"Whitmore Elementary."

"I'll look up the address."

"Okay. School ends at three."

"I figured."

As they ran out of small talk, their gazes met, and the air sizzled between them. It would be best if he said nothing, but he hadn't been making the best decisions all day. "What happened in the kitchen—it wasn't an experiment, Grace; it was a need. But you already know that, don't you?"

"Yes. I wanted to kiss you, too," she admitted. "But we're both smart enough to know that this isn't going anywhere."

"Not everything has to go somewhere."

"But it always does—whether it's a dead end or happily ever after." She cocked her head to the right, giving him a thoughtful look. "You probably don't believe in happily ever after...that's a little too close to miracles and Santa Claus for you, isn't it?"

"I might be more cynical than you, Grace, but I believe in being happy. Whether it's forever..." He shrugged. "Who knows? There are a lot of variables to the *ever after* part. And considering the state of your parents' bitter divorce, I'm surprised you believe in marriage."

"It doesn't totally make sense, I agree. Their divorce made me wary and probably overly suspicious of every man's intent, but I still want what my grandparents had, what my grandmother called a *great love*. She told me so many stories about the love she and my grandfather had. They'd write each other poetry. It was amazing. Obviously, my parents went down a different path, but who's to say I can't follow in my grandparents' footsteps instead?"

"No one."

"What's life if you can't have your dreams?" she added. "I know you have dreams, too, Ian. They might not be about love, but they're still part of you."

"That's true," he murmured. "Although, my dreams are…changing…"

"In what way?"

"I'm not sure yet. I've hit one of those walls where I need to bounce off and figure out where to go next. I've had my head down, pedal to the metal, going full steam after the prototype filtration system I just finished. Now it's done, or at least my part in it. I'm trying to figure out what's next."

"What will be next?" she asked curiously.

He shook his head. "I have no idea. I thought I might get some inspiration this week."

"From the conference?"

He nodded, but at the moment all of his inspiration was coming from her. He told himself that would change when he got back to the hotel, when he immersed himself in science talk with science people.

"Then you should get to it," she said, opening the door.

He knew he should; he just didn't really want to. He was having a hard time forcing himself to walk out of her house. He stalled one more second. "If you have any more problems tonight, call me."

"If I have any problems tonight, I'll call the police."

"Good idea. Then call me." On his way out the door, he stole one last kiss. Her surprised lips parted under his, and he wanted to linger, but he heard Tyler coming down the hall.

"Good-bye, Ian," she said, her green eyes sparkling bright again.

"Just good night, not good-bye. You and I—we may not know where we're headed, but I know we're not done yet."

Nine

After returning to Silverstone's, Ian took a cold shower, spending at least fifteen minutes under an icy stream of water until he cooled down. It wasn't easy. He kept reliving one of the best kisses he'd ever had. What had started out as a challenge had turned into a hell of a lot more.

He'd known Grace would be passionate, but still he'd been jolted by the need that had swept through him. He'd never felt like he had to have a woman until today. *But Grace?* Could he have picked someone more problematic?

Grace was not a woman who lived on the surface of life; she was complex, stubborn—sometimes ridiculously so—but that just made her more interesting. She could be bitter and cynical but she could also be idealistic and optimistic, as evidenced by her kindness to Tyler, her belief in Santa and miracles.

She might judge scientists by her father's standards, but even to scientists—like him—she could also be amazingly generous, allowing a perfect stranger to spend the night in her house because of a snowstorm.

And all those complicated traits aside, she was funny, sharp, and interesting to talk to. She was a challenge, no doubt about that. *A challenge he should walk away from.* But he'd already committed himself to seeing her at least one more time. So, he'd have to walk away after tomorrow's get-together. There was no way he was letting Tyler down just because he had the hots for the kid's babysitter.

He stepped out of the shower and dried off, then got dressed for the conference cocktail party in black slacks and a light-gray dress shirt, his thoughts turning to the upcoming event.

Science was his game, and the people downstairs were the players. They were his people—the people he should be concentrating on instead of one very pretty redhead with dazzling green eyes and a smile that always made him breathe a little faster. He definitely needed to get his focus back to what mattered most, and that was his career—at least it always had been.

When he got downstairs, the grand ballroom was packed with several hundred men and women: scientists, tech experts, CEO's, investors, and politicians. The level of noise was high as everyone battled to get their opinion heard.

He hesitated inside the door, having the strangest desire to turn around and leave. Did he want to get back onto this spinning wheel? He loved actual science, but this part of the job had never been his strength or his interest. Networking was essential to funding and to collaborative projects, but it often felt fake, and he'd never been good at pretense.

Deciding to work his way slowly into the room, he headed toward one of the nearby bars for a fortifying drink. At the back of the line was a man he hadn't seen in six or seven years, but a man he'd once known very well—his grad school roommate, David Pennington.

He'd met David ten years ago when he was twenty-two years old and starting grad school at Stanford. They'd shared an apartment with two other guys for the next three years, and his friend hadn't changed much since then. He still had a big, wide smile, blond hair, brown eyes, and a long, skinny frame that took him up to about six foot four. While David had a brilliant mind, his work ethic was nowhere close to Ian's, but he'd been good at getting Ian out of the library and into a bar once in a while.

"Ian?" David asked, surprise spreading across his face as their gazes met.

"David. What are you doing here?" Last he'd heard, David had walked away from his job to travel the world after the death of his father three years earlier. There hadn't been a funeral, so he hadn't actually seen David at that time, but he had spoken to him on the phone and sent him a few texts. Now, he realized just how many years had passed since they'd actually seen each other, and he felt guilty for not having followed up with David since then. "I thought you were in India doing yoga and meditating," he added.

"I was," David said with a small smile. "Until about six months ago. That's when I met Ahmed Mehati when I was in Mumbai. I'm sure you've heard of him."

"The man who founded Vipercom? Of course, I've heard of him."

"He offered me a job, and I decided it was time to put my passport away for a while, and get back to the nine-to-five grind."

"How's that going?"

"It's all right. I'm better now." He gave Ian a pointed look. "We both know I was a shit-faced mess a few years ago."

"You'd had some rough times. I'm glad you're feeling better."

"I am. My father's death was really just the tipping point. I was burning out on work even before he died, and afterward I just couldn't go back to it. Traveling the world gave me some new perspective. It made me see everything in a different light."

"I can imagine it would. Where did you go?"

"Everywhere. Well, not quite everywhere, but close. What about you? I hear your water project is going to be a game changer."

"That's the plan, if we can get the delivery channels to work, which is a major challenge."

"I hear there's some interest in buying your company."

"It's something I'd consider if it meant bringing down manufacturing costs and allowing us to distribute around the world. My partner is working on that end of things."

"Leaving you to work on what?" David asked with a quizzical look.

He shrugged. "I have a few ideas in mind. I haven't settled on anything yet."

"All water related?"

"It is one of the biggest problems of our time."

"You don't have to convince me of that. But I can see your brilliance being helpful in a lot of areas." He paused as they moved forward in the line. "Are you seeing anyone right now?"

His mind shot to Grace, but he could hardly call their brief acquaintance a relationship. "No. What about you?"

"Very single at the moment, but thinking there might be some opportunities here." He tipped his head toward two attractive women standing near the bar. "Want to be my wingman—like the old days?"

"Not a chance in hell," he said with a laugh. "It's a thankless job."

"Hey, I did the same for you on a few occasions."

"Very few."

"Whoa!" David said suddenly, looking past him. "Isn't that your ex-girlfriend, Brenna Pruitt, talking to Westley Ferguson?"

He turned his head to see his grad school girlfriend in conversation with Westley. He'd dated Brenna for almost a year when he was twenty-four years old. She'd been similarly engaged in pursuit of a PhD, and they had seemed like a good match at the time. But in some ways, they'd been too alike, too single-minded and self-absorbed. Their break-up hadn't been overtly emotional; in fact, their relationship had just faded away. He hadn't seen Brenna in years.

"She looks good," David added. "Feel any old sparks?"

He actually felt completely dispassionate as he looked at

Brenna. She was still a very attractive blonde, with a great figure displayed in a skintight dress and high heels, but he didn't feel anything else. His head was still caught up in a sexy redhead who was having pizza with a seven-year-old right now.

"Ian?" David prodded.

He shook his head. "No sparks."

"Then I'm guessing that despite your claim to not be in a relationship, that there's someone else lighting up your life. Because Brenna is hot."

His thoughts immediately flew back to his kiss with Grace. There hadn't been just sparks with her but a blazing inferno of heat.

"I'm going to take that as a yes," David said with a laugh.

"Take it any way you want." He stepped up to the bar and ordered a beer as David requested a gin and tonic. After they got their drinks and moved away from the bar, Brenna saw them. Her eyes lit up with recognition, but along with that gleam of familiarity, something else passed through her gaze. She pulled her arm away from Westley, as if she'd been caught cheating, which was a ridiculous idea. She'd probably been with half a dozen men since him.

"Ian," she said, coming over to speak to them, Westley following behind. "I had no idea you were going to be here."

"It was a last-minute decision," he replied. "Nice to see you, Brenna."

"You, too," she replied, then glanced at David. "How are you, David?"

"Great. You look good." David added.

Brenna seemed a bit flustered by the compliment, which was odd, since she'd never been uncomfortable with male attention. As a female scientist, she often found herself in male-dominated circles, and he'd always thought she enjoyed it.

Clearing her throat, she said, "Do you both know Westley Ferguson?"

"Westley and I are acquainted," he said, giving the other

man a nod.

David stepped forward to offer his hand to Westley. "I've long been an admirer of your father; I'm David Pennington."

"It's good to meet you," Westley said. "Brenna mentioned that you're working with Ahmet now."

"I am."

"Is he here?"

"Somewhere. I haven't seen him yet."

"I'm looking forward to the panel he's giving with my father."

"Two people at the top of their game," David said with a nod. "I'm not going to miss it."

"I'm going to get a drink," Brenna interjected.

"Let me buy you one," David said. He glanced at Ian. "Are you good?"

"I'm fine for now."

"So how well do you know Grace Donelan?" Westley asked him as Brenna and David left to get in line at the bar.

"It's actually Grace O'Malley. She changed her name after her parents divorced," he said, not sure why he felt the need to explain that.

Westley raised his brows in surprise. "She hates her old man that much?"

"Something like that."

"I guess it makes sense. Her father cheated on her mother. He also stole some of my father's intellectual property when he left our company. Seamus Donelan is not the good guy everyone thinks he is." Westley paused, his gaze sharpening. "How do you know Grace? I thought you might have met through her father, but if she's estranged from her dad, that seems unlikely."

He didn't think it was any of Westley's business how he'd met Grace. On the other hand, he didn't want to make more of it than it was. "I met with Seamus in Ireland, and he asked me to give something to Grace when I came up here for the conference. So I did. That's how we met."

"Really? So that was just a few days ago? You seemed

friendlier than that."

He saw the speculation in Westley's eyes and wondered where it was coming from. "I understand you and Grace used to know each other when you were kids."

"Grace had a big crush on me," he said with a smug smile. "Back then I was only interested in her older sister, but I have to admit Grace grew up all right. She's one fine-looking woman these days. I'm hoping to get reacquainted. Unless there's someone who has a claim on her?"

He felt irritated at Westley's words, and he didn't quite know why. "You'd have to ask her," he said shortly.

"Maybe I'll do that. I wouldn't be getting in your way, would I? If you're hitting on her, just say the word."

"Hitting on who?" David interrupted as he and Brenna rejoined the group.

"Grace Donelan," Westley said.

"Are you talking about Seamus Donelan's daughter?" David asked, an odd note in his voice.

"Yes," Westley replied. "Grace lives here in Tahoe, and Ian was with her earlier today. I was just asking him if he was interested in her, because I definitely am."

David shook his head, confusion in his eyes. "Wait a second. You're talking about dating Donelan's daughter? Isn't the timing a little odd after what happened? I'm surprised she's here and not with her father."

"Why would you say that?" Ian asked sharply. "Why would she be with her dad? She and her father are estranged."

"Oh. I didn't know that, but still, he might not make it, so I just thought that—"

"Wait, what are you talking about?" he interrupted, uneasiness straightening his spine. "Has something happened to Seamus?"

"You haven't heard?" David asked in surprise. "Seamus Donelan was attacked in his university office almost a week ago."

"No. Are you sure?" he asked in disbelief. "I haven't seen anything in the news about that."

"I don't know how much coverage it got here in the States, but Ahmet told me about it a few days ago."

"How badly was he hurt?" Westley asked. "I can't believe this hasn't been on the news."

"He's in a coma and the prognosis isn't good," David said somberly.

"Who did it?" Brenna asked. "Who attacked him?"

"No one seems to know. Apparently, the cleaning crew found him, and one of the men said they saw someone running down the hall, but there haven't been any arrests."

"That's terrible," Brenna said. "Who would want to hurt him? He's a college professor."

"He has a long past," Westley put in, an odd gleam in his eyes. "Who knows who Seamus has pissed off over the years? I bet the list is longer than anyone realizes."

David looked at Ian. "I'm surprised his daughter didn't say anything to you."

"She doesn't know," he replied. "Like I said, they've been estranged for years."

"Still, you'd think someone would have called her," David said.

"How do you know her?" Brenna asked curiously.

"I met with her father in Ireland a few months ago; he asked me to take her something," he said, repeating what he'd told Westley.

"What was that?" Brenna asked.

Three pairs of interested eyes turned in his direction. "I don't know what it was. She didn't open it in front of me. I'm sure it was personal." He really didn't want to discuss Grace with any of them. "Will you excuse me? I see someone I need to speak to. We'll catch up later." As he walked away, he realized his abrupt departure had probably only created more interest in his relationship with Grace, but he didn't care. He needed a minute to think.

He left the ballroom and walked into the adjacent hallway. He paused by the window, debating what to do. Should he call Grace and tell her about her dad? But did he have enough information? He needed to find out exactly what condition Seamus was in.

He opened up the Internet on his phone and put in Seamus's name, pulling up an article from a UK news source about the assault. He realized he'd been so caught up in his work, followed by Thanksgiving, and then Grace the past few days, he'd paid little attention to the news. But there actually hadn't been much news, which surprised him. On the other hand, he sometimes forgot that the scientific geniuses in his world were not of that much interest to the general population.

As he ran down the search items again, he felt both a burning need to tell Grace what had happened to her dad as well as a desire to protect her from more pain. How was she going to feel if her dad died with this distance between them? She might try to say it didn't matter, but she was too kindhearted for it not to matter.

Thinking about Grace reminded him of David's question. *Why hadn't anyone notified her of his accident?* She and her father were estranged, but she was still a relative. Had they spoken to her mother? Or perhaps Seamus had another woman in his life, maybe the woman he'd had an affair with?

Another disturbing thought entered his mind. *Could the open door at Grace's house be related to Seamus's accident?* As a scientist, he didn't believe in coincidence but rather cause and effect. Now the incident seemed like something that needed to be investigated further.

He punched in Grace's number. He wanted to find out where she was so he could talk to her. If she'd already gone to Tyler's house, he'd meet her there. Unfortunately, his call went to voice mail, and he did not want to leave a message.

He slipped his phone into his pocket with a frown. As he turned to go back into the ballroom, he saw Brenna coming out the door.

"You left rather abruptly," she said, a concerned look in her eyes. "Everything okay?"

"I had to make a call."

"To Donelan's daughter?"

"As a matter of fact—yes. She should know about her father."

"I thought you said they were estranged."

"Still…"

"I hope he'll be all right. He would be a tremendous loss to the science community."

"He would."

"So," she said, looking suddenly nervous. "I'm glad we have a chance to talk—just the two of us. I've thought of you over the years, Ian, especially as I watched your career take off. You've done some amazing work, but I'm not surprised. I always knew you would achieve whatever you set your mind to."

"Thanks. What have you been doing, Brenna?"

"I was working at Janus Tech until a few months ago. I just joined Draystar, Westley's company."

He was surprised. "But you're a chemist. Why would you work at Draystar?"

"They're expanding into some new technology," she said with a vague smile.

"Congratulations."

"I hope it will be a good move. It's a little too soon to tell." She gave him a nervous smile. "You look really good, Ian. I'm surprised you came to this, though. You used to be too busy for networking cocktail parties. You said they were unimportant—that the real work was not done over martinis."

"That does sound like me," he admitted. "Unfortunately, since we were in grad school, I've learned that the people who control the funding do require these martini events, so I occasionally show up."

She smiled. "I've missed you, Ian. You were always so real, so honest and substantial. There was never any bullshit with you. I don't think I appreciated that as much as I should have."

He didn't know what to say to that. "Thanks."

"Is there a woman in your life now?"

"No. Not really."

"That sounds like two answers: *no* and *not really*. Can't decide?"

Brenna had always had a sharp mind. He shrugged. "What about you?"

"I was married for two years. I got divorced nine months ago. It was a bad scene," she said, a bitter note in her voice. "I always thought I was smart, you know. Whatever other faults I had, I could always rely on my intelligence, but I was excruciatingly dumb when it came to picking a husband."

"Relationships are based more on emotion than logic."

"I suppose." She paused for a moment. "I don't really remember why we broke up. Do you? It's not like we had a big fight or anything."

"Does it matter? It was years ago." He cleared his throat. "We should head back inside. I'll buy you a martini."

She smiled, and her tension seemed to ease. "All right. I'll let you."

After sharing a large pizza and playing a half hour of arcade games at the pizza parlor, Grace took a weary Tyler back to his house a little before eight. He was thrilled to be going home to his room and his toys.

As Tyler got ready for bed, she went into the living room and unzipped the large tote bag she'd brought with her. She'd thrown in PJs and something to wear for work tomorrow, along with some toiletries. At least, that's what she'd thought she'd thrown in, but as her gaze landed on the puzzle box her dad had sent, she realized she'd somehow picked that up, too.

Apparently, she wasn't quite as eager to send the puzzle box back as she should be.

Her fingers played around the edges of each Celtic knot. Old memories teased at the back of her brain—happier thoughts about her dad. Did she dare let them in?

Just holding the puzzle box felt like a betrayal to her

mom and her sister—to the family who'd loved her versus the father who hadn't.

She set the box on the coffee table and sat back on the couch, pulling out her phone. She punched in her sister's number.

"Hey, Jill," she said, propping her feet up on the table. "How are you?"

"I'm sore. I just got back from Pilates."

She wasn't surprised to hear that. Jillian had been a fan of workout classes her entire life. If she wasn't doing Pilates, it was yoga, Zumba, or Tai Chi.

"What's up?" Jillian asked.

"Nothing. Just checking in."

"Really? It sounds like you have something on your mind, little sister."

"Maybe," she conceded.

"You know I can read you like a book. So, talk. What's going on?"

She took a breath and then jumped into dangerous water. "Do you ever think about Dad?"

Silence met her question. "Why would you ask me that now?" Jillian finally said, an edge to her voice.

"He sent me a package."

"So send it back the way you've always done; the way I always do."

"Did he send you anything?"

"No, not in several years, but then I wasn't Daddy's little girl like you were."

"I wasn't that, either," she denied. "He was absent for me, too."

"Not when you were little. It's okay to admit it, Grace. You were closer to him than I was. You have a curious mind like he does. He recognized that in you. He and I had nothing in common. So he liked to spend time with you over me. It was what it was."

She didn't have that much of a curious mind, considering it had taken her more than a day to open the package, and she still hadn't actually tried to work the puzzle pieces. On the other hand, she was tempted to open it. Part of her wanted to know what was inside.

"I was just thinking," she said slowly, "that maybe we didn't recognize that Dad's devotion to work actually had a positive impact on a lot of people. It's not like he just left us to go to a bar. He did work long hours."

"You mean when he wasn't having an affair and fathering another kid?" Jillian asked bitterly.

She let out a sigh. "I know he did some terrible things."

"Exactly. So, what's going on, Grace? Why are you trying to excuse his bad behavior now?"

"I'm not doing that, but Dad didn't send me the package in the mail; he had someone deliver it personally, along with a message of how much he cared about us and regretted his actions."

"Nothing you haven't heard before."

Her sister was tough. There wasn't a hint of weakening in her voice.

"Hearing someone else say it was different," she said defensively. "The man who delivered the box is a scientist like Dad. He's a big admirer of our father, in fact. He made me wonder if I was too quick to cut Dad completely out of my life. I mean, we changed our names; we acted like he didn't exist, and he was our father. How many kids do that after divorce?"

"He wasn't around for us, Grace. And we changed our names for Mom. She was the one who took the time to raise us, to love us. He left us. She didn't. It was important to her that we use her maiden name, and I haven't regretted it." Anger ripped through Jillian's voice. "Whatever this guy said should not change the opinions you've held your whole life."

Jillian was right. On the other hand—were they really *her* opinions?

She licked her lips, as she continued a conversation she knew would annoy her sister, who'd already made her point of view clear. "He left Mom, Jillian. We made it about us, but wasn't it really Mom he left? Dad wanted to see us. He wanted to keep in touch. She wouldn't let him. At the time, I was so hurt and angry that I went along with it, but now I kind of wonder if it was the right decision."

"Look, I don't know what you want me to say," Jillian said in a grumpy tone. "You can't rewrite history, but if you want to open what he sent you, then open it. If you want to talk to him, talk to him; it's your choice, Grace. It's your life."

"Mom would hate me."

"Well, you don't have to tell her."

"How would you feel about me making contact? Are you going to hate me, too?"

"I'm not thrilled with the idea, but like I said, it's your choice. I do feel like he left us as well as Mom, and I was always closer to her. But you're an adult. You can do what you want."

"Do you remember those puzzle boxes Dad used to do with us?"

"You mean with you? Yes. You spent hours on those things to find some secret silly message hidden inside. Why?"

"That's what he sent me. I don't remember how to open it. I'm not sure I want to try."

"Obviously, you want to try, Grace."

"It was easier to send things back when I didn't know what they were." She paused. "I wonder how he got my address. He sent me packages and letters when I was in San Francisco that I always sent back, but this is the first time he sent anything here."

"I don't think you're that difficult to find."

"I guess. Do you think that Mom intercepted letters and packages that Dad sent to us when we first left?"

"Probably. She was devastated and furious. She wanted no reminders of him."

She remembered the painful cloud that had hung over all their lives those first few years. "It has been more than ten years now. She's fallen in love again; she's remarried. Do we need to keep the anger going?"

"Look, if you want to open the puzzle box, then open it. But the worst thing you can do is just stew about this," Jillian said practically. "Either send it back or open it, but don't let it just sit there. It's going to drive you nuts."

"That's probably good advice."

"My advice is always good, and you rarely take it," Jillian retorted.

"I do listen to you."

"Not very often."

She smiled to herself, realizing how much she'd been missing her sister. They might have very different personalities, but they'd always had a deep bond that could never be broken. And no matter how much they disagreed, they'd always be there for each other. "So what's new with you, Jillian? Any men in your life?"

"Two actually," her sister said, a lighter note in her voice.

"I'm impressed. You usually can't find one guy you like, much less two. But that sounds like a juggling act."

"Unfortunately, I don't really like either one of them that much. They're both nice in different ways. They just don't make me want to drop everything to go out with them. They don't get my blood pumping, you know?"

She did know, having recently been reminded just how wonderful it was to kiss a man who got her blood pumping in a really good way.

"Grace?" Tyler's voice wafted down from the upstairs bedroom. "I'm ready for my story," he yelled.

She put her hand over the phone. "I'll be there in a few minutes." Then she said to her sister, "I have to go."

"Who was that? It doesn't sound like you're alone tonight."

"I'm not. I'm with a very demanding male."

"That sounds interesting."

She laughed. "Not really; he's seven. I'm babysitting one of my students."

"Oh, Grace, you really need to get a life."

"I'll talk to you later." She set down the phone, but before she could get up from the couch, it rang again. Her heart sped up as she saw the number—Ian. She hadn't thought she'd hear from him until tomorrow. "Hello?"

"Grace, I need to talk to you."

There was an urgency in his voice that made her nervous. "About what?"

"I can't do it over the phone. Are you at Tyler's house?"

"I am. I'm about to read him a bedtime story. Can this wait until tomorrow?"

"It really can't. Can I come over?"

She hesitated, not sure what was on his mind. "Ian, we just said good-bye a few hours ago. It's late, and I'm tired, and I don't think it's a good idea."

"It's about your father," he said, surprising her with his words.

"Now I really don't want you to come over."

"Grace, I wouldn't ask if it wasn't important."

She couldn't imagine what he had to tell her about her father now, unless it was something he'd learned at his conference. "Fine. But give me a half hour. I want to get Tyler to sleep first. He's exhausted, and he has school tomorrow."

"Sure, of course."

She gave him the address and said she'd see him soon. Then she went upstairs.

Tyler wasn't in bed; he was sitting on the window seat, staring out at the night sky.

"Hey, you're supposed to be in bed," she told him.

"I was looking for Santa and his sleigh, like Madeline did in the book."

She gazed out the window and saw nothing but tall, shadowy trees and some really shiny stars. It would be something to see Santa and his reindeer streaking across the sky, knowing he was going to make some wishes come true, wishes like Tyler's—to see his dad come home again. She wanted to believe that as much as Tyler did.

She hadn't heard from Carrie all day and nothing more

from Tyler's grandparents. She kept telling herself that no news was better than bad news, but it was difficult to believe that.

"Come on, let's get you into bed, and we'll read a different story," she said. "We have an early morning tomorrow. No more snow days. It's back to school."

"Just a few more minutes?" Tyler pleaded. "I don't want to miss Santa."

"I don't think he's working tonight. It's weeks before Christmas. He's probably still at the North Pole finishing up with his toys."

Tyler gave her a thoughtful look. "But you don't know for sure, do you?"

"One thing I do know for sure is that Santa wants little boys like you to get lots of sleep."

He sighed. "Okay."

"What do you want to read tonight?"

He scrambled off the window seat and led her to the bed, where he had three books out. "I want to read these."

"All three?"

He nodded vigorously.

"Then we better get started."

He climbed under the covers, and she sat down next to him. "You begin, and I'll help you," she said, wanting to encourage his reading skills.

Tyler started out strong, but his eyelids started to droop, and she found herself finishing off the first story as he fell asleep.

She waited a few moments and then carefully got off the bed. She tucked in the covers and put all the books on the night table.

Tyler was a little angel, she thought, her heart stirring with both love and a little fear for Tyler's future. She wanted only good for him, and that meant both of his parents had to come home.

She walked to the door and turned off the light just as she heard a car pull up out front.

Her nerves immediately jumped, and she moved quickly downstairs. She had no idea what to expect from Ian, but she had a feeling something important was about to happen.

She didn't know what Ian had to tell her about her father, but that wasn't the only thing she was worried about. It was seeing him again. It was the kiss she could still taste on her lips. It was the way his eyes looked into her soul. It was about how much she wanted to kiss him again, to touch him, to be in his arms.

Oh, Lord, she really needed to get a grip. She drew in a breath and came up with a plan. She'd hear what he had to say and then she'd send him away—without a kiss, she told herself firmly.

But as soon as she opened the door and looked into his striking blue eyes, she wanted nothing more than to fling herself into his arms.

His words stopped her.

"I'm afraid I have some bad news," he said, stepping inside the house and shutting the door behind him. "Where's Tyler?"

"He's upstairs. He's asleep. What's the bad news?" Her heart was now beating faster for another reason. "Has something happened?"

"I'm afraid so. I was at the conference cocktail party, and your father's name came up."

Her muscles tightened. "I don't want to hear about my dad."

"You have to hear this, Grace. Your dad was attacked in his office last week. He has serious head injuries. In fact, he's been in a coma for a week."

"What?" she gasped, putting a shaky hand to her mouth. "I—I don't understand. Someone told you this?"

"Yes, and then I looked it up online. I probably would have seen it sooner, but I haven't been on the Internet much the last few days."

"Is he going to be all right?"

His gaze was honest and grim. "I honestly don't know."

"You said someone attacked him in his office at the university? Who would do that?"

"I wish I had an answer for you. I thought you should know."

She felt suddenly weak, dizzy, unstable. She might have gone down if Ian hadn't put his arms around her.

"I've got you," he said, his husky voice in her ear.

She put her head against his chest. He felt solid and safe. And she wanted to stay there forever. But she couldn't. She had too many questions. She lifted her head and looked into his eyes. "What should I do?"

Ten

Ian usually liked questions. He prided himself on being able to solve problems that baffled others, but Grace's question was different. It was filled with emotion and drama, and the right answer eluded him, but her green eyes were frightened and pleading, and he couldn't resist trying to help. "You could call the hospital."

"I changed my name. I'm not a Donelan anymore."

"That doesn't make you any less his daughter, Grace."

She licked her lips. "It's the middle of the night there now."

"There's always someone awake in a hospital." He paused. "Or you could call your mother—your sister—see if one of them will do it."

"I just talked to Jillian. She's still really angry with my dad. And my mom..." She shook her head. "It has to be me." Then she frowned. "Why didn't anyone call me? Why didn't the hospital or the police? I know Jillian doesn't know. She would have said something."

He shrugged at another question he couldn't answer. "Maybe they didn't know where any of you are."

Guilt ran through her eyes. "We did cut all our ties."

She pulled out her phone, her hand shaking. "I don't

know which hospital. I don't know the number. I don't know—"

He cut her off, taking the phone out of her hand. "What's the hospital nearest the university?"

She blinked a few times, then said, "St. Mary's."

He searched for the number, then punched it in and handed her phone back as the call rang through on speaker.

She drew in a deep breath. "Hello," she said as the operator answered. "I'm—I'm looking for information on my father's condition."

"One moment," the woman replied.

The next person to come on the line said, "Patient Services."

"I'm looking for information on my father's condition," Grace repeated. "His name is Seamus Donelan. He was admitted last week."

"And your name?"

"Grace Donelan; I'm his daughter."

"I'm going to transfer you to the nurse's station; they'll be able to answer your questions."

Ian stayed close as Grace swayed a little. "Do you want to sit down?" he asked, while they waited for the call to go through.

She shook her head. "I'm okay." She straightened as another voice came on the line.

"You're asking about Seamus Donelan?" the woman questioned.

"Yes. I'm his daughter, Grace. Can you tell me how he's doing?"

"His condition is unchanged. He suffered a serious head trauma. He's been unconscious since he was brought in."

"Is he..." Grace licked her lips. "Is he going to be all right?"

"I'm sorry. We don't know yet. Until the swelling goes down, and he wakes up, we won't be able to determine the extent of the damage."

"Who is his doctor? When will he be in? I'd like to speak

to him. I don't know why anyone in the family wasn't notified."

"Alan Merrick is his physician. He'll be in at eight. I can have him call you. However, Dr. Merrick did relate all pertinent medical information to your mother several days ago."

"What?" Grace asked in astonishment. "He spoke to my mother?"

"He spoke to Patricia Donelan Carmichael. Is that your mother?"

"Yes, it is. I—I didn't realize. Thank you."

"No problem."

She disconnected the call and looked back at him through confused eyes. "I don't understand. My mother was notified, and she didn't tell me or Jillian. At least, I don't think she told Jillian. Maybe my sister was in on keeping the secret, but on the other hand, she's not that good at keeping secrets, and I just talked to her."

Anger joined her bemusement, and he had a feeling her sister and mother were about to get an earful.

"My father could be dying, and no one told me," Grace added. "How could my mother not say anything?"

"When did you last talk to your mom?"

"Thanksgiving. We didn't spend the holiday together. She was in Hawaii, and Jillian went skiing with a college friend, so we all did our own thing this year. But I wished her a happy holiday, and she never said a word about my dad."

"Maybe she didn't find out right away."

"But she's known for a while, and she knows how to reach me."

"Is it that surprising? From what you've told me, your mother has never wanted you to have a relationship with your father. She probably didn't want to worry you or get you involved."

"I'm sure that would be her reason, but it's not right."

She walked into the living room and sat down on the couch. She drew in a breath, then blew it out as he took a seat across from her.

"Sorry to be the bearer of bad news," he told her. "I debated whether or not I should tell you tonight or tell you at all."

"You were right to tell me. I needed to know."

He was immensely relieved that she felt that way. "Okay, good."

"But what do I do now? Do I go there? Do I stay here?" She paused. "What if he dies? What if he never wakes up? What if I never see him again?" She jumped back up to her feet, obviously too agitated to sit.

He sat back in his chair as she paced around the room. He let her walk off the adrenaline. There was nothing he could say to talk her down; she needed to get there on her own.

Finally, she came back to the couch. "You probably think it's weird that I'm so upset when I've spent the last couple of days telling you how I don't need him in my life, that I cut him off a long time ago, that I didn't even want to open the package that he sent me."

"I think that your relationship is complicated."

"That's an understatement. I don't really know how things got so tangled up."

"Maybe you'll be able to figure that out once you untangle them."

"How do I do that now? He's in a coma. He has a brain injury. Even if he wakes up, he might not even know who I am."

"True, but he's only part of the tangle."

"You're talking about my mother."

"She seems like a good place to start," he admitted.

Grace glanced down at her watch. "She hates when I call her after nine, but I need to talk to her."

As she grabbed her phone again, a noise came from upstairs, like someone had knocked over something.

Grace immediately frowned. "Tyler is supposed to be asleep."

"I'll check on him. You make your call."

"You come right back if something is wrong," she ordered.

"I promise. Tyler probably just got out of bed to go to the bathroom."

He jogged up the stairs and down the hall, passing Tyler's parents' bedroom on the way. When he entered Tyler's room, the lights were out, but he could see the little boy sitting in the window seat, looking out the window. He stepped back into the hall and yelled downstairs. "Everything is fine, Grace. Ty is just looking at the sky."

"Thanks," she yelled back. "Tell him to go to bed."

He returned to the bedroom, walking over to the window. "Grace said you're supposed to be in bed, Ty."

"I woke up and I thought I should look for Santa one more time," Tyler told him, an earnest look in his eyes.

He sat down on the window seat next to him, the moonlight showing the worry in Tyler's eyes. He wished he could find a way to erase it.

"Christmas is weeks away, buddy," he said.

"I know, but the book said if you see Santa before Christmas, you'll get your wish."

"You know that's just a story."

"But it could come true. Have you ever seen Santa?"

"No, I never have." At least he could answer that question honestly.

"Well, I will," Tyler said, a little defiance in his voice. "I have to. I have to get my wish."

"I think..." He chose his words carefully since he was stepping into territory that was foreign to him, but he felt compelled to go there to save Tyler from more worry, more fear, more pain. "I think wishes are heard no matter where you are and what you see. They come from the heart. They go out to whoever needs to hear them."

Tyler stared back at him, considering his words. "So if I don't see Santa, I'll still get my wish?"

"I think Santa knows what your wish is," he said, trying

not to lie but also not to lead Tyler too far down another path.

"I want my dad to come home, Ian."

"I know."

"He told me that when he looks at the stars at night—wherever he is—he can picture me sitting in this window looking at the same stars. It's like we're together."

His heart tore at Tyler's words. "Then you're together right now."

"But I wish he was here. It's been forever."

"Your dad wishes that, too," he said quietly. "He'd probably also wish for you to be in bed, getting your sleep, because you have school tomorrow. And we have to finish our volcano after that, so you've got a busy day ahead of you."

"Okay. Where's Grace?" Tyler asked, as he got up from the window seat and walked over to his bed.

"She's on the phone. She's right downstairs."

"Are you going to tell her I got out of bed?"

"I'll tell her you're back in bed, and you're going to stay there. How about that?"

Tyler gave a happy nod and then slid under the covers. As Ian said good night and turned out the lights, he was assailed with the oddest feeling. It felt almost *wistful*.

He'd never thought much about having a wife or children. He wasn't against it, but it wasn't in the immediate cards. Work was always at the top of the list. But being with Tyler was making him wonder what kind of father he would be. As he walked down the stairs, he could almost see himself in that role, which then made him think about being a husband—but who was his wife?

A beautiful redhead flitted through his mind.

He paused at the bottom of the stairs, hearing Grace's voice on the phone. And for more than one reason, he decided to give her a little space. Turning down the hall, he headed into the kitchen for a cold drink.

"Mom, we have to talk about something important," Grace said forcefully. The first five minutes of the call had been all about her mother's annoyance that she was calling so late and then she had segued into her additional annoyance about some lost necklace that she was sure someone from the airlines had stolen during their recent trip to Hawaii. Her mother had always had a lot to say about everything, and Grace usually had more patience for her problems, but not tonight. "Mom, stop," she said, cutting off her mother in mid-sentence. "You have to tell me what's going on with Dad."

Silence followed her words. *Well, she'd finally found a way to shut her mother up.*

"What are you talking about?" Tricia asked warily.

"You know what I'm talking about. Dad was assaulted. He's in the hospital. They told me they filled you in on his condition days ago."

"How did you hear about it?"

"I heard the news from someone who knows Dad. I should have heard it from you. Why didn't you call me?"

"I didn't want to upset you until I knew what was going to happen."

"What was going to happen?" she echoed. "It already happened, Mom. Dad is hurt and apparently badly. He might not wake up." Her stomach clenched at the thought.

"I was trying to protect you, Grace. Your father hurts you, and I bandage you up. That's what I've always done."

That was a pretty big generalization, but at the moment she was more concerned about her father's condition. "What exactly did the doctor tell you? Is Dad going to survive? Will he be all right? Will he have any—any brain damage?"

Her mother drew in a swift breath. "I don't know. There's swelling on his brain. They won't know the extent of his injury until it goes down."

That didn't sound good. "What about the assault? What happened? Did you talk to the police about it?"

"Yes, a detective called me a few days ago. He said that the university cleaning service probably saved your father's life, because whoever attacked him went running when they came down the hall."

"Did they see who it was?"

"Just a man in dark clothes and a cap or a hood, no other identification. There was nothing caught on the security cameras in the building; in fact, two of them were disabled."

"Disabled? That doesn't sound like the work of a disgruntled student."

"I honestly don't know what your father was involved in. I told the police I hadn't spoken to him in more than ten years."

"But he was just a teacher—a professor. What would he be involved in?"

"He's a teacher now, but over the years…who knows?"

She frowned at her mother's words. "It sounds like you actually know more than you are saying."

"I really don't, Grace. Obviously, I never knew your father well. If I had, I might have realized he was cheating on me and that he had another family tucked away. I told the detective that he should speak to Seamus's mistress, not me, but apparently, she's no longer in Waterford."

"So they're not together?" She'd wondered over the years if her father had ended up with his lover and their child. She'd even been a little curious about that child, the brother she'd never known.

"I have no idea," her mother said. "The detective said he spoke to her over the phone, but according to her, she hadn't had any contact with Seamus in several years."

"I always thought he was with her—all these years," she murmured. "I thought he was with *them*."

"Yes, well, I'm not surprised he ended up alone. The only person Seamus really cared about was himself. I'm sure she figured that out at some point."

"I don't want this to be the end, Mom," she said, suddenly terrified by that thought. "I know he did some terrible things, and he hurt us all, especially you, but I don't want him to die."

"There's nothing any of us can do, Grace."

"Do you think I should go see him?"

"No," her mother said with vehemence in her tone. "I don't want you near whatever got him hurt. Someone attacked him. Who knows what kind of trouble your father is in? And there's no point anyway. He's unconscious; he wouldn't know you were there. Promise me, you will not get on a plane to Ireland."

She hesitated and then said, "I won't do it unless I feel I need to."

"No, Grace, you can't go."

"I don't know what I'm going to do, but there's one thing that has to happen: you need to tell Jillian, or I will. She has a right to know." She didn't think Jillian would want to rush to her father's side, but her sister should have the opportunity to make that decision for herself.

"I'll tell her tomorrow," her mother said with weary resignation.

"And you'll let me know immediately if you hear something else? No more hiding information to protect me. I'm a grown woman now."

"I know, but you'll always be my baby. How is everything else going, Grace? Are you going to be able to come home for Christmas?"

She didn't want to tell her that the new house her mother shared with her second husband didn't feel at all like home. "I should be able to come down to San Francisco for Christmas," she said. "Jillian and I were talking about getting a hotel room in Union Square for Christmas Eve."

"Don't be ridiculous. You can both stay with me."

"We'll see. We'll talk before then."

"Please don't be mad at me, Grace," her mom said. "I did what I did out of love. I hope you know that."

"I do know that," she said, although inwardly she couldn't help thinking that love wasn't really a reasonable defense for every action, but she was too worked up about her father to start something with her mother. "I'll talk to you tomorrow." As she set down her phone, she saw Ian hovering in the hallway, and she motioned him into the living room.

He sat down next to her and handed her a cold bottle of water.

"Thanks," she said, opening the bottle and taking a much-needed sip.

"What did your mom say?"

"She didn't have much additional information to give me. She did tell me that apparently my father doesn't see his mistress or his son anymore. I guess he really is alone now." She knew she shouldn't feel one iota of sympathy for him, but somehow she did.

"What about the attack? Did the police tell your mother what happened?"

"Not really. They said his life was probably saved by the cleaning service, who apparently interrupted the assault. There was a man spotted running away, but the security cameras were broken, and he got away."

"That's not good."

"No," she said, as fear crept up her spine. She couldn't imagine why someone would want to hurt her father. "I don't understand why this happened. It doesn't feel random."

"Oh, I don't think it's random, Grace."

She frowned, wishing there was more doubt in Ian's voice. "But who would want to hurt him?"

"Maybe that wasn't the goal—just the consequence."

"You're saying that they went into his office for another reason?"

"It was after hours, late in the evening. It's possible they thought he would be gone by then."

"Which would imply they were looking for something in his office." She paused. "When I said to my mother that Dad was just a teacher, she made some comment about now he was a teacher, but before that who knows what he was involved in. Do you know what my dad used to be involved in, Ian?"

"I know some of his work, but he's been out of the public

eye for almost as long as you've been estranged from him. It's difficult to imagine what he would suddenly have now that he didn't have years ago."

"That's true." She thought for a moment, surprising herself with where her mind was going. "What if we looked into it?" she said slowly, meeting his gaze. "What if we talked to some of Dad's friends? Some of them are here in Tahoe. I could ask Harry. He probably knew my dad better than anyone. He and Westley said my dad betrayed them. I should find out exactly what he did to them."

"That could be a place to start."

Her brows drew together as she thought about the Fergusons. "Did Harry tell you about my dad's attack?"

"No, that was an old friend of mine—David Pennington. Westley was also there and seemed just as surprised as I was. I think the news is just now getting out in the science community."

"Why did it take so long? I thought you said my dad was a superstar."

"I also said he's been off the public radar for a while."

She sat back against the couch and blew out a breath. "I feel like I just ran a marathon, but it was all in my head."

Ian smiled at her, that warm, sexy smile that made her breath catch in her chest. She'd told herself earlier that she needed to keep her distance, but here he was again, and the last thing she wanted to do was send him away.

He looked good, too, in his cocktail attire, his face cleanly shaven, his skin hinting of a musky cologne. The other women scientists were probably fighting over him. And that's the kind of woman he should end up with—someone from his world, someone he could really talk to, someone who might even work with him. He certainly wasn't going to settle down in Lake Tahoe with a second-grade teacher who didn't respect his profession.

But she did respect him. How could she not? He wasn't just smart; he was also generous, compassionate, and kind. He'd left his own party to tell her something she needed to know, and she appreciated that so much. She was tired of other people deciding what she should and shouldn't know—like her mother had always done, and even Jillian, to some extent. But Ian had given her the truth.

She licked her dry lips, drawing his gaze to her mouth.

Not the best idea.

She cleared her throat, feeling a different sort of tension now. "You should go back to your party, Ian."

"It's probably over by now."

"What do you have going on tomorrow?"

"The keynote speech is at nine. Then there are some group meetings, demonstrations, talks—usual conference stuff."

"Sounds boring."

His eyes sparked with amusement. "Actually, it's quite interesting—if you like that kind of thing, which I do."

"I know." She let out a sigh. "Maybe after I get Tyler situated with his grandparents, I can talk to Westley about what he's heard and what he might know."

Ian frowned. "You should be careful."

"Around Westley? Why? I've known him since I was a kid."

"Actually, you haven't known him *since* you were a kid. I don't like him or trust him."

She frowned. "He's the best contact I have. I'm likely to get more information out of him than his father. Why don't you like him?"

"Gut feeling."

"I thought you scientists went by facts, not by gut feelings."

"Instinct can also be important. And my instinct where Westley Ferguson is concerned is ringing alarm bells."

"Well, I don't think he's so bad."

"You still have a crush on him?" he asked, not looking too happy about that possibility.

"Don't be ridiculous," she said.

"Why not? He's single. You're single. And you had a

thing for him."

"When I was twelve. I'm not interested in dating him, just getting some information on my father."

"I'll see what information I can find at the conference tomorrow. We can touch base after school when we meet up to finish the volcano."

"You're still going to do that?"

"I made Tyler a promise. I don't break my promises."

"I appreciate that. He really likes you. And you're keeping him distracted while his mom is gone."

"I like Tyler. And I like you, too, Grace."

She drew in a quick breath. "You always surprise me with how honest you are, Ian."

"I know. I can't seem to stop crushing kids' dreams or telling the truth," he said with a wry smile. "It's a bad habit."

"Actually, it's refreshing. It's probably why I like you, too."

"So what do you want to do about it?" He put a hand on her shoulder, the heat from his fingers burning through her top.

"So many things," she said a little breathlessly. "Some good. Some bad. Some crazy."

"Sounds intriguing. Tell me more."

She shook her head. "I shouldn't."

"If you don't want to tell me, show me." He covered her mouth with his as her lips parted in protest.

She meant to push him away, but she just couldn't. After a quick breath of surprise, she went all in on the kiss. *Had it only been a few hours since they last kissed?* It felt longer than that.

Need burned through her, overwhelming all the confused emotions of the last hour. It was just her and Ian. His mouth. His hands. His body so close to hers. She didn't want to think about anything else.

She cupped his face with her hands as she kissed him, then ran her hands down to his shoulders as she pulled him closer.

"God, Grace," he whispered. "You're on fire."

"I think that's you."

"Or it's us," he murmured, coming back for another passionate kiss.

His hands slipped under her top, his fingers roaming across her bare back, and she wanted that same touch on her breasts, her stomach, her thighs, the most tender part of her body. But as their kisses grew more passionate, the narrow couch became too small, and suddenly she was falling off the couch with Ian landing next to her.

She stared at him in shock.

He had the same bemused expression on his face.

She smiled and then started to laugh.

He grinned back at her. "The floor works for me, too."

"Not for me," she said, pushing against his chest as he came in for another kiss. She scrambled away from him and got to her feet. "Tyler is upstairs. This isn't my house. I don't know what I was thinking."

He rose more slowly. "You're killing me, Grace."

She drew in a breath and let it out. "I know, but this isn't the time."

"You're right," he said. "But you didn't have to shove me off the couch to get my attention."

"I didn't push you off the couch. That was just a little too much—enthusiasm."

A smile played across his lips. "I liked your enthusiasm." He gave her a kiss so quick she couldn't complain. "I'm going to go now."

"I think that's best," she said, her body still telling her brain to shut up and have some fun.

But Ian was already moving away, and she had to let him go. He paused at the door. "I'll see you tomorrow, Grace. If you need me before then, call me."

As he walked out of the house, she was tempted to grab her phone and punch in his number right this second, because every nerve ending in her body said she needed him.

She had to fight hard to get past that urge. She told

herself it was better this way. A little frustration now was better than pain later. She needed to remember that he was always going to leave, no matter how long he stayed. It was never going to be forever.

Eleven

※

Grace went to bed with Ian's image in her head, but somewhere along the way, her dreams moved into the past.

It was a Saturday night. Her parents were young and having a dinner party with their friends. The Fergusons were there, Harry and his wife Pauline. The Conovers from next door—Bryce and Lila—were also present. She and her sister Jillian had snuck downstairs to spy on them. The adults were drinking wine and laughing. Her father gave her mother a playful kiss on the cheek.

There'd been love between them then. When had it ended?

The images in her head grew dark, desolate. She heard her mother pacing the floor late into the night. Finally, the slam of the front door, her mother's voice raised in anger, her father's voice raised in weariness.

There were accusations, then the sound of agonizing sobs. She'd been torn between burying her head under the covers or going to her mother. In the end, she hadn't left her room. She hadn't wanted to know the result of another fight. She'd been too afraid of an end she'd been fearing for years.

It came the next morning.

They'd packed up their rooms and gotten on a plane and

gone to her grandparents' house in San Francisco. She'd barely had a chance to say good-bye to her friends. While she'd been to the city before to visit her mom's family, it had still been a culture shock. She'd been hurt, angry, unsure, lonely, homesick...so many emotions had filled that first long, terrible year.

Eventually, she'd made friends, gone to college, gotten a teaching credential and built a life for herself. Three years ago, she'd moved up to the mountains and found a cute house to rent and more friends and felt like she was finally happy, finally free of the past.

Then Ian showed up.

Now Ian was back in her dreams, looking handsome, sexy, and desirable. And now she tossed and turned for another reason. She remembered the feel of his hands on her body. She could still taste his mouth on her lips and inhale the sensual scent of his cologne.

She kicked at the covers, feeling a desperate need in her body that made her restless and angry with herself. *Why had she sent him away? Why did she always play it safe?*

She could have had him tonight. But when they'd tumbled off the sofa, the hard floor had shocked her brain into working again. If that hadn't happened, maybe she would have kept going.

But she would have regretted it—wouldn't she?

Or would it have been an amazing night? Possibly, the most amazing night of her life?

Her subconscious brain put them in bed together now. She could feel him beside her: his strong, fit body, pressing her against the mattress, his compelling eyes creating an irresistible pull, his possessive hands roaming her body, his greedy lips on hers.

She tightened her fingers around the sheet, wishing it were real, but it wasn't, and as light pressed against her lids, her eyes finally opened.

It was morning. She felt a wave of relief despite her still racing heart and unfulfilled needs. Reality was back. Today would be a normal day. She'd be in her classroom, teaching her students. Later tonight, Tyler would be with his grandparents, and she would be free.

The thought of not having her little chaperone was both exciting and terrifying. She wouldn't be able to use Tyler as an excuse...

But who was she kidding? Today would also be a normal day for Ian. He'd be networking with his science friends and getting ready to change the world in some way. She trusted that he'd keep his promise to finish Tyler's volcano after school. But after that, his commitment would be done. They'd say good-bye, and that would be it.

Exhausted by all her thoughts, she rolled out of bed, showered and dressed and changed the sheets on the bed for Tyler's grandparents. Then she went down the hall to Tyler's bedroom.

Tyler was still asleep. He was half in and half out of the covers, as if he'd also had a restless night. She'd checked on him before she'd gone to bed last night and he'd been asleep, but she had no idea if he'd woken up and spent more hours looking for Santa through the windowpane. She hoped not.

She decided to give him a few more minutes, so she went downstairs into the kitchen and started the coffeemaker.

Her phone rang, and Carrie's number flashed across the screen. "Hello? Carrie?"

"Hi, Grace," Carrie said, a deep weariness in her voice.

"How's Kevin?"

"He's not out of the woods, but he's holding his own at the moment. It's really touch and go, Grace. He lost a lot of blood and there's internal damage. They keep thinking they've fixed everything and then something else comes up. But he's too weak for more surgery, so he has to stay stable. The next twenty-four to forty-eight hours will be critical."

Her heart went out to her friend. She couldn't imagine what Carrie was going through. "Kevin is a fighter. He's going to beat this."

"That's what I keep telling myself. I have to keep the

faith."

"You do."

"How's Tyler? How's my baby boy?"

"He's great. We went sledding yesterday, and Ian helped him get started on the volcano project."

"So the sexy scientist is still hanging around."

"Yes. Tyler really likes him. I hope you don't mind. Ian is good with Tyler, and the volcano is coming along nicely."

"I trust you, Grace. If you like him, I'm fine about him being near Tyler. My parents said they should get there tonight. They'll take over for you. I really appreciate you putting your life on hold for me."

"I was happy to do it. I think Tyler would really love to talk to you. Can I wake him up?"

"Is it too early? I'm all mixed up on the time."

"No, I was going to get him up in a minute anyway," she said, heading for the stairs.

"Thanks again for everything, Grace. I owe you."

"You don't owe me a thing. Just bring Kevin home with you."

"Believe me, I'm trying."

As she walked into Tyler's room, he gave her a sleepy look.

"Hey, Ty, your mom is on the phone."

His eyes widened, and he immediately sat up as she handed him the phone. "Hi, Mommy," he said.

She smiled to herself as Tyler launched into a litany of everything he'd been doing. While he was talking to Carrie, she went downstairs and started breakfast. Before too long, Tyler came downstairs and handed her the phone.

"Mommy had to go," Tyler said. "She told me Nana and Papa are coming today."

"Tonight," she said. "That will be fun, won't it?"

"But Ian is still going to help me finish the volcano, right?"

"He said he'd meet us after school."

"Oh, good," Tyler said with relief.

She had a feeling Tyler was going to have as hard a time as she was saying good-bye to Ian. "What do you want for breakfast? Eggs, cereal?"

"I want cereal," he said, walking over to the table.

"Great."

A few minutes later, she set down a bowl of cereal with some sliced bananas and blueberries on top. He didn't immediately start eating, and she could see something was on his mind.

"What's up, Ty?"

He looked up at her. "Is Mommy with Daddy?"

Her heart skipped a beat. "Why would you ask me that?"

He shrugged. "Why don't they want me to be there, too?"

"Your mom is not with your father right now," she said, hoping she'd be excused for the lie, but she could tell that Tyler was feeling left out. "But I know that she wants your dad to come home as much as you do."

"It's taking too long," he complained.

"I know." She leaned against the counter as Tyler ate his cereal, thinking back to all the times she'd wondered where her dad was and when he was coming home. But that had been completely different. Her father wasn't a soldier; he could have come home any time he wanted to. Although, he was someone who had tried to make the world a better place. And now he was hurt, lying alone in a hospital bed in Ireland.

Her mother would say that he deserved to be alone, that you reap what you sow, but she felt torn, conflicted about what she should do. Her mom didn't want her to go to Ireland, and certainly she had a job to keep and Tyler to watch over for at least today, so there was nothing she could do right this second. She'd think about her options later.

Right now, she just really wanted to have a normal, predictable day. But somehow she didn't think it was going to be that way. There'd been nothing predictable about her life since Ian had shown up.

⇒◄⇐

Ian woke up with the dawn and jumped on to his computer, his research target Seamus Donelan. He'd been thinking all night about Seamus. If his attack wasn't random, then it had to be tied to something Seamus had been involved in.

He brought up every article he could find on Seamus and by eight a.m., he'd discovered that Seamus owned seventeen patents, had started five companies, served on the board of directors for three other organizations, and worked as a consultant for another half-dozen businesses. His inventions and interests had ranged from biogenetic engineering to robotics, stealth technology, astrophysics and nucleonics, the study of atomic nuclei.

Frowning, he thought any one of those cutting-edge technologies could have gotten Seamus into trouble. Looking at the list of companies, he saw some familiar names, many of whom were at the conference including Draystar, owned by Harry Ferguson; Janus Tech, the company Brenna had worked at until recently; and Vipercom, where David worked.

There were other names he recognized as well, probably some of whom were at the conference. But he couldn't quite wrap his head around the fact that one of his colleagues, one of the people he admired and respected, could have been involved in an attack on Seamus Donelan. And why now? Seamus had been in academia for ten years. He'd quit everything after losing his wife and kids. So what had happened to suddenly put him in danger?

Whatever it was probably couldn't be found on the Internet, or it would be all over the news. No, it had to be something that only Seamus or a few other people knew about.

His mind drifted back to Grace's open door, her gut feeling that someone had been in her house and gone through her drawers. Had there been someone who'd gone through her home, looking for something that they might or might not have found in Seamus's office?

Uneasiness ran through him. He glanced down at his

watch. Grace would be at school now, surrounded by her students. She wasn't in any danger, he told himself. In fact, he could be completely wrong. The open door could have just been a coincidence—only he didn't believe in coincidences.

He'd just gotten up from his chair when his phone buzzed and Brenna's name flashed across the screen. It had been a long time since he'd gotten a call from her. "Hello?"

"Hi Ian. I was wondering if we could talk."

"Sure. I'm heading downstairs in a minute."

"Can I catch you before that? It's so crowded down here, and there are a lot of people listening in on conversations. I can come to your room."

He frowned, not sure why Brenna felt the need for a private conversation, but he was fairly certain it wasn't a good idea. Still, what could he say? He was somewhat curious. "Fine. I'm in room 1242."

"Great. I'll be there in a few minutes."

He glanced around the room, grabbing his wet towel off the bed and throwing it over a hook in the bathroom. He shoved his suitcase into his closet and closed the door. He'd barely done that when he heard her knock.

He opened the door, and she gave him a bright smile that for some reason felt a little forced. He waved her inside. She wandered over to the window and looked out. "You have the mountain view. I have the lake."

"I didn't think I'd be spending much time gazing out the window," he said.

She turned back to him, and he thought she seemed nervous, which was unusual, because Brenna had always been one of the most confident people he knew.

She did look good, he thought, dressed in a red knit dress that demanded attention, her blonde hair pulled back at the base of her neck, her face perfectly made up, and her blue eyes framed with long lashes. She was certainly more put together than she'd been in grad school, but those days they'd spent more time in jeans and lab coats, living off endless streams of coffee, and the belief that one day they were going to change the world.

"You're staring," she said. "What's the verdict—better or worse?"

"Great as always," he returned with a small smile. "But you already knew that."

"Still—nice to hear, especially from you, Ian. You were never less than honest with me. I don't think I really appreciated that until I met men who were anything but honest."

He didn't want to touch that comment. "So, what's up?"

She hesitated, then said, "I wanted to talk to you about Seamus Donelan."

"What about him?"

"There are some rumors floating around that he stole technology from Draystar."

"What kind of technology?"

"I don't know. I asked Westley; he said he couldn't tell me. But I don't know if that's because he doesn't know or doesn't want to say. Since Seamus was attacked, and Draystar is my new employer, I feel a little uneasy. Is there something I should know about Draystar—about the Fergusons? Did Seamus tell you anything about them or any trouble he was in?"

He was taken aback by her questions. He didn't believe for one second she was worried about her job at Draystar, so what was really driving this conversation?

"Seamus and I didn't talk business," he said. "At least, not in a specific way."

"So he didn't mention Draystar?"

"No, nor did he mention Janus Tech, the last company you worked for, another company Seamus had a relationship with, but I'm sure you knew that."

"But he didn't have a problem with the people at Janus. He was well-loved and very well-respected by the owners of the company. They talked about him quite reverently. Of course, I wasn't there when he was, so I never met him personally." She paused. "How did you come to talk to him anyway?"

"Seamus knew my Irish grandmother. She set up the meeting for us. We spoke about Ireland and education. My great-grandfather was actually one of Seamus's teachers."

"Really? That's interesting and unexpected."

"It surprised me, too." Folding his arms across his chest, he said, "What do you really want to know, Brenna?"

"I told you."

"If you're nervous about working with the Fergusons, then quit. You're brilliant in your field. I don't even know why you'd go to Draystar in the first place."

"I told you they're expanding, and they offered me a lot of money. It was too good of an offer to refuse. Their company is on the rise."

"I don't know what else to tell you."

"I'm probably just imagining things. Despite whatever went down between Seamus and Harry, they were friends for years. Maybe it was just a misunderstanding and has nothing to do with Seamus's attack. He probably had other enemies. People that smart tend to make others nervous, especially when they're working on classified, highly advanced technology."

"Like I said, I really don't know."

"So what is Donelan's daughter like?" she asked, changing the subject.

He shrugged, not sure how to answer that. He certainly wasn't going to tell an ex-girlfriend that he thought another woman was hot. "She's nice. She's an elementary school teacher."

"It doesn't sound like she's as ambitious as her father. Seamus was a star by the time he was twenty-three."

"Seamus had—has—a brilliant mind," he said, not wanting to think of Seamus not surviving the attack. "Why don't we go downstairs? The keynote is starting shortly. I'm sure your new boss would want you to be there. Harry has always liked an audience."

"That's true."

He grabbed his key off the counter and ushered her out of his room. When they got onto the elevator, they ran into Westley.

He gave them both a surprised look. "Good morning," he said.

"Morning," Ian muttered, realizing that Westley was looking at him and Brenna and quickly coming to the wrong conclusion—like maybe they'd spent the night together. But what did he care what Westley thought?

"I'm excited to hear your father speak," Brenna put in as the elevator whisked them down to the lobby.

"That makes one of us," Westley said dryly. "But I'd be disinherited if I missed one of his many speeches." He gave them a speculative look. "So, David told me you two used to be a couple back in grad school."

"That's right," Brenna said.

"What broke you up?" Westley asked, turning his gaze to Ian.

"Nothing in particular," he replied.

"Do you have the same story?" Westley asked Brenna.

"We wanted different things," she said, giving him a bit of a sad smile. "I don't think I realized how great we were together until years later."

"You're both single now," Westley put in. "Isn't that true?"

Thankfully, he was saved from answering as the elevator doors opened on the lobby level. They were immediately thrust into a group of conference-goers, and he was happy when the three of them were separated by the crowd.

As he joined the throng of people heading to the keynote, he said hello to some friends and acquaintances, but his mind was still back on his odd talk with Brenna. Had her questions really been about the Fergusons? Or had she been sent as an old friend to find out what he knew, what Seamus might have told him?

He'd never distrusted Brenna before; he'd never had a reason to. But she'd been acting odd in his room. He didn't know exactly why she'd come, but he was almost certain it had nothing to do with what she'd actually told him. While she'd tried to use Draystar and the Fergusons as bait, he wondered if she was really digging around for information related to her former employer Janus Tech.

Maybe there was someone from Janus Tech at the conference that he could speak to. He had a feeling it was going to be a busy day.

Twelve

Grace felt good to be back in her classroom where she was in charge of her world and everything made sense. She concentrated on her lesson plans and keeping the kids engaged in learning, forcing thoughts of her father and Ian out of her head. The children were in good moods after their unexpected snow day, so she had few behavioral problems. She wished all days could be this easy.

But as the clock neared three, she suspected her stress-free day was going to get more difficult. In fact, it started as soon as the bell rang. She'd just put Tyler in charge of cleaning up some paintbrushes in the back of the room when her phone rang. It was her sister, and she had a feeling she knew just what Jillian had to say.

"I can't believe it," Jillian said, anger in her voice. "Mom just called me. She told me Dad is in the hospital."

"I know. I found out last night. I couldn't believe she didn't tell us before now. She's known for days."

"She said you forced her hand. She didn't want to tell us at all."

"It was wrong of her to keep the information from us."

"She was trying to protect us," Jillian said, her anger turning to defense.

"We're adults. We had a right to know." Her hand tightened on the phone. "He might die, Jillian. Do you realize that?"

Her sister let out a sigh. "I don't know what to think about any of it. It doesn't even seem real."

"But it is real. Our father was attacked, and he's fighting for his life alone in a hospital, thousands of miles away from here."

"Are you going to see him?"

"I've been thinking about it. I'm tied up at the moment watching my friend's child. It's a long story, but I probably can't do anything before Friday at the earliest. I'd have to get someone to cover my class and get a plane ticket. I wish I could just jump on a plane, but it's not that easy."

"Maybe you don't want it to be easy, and you're looking for reasons not to go. I don't blame you."

"That's not it at all," she said. "I'm not looking for excuses. I just have responsibilities."

"Well, it probably doesn't matter. Mom says he's unconscious. Even if you go, he won't know you're there."

"He might wake up."

"And if he doesn't? What are you going to do? Sit by his bed and talk to him? What would you even say? Are you going to tell him you're sorry for leaving, for not answering his letters? Are you going to let him off the hook for everything he did to Mom?" While there was anger and bitterness in Jillian's voice, there was also fear and frustration.

"I don't know," she murmured. "It's all so complicated."

"Look, I'm sorry about what happened to him. But it doesn't erase everything that he did or didn't do, like love us, care for us."

"He did love us," she argued. "He made a lot of horrible mistakes, but I think there was love."

"You always want to think there's love," Jillian said harshly. "You're such a romantic, and I don't know how you can be after witnessing all the anger and pain of our parents' relationship."

"There were some good times early on. I've been remembering them lately. I was thinking last night about the parties they used to have. We'd sneak down the stairs to spy on them. They would drink champagne and gossip about their friends with the Fergusons and the Conovers and then they'd put on music and dance until midnight."

"God, Grace, that was so long ago."

"But it happened. It was real. They loved each other for a while."

"Until Mom saw Dad for who he really was."

"She didn't have to cut him off from us. She didn't have to urge us to get rid of his name."

"Is that what this is about, Grace? You feel guilty for shutting him out of your life?"

"He did end up alone."

"Because of his actions, not yours. You didn't do anything wrong, Grace. You didn't deprive him of a father-daughter relationship that he never actually wanted to have. We didn't leave until we were teenagers. There were a lot of years in there where he could have been a good parent."

Her sister was right about that.

"I don't want you to feel guilty, Grace," Jillian continued. "You didn't put him in that hospital bed. You didn't destroy the family. You didn't betray him by choosing Mom. None of this is on you."

"I wish it were as black and white as it used to be," she said. "But lately, I'm questioning everything."

"So, what are you going to do, Grace? Are you going to Ireland?"

"I'm still thinking about it."

"I can't believe I'm offering this, but do you want me to go with you?"

She was shocked at her sister's words. "But you just said—"

"I know what I said. But you're my sister. If you need me to go with you, I will."

"Well, I appreciate that. I'll be done with babysitting later tonight. Then I'll decide."

"Let me know."

"I will." She set down the phone as Ian appeared in her doorway, wearing dark jeans and a gray sweater under a black coat. God, he looked good. Her mouth literally watered when she saw him, and she had to force some air back into her chest. "Hi."

He smiled. "Am I too early?"

"No, you're right on time. Tyler is in the back, washing the paintbrushes."

As he entered, his gaze swept the classroom. "Your room is very...colorful."

She laughed. More than a few of the other teachers had told her that her classroom put theirs to shame, but she just couldn't help herself. She loved putting up the students' artwork, whether it was paintings on the wall or rainbow streamers from the ceiling, or math puzzles and alphabet blocks on the chalkboard.

There were also books and books and more books, everywhere the eye could see. She'd created a reading corner for afternoon free reading time that was filled with cushions and bean bag chairs. In the opposite corner was an art area where budding creators could express themselves through paint and clay and other mediums.

"I know it's a little much," she said. "I can't seem to stop myself. I see something cute or fun and I want to put it up. But trust me, the kids do some serious learning here, too. There's nothing I like more than opening their minds to something new and interesting."

"Including science?"

"Of course. I'm really not that narrow-minded, at least not when it comes to seven-year-olds and their science curriculum."

"Glad to hear that. We can always use more brilliance coming through the ranks."

"I bet there was a lot of brilliance at your conference today."

"Definitely. Also a lot of blowhards, but don't tell anyone I said that."

She liked that while Ian obviously took his work seriously, he could also be dry and sarcastic. "Your secret is safe with me."

As his gaze settled on her face, her stomach fluttered, and she was right back to where she'd been the night before—wanting to kiss him, wanting to touch him. But just like before, Tyler was really, really close. In fact, he was coming out of the back room, a smile lighting up his face as he saw Ian.

"Ian," he said, running across the room.

Ian looked a little surprised when Tyler literally jumped into his arms. But he caught him and held on. Ian might think of himself as a dedicated scientist, but he looked like a family man right now...*a man she might want in her family.*

"Hey, buddy. How was school?" Ian asked.

"It was good, but I want to finish my volcano now."

"So do I. I've been thinking about it all day." He paused. "Where is the volcano? At your house or Tyler's house?"

"Tyler's house. I took it there yesterday."

"Great. Are you ready to go? I'll follow you there."

"You could have just met us there," she said. "Since you were there last night, you knew the address."

"I wanted to see your classroom."

"Really? Why?"

"I was curious."

"And..."

"It looks like you—warm, welcoming, creative, a little chaotic. It feels like a place where dreams start, and I can't imagine any better environment in which to teach children."

She was actually touched by his description. "Thanks. Let me just check the back room, and then we can go."

"Take your time."

She made sure everything was in good order, then returned to her desk, grabbed her bag, and headed out to the parking lot with Tyler and Ian. Tyler was talking a million miles an hour to Ian, who seemed able to follow the random conversation enough to give an answer when required.

"Sounds like you had a busy day," Ian told her as she got Tyler into the backseat of her car.

"We did accomplish a lot. I think the snow day was a good break. Everyone returned with new energy." She paused. "So you'll follow me?"

"I won't take my eyes off you," he promised.

She flushed at his words, her toes curling at the look in his eyes. Thank goodness she still had Tyler—for at least a few more hours anyway.

True to his word, Ian didn't take his eyes off Grace's car on the short drive to Tyler's house. Nor could he stop looking at her while they shared an afternoon snack at the kitchen table and finished off the purple volcano and its surrounding terrain. Despite the amount of attention that Tyler required, his gaze kept drifting back to Grace.

Unlike yesterday, she was an eager contributor to the science project, and he was impressed with not only how creative she was, but also how often she encouraged Tyler to understand what he was actually building. She was determined to make it a learning project and not just art, and he appreciated that.

They ordered in Chinese takeout for dinner, and while the volcano was drying, they moved on to the rest of Tyler's homework.

He really wanted to talk to Grace about Seamus, but that would have to wait until Tyler was off to bed or his grandparents arrived. Grace had told him that the last text she'd gotten hours ago had said their plane was delayed.

He felt a little guilty hoping that that delay wouldn't prevent them from arriving tonight. He wanted to get Grace on her own, and it wasn't just to talk about her father.

At a little before eight, they heard a car outside, followed by the doorbell. Grace went to get the door, and a few moments later, Tyler's grandparents entered the room. Sally was a short, plump blonde. Her husband, Burt, was a balding man with a big smile. Tyler let out a squeal of delight and jumped off the couch, launching himself into their arms.

As the three of them hugged, Grace looked over at Ian, and he could see how touched she was by their emotional reunion. He knew she wasn't just thinking about Tyler seeing his grandparents; she was imagining the same kind of scene with Tyler's parents. He really hoped that would happen one day very soon.

They spent the next half hour talking with Sally and Burt, but eventually Grace said good night to Tyler, told him she'd see him at school, grabbed her bag, and then followed Ian outside.

Her car was parked in the driveway; his was on the street. He stopped by her vehicle as she opened the back door and tossed her bag onto the seat.

"What do you want to do now?" he asked. "Go back to your place?"

She hesitated, then glanced at her watch. "It's eight thirty. It's not that late. I was thinking maybe I could try to find Westley. Unless you already spoke to him today? I've been wanting to ask you all day if you found out anything about my father, but I didn't want to bring it up in front of Tyler."

"I know. I felt the same way. I saw Westley, but I didn't talk to him about your father. Harry was mobbed after his keynote, so, unfortunately, I didn't get to him, either, but I did do some research into your father's activities before he went into academia."

"Did you find out anything?"

He really wished he didn't have to crush the hopeful gleam in her eyes. "I know he worked with at least a half-dozen people who are here at the conference. I've been told, as you have, that there's bad blood between your dad and Harry Ferguson. But, honestly, any number of his projects could have put him in danger, if that's even what happened.

We still don't know if the attack was work-related or tied to a disgruntled student."

She sighed. "So we're not getting anywhere fast."

"Well, it's possible the police investigating the accident might have more information. Maybe you should try to talk to them."

"I did actually call there this afternoon, but I was told that the detective was out, and he hasn't gotten back to me yet. Hopefully tomorrow."

He nodded. "I hope so. I'm sorry I didn't get you more information."

"Don't be. This is not your problem."

"I want to help."

"I would still like to speak to Westley. Do you think he's hanging around the hotel?"

"Most people seem to be at the bar every evening."

"Then let's do that."

"Okay. I'll follow you there."

"Still keeping your eye on me?" she asked with a smile.

He smiled back at her. "I can't seem to stop, Grace."

-->>-<<--

Grace felt reassured by Ian's headlights in her rearview mirror. True to his word, he stayed right behind her until they parked about five spots away from each other in the hotel lot. He met her as she got out of the car. She shivered in the cold night air, taking a moment to zip up her coat. It wasn't snowing, but it was freezing, and they walked quickly into the hotel.

It wasn't until they neared the lobby bar that she realized her black boots, leggings, and dark-green sweater under her gray coat were well-suited for teaching seven-year-olds, doing yard-duty at recess and building a volcano for a science project but not so much for having cocktails in the fancy bar at Silverstone's.

She paused in the doorway. "I should have changed my

clothes," she muttered.

"You look great," Ian said.

"I don't look like anyone in here." She tipped her head toward the crowded bar area, where many of the women were wearing cocktail dresses.

"Oh, well, some people went out to dinner, but you're fine." He gave her a reassuring smile. "You're actually the most beautiful woman in this room."

"I thought you said you didn't lie," she retorted.

"I'm not lying. When I look at you, that's what I see."

Heat warmed her cheeks. "You can be very charming, Ian."

"And you can be far too modest. Hold your head up. No one holds a candle to you in here."

She couldn't help but be flattered by his appraisal. Did he really see her that way? Or was he just trying to boost her confidence? In the end, it didn't matter. She wasn't here to mingle but to get information on her father.

"Grace?"

She spun around at the sound of her name, seeing Westley approaching. He looked very sophisticated and handsome in his obviously expensive suit and silk tie.

He kissed her on the cheek. "I'm so glad you came over. I still owe you a drink."

"Uh, all right." She gave Ian an apologetic smile and allowed Westley to escort her to the bar.

Out of the corner of her eye, she saw an attractive blonde and another handsome man join Ian. She felt marginally better for abandoning him the way she had.

"What's your pleasure?" Westley asked.

"A glass of chardonnay would be great."

He ordered the wine for her and a shot of whiskey for himself. After the bartender handed them their drinks, he found two open barstools. Clinking his glass against hers, he said, "To you, Grace. To old friends getting reacquainted."

She nodded and took a sip of her wine.

"So how are you?" he asked. "I heard about your father

last night. I'm sorry."

"You don't even like my dad, do you?"

"I still wouldn't want something to happen to him."

His words felt genuine and maybe they resonated, because she felt a little the same way. "I appreciate that, Westley."

"How's he doing?"

"He's unconscious. I don't know much more than that."

Westley nodded. "Do they know who attacked him?"

She shook her head. "No. I feel like it must have something to do with work he did before he started teaching. You mentioned that my father betrayed yours. Can you tell me what happened?"

Westley stiffened. "You don't think my father had something to do with the attack on your dad, do you? Because that is ridiculous."

"I—I don't think that," she said quickly. "I'm just trying to understand what kind of person my dad was. I always heard he was brilliant and well-respected, but I didn't know that guy. And when I heard the other day that my dad had had a falling out with yours, I wondered what that was about."

"I don't know the details, Grace, but my father said Seamus took something from Draystar that belonged to the company and not to him. And he's been trying to get it back for years, but your father claims it's his intellectual property. It's a he-said, he-said kind of situation."

"So your dad never tried to get this back through legal channels?"

"No. He always told me it was a private matter, but that I should never trust anything Seamus Donelan had to say. Quite frankly, I was shocked at the anger and animosity my dad held toward your father. They used to be best friends. On the other hand, your parents used to be married, and I always thought they were good together, so what did I know?"

"I guess no one knows what a relationship is about except for the people who are in it," she said, sipping her wine.

"Ian said you don't talk to your dad."

"Not in ten years."

"But he sends you things?"

"Yes, most of which I send back unopened. I suppose it's his way of reaching out to me." She paused. "Do you know of anyone else who might have a grudge against my father?"

"I have no idea, Grace. Your dad was brilliant, but he was ambitious. You step over people on the way up, sometimes they take you down when they catch up to you."

"I never pictured him as that ruthless."

"Oh, he was—he definitely was."

She didn't really know why she would be surprised by his words. Her mother had said much the same thing. It had just never jibed with the man she knew.

"Let's talk about you," Westley continued. "You're a teacher now?"

"Yes, second grade. I love it."

"You were always good with kids. That summer we spent together, you used to play with the younger children in the sand, helping them build sand castles."

"That's because they let me play with them, whereas you and Jillian used to ditch me."

He smiled. "Sorry about that. How is your sister?"

"She's fine. She lives in Sonoma."

"Wine country—nice. Is she married?"

"Nope, still single."

"Hard to believe no one has taken either of you off the market."

"I don't think of myself as *on the market*, Westley."

He laughed. "Sorry, didn't mean to offend."

"Tell me about you. What's your life been like?"

As Westley happily launched into a monologue about himself, her gaze drifted across the room to Ian. The blonde had vanished, but he was now sitting at a table with a man who looked to be about his age. They seemed to be joking with each other.

The more Westley droned on, the more she wished she

was at Ian's table. She'd had such a huge crush on Westley as a preteen, but while he was still attractive now, she wasn't feeling the tingle in her spine anymore. That seemed to be reserved for Ian.

She really didn't know what she was going to do about him. Fate had put him in her path—actually, that wasn't fate; that was her father. She'd always sent back whatever her father had sent her, but Ian—Ian was different. She didn't know how it was going to feel when he left, but she had a feeling it was going to suck.

"Grace?"

Westley called her attention back to him. "Yes?"

"I asked you if anything was going on with you and Ian Callaway. You came in together tonight."

"We're—friends."

"I've heard that before," he said, sipping his drink, doubt in his eyes.

"What do you think of him?" she asked, curious as to his answer.

"Professionally, he's at the top of his game."

"And personally?"

Westley shrugged. "A little too serious and single-minded for me. He's boring."

She found Ian anything but boring. But since Ian wasn't a fan of Westley's, she couldn't really expect Westley to be a fan of his. She set down her empty glass. "It was nice to catch up, Westley."

"But you're going back to Ian. All the women like Ian," Westley drawled. "You know he's more interested in water filtration devices than relationships, don't you? Do you really want to follow in your mother's footsteps?"

"I wouldn't be doing that," she said defensively. "And, as I said, we're friends."

"Let's keep in touch, Grace," he said, as she got to her feet.

"Why? I live here in Tahoe, and you live—where do you live?" she asked curiously.

"I'm based out of New York, but we have offices in London, San Francisco, and Los Angeles, so I get out to California fairly frequently."

"Well, I don't get anywhere, so you know where I'll be."

"Good to know."

"Good night, Westley." She walked across the bar to Ian's table.

He pushed out the chair next to his. "Have a seat, Grace."

"Am I interrupting?"

"No. This is my old friend David Pennington. David, this is Grace."

David got up and shook her hand. "I'm sorry to hear about your father."

"Thank you." She sat down. "So you and Ian went to school together?"

"Grad school at Stanford," David replied with a sparkling smile. "I was a bad influence on him."

"That's true," Ian agreed. "If there was trouble to be found, David usually found it."

"It found me," David argued. "But when I did get you out of the library, you could usually keep up with me."

Grace watched with amusement as David and Ian bantered back and forth. She liked seeing Ian with his friend. Unfortunately, every new thing she learned about him only made her like him more.

"So, how do you like living in Tahoe?" David asked her.

"I love it. Boating in the summer, skiing in the winter, long hikes in the fall and spring. It's great."

"We should all go skiing," David suggested. "I was thinking about tomorrow afternoon. There's a break in the workshop schedule. What do you say?"

"I work until three thirty," she said. "It's pretty late to head up the hill for me. You guys should go."

"What do you think, Ian?" David asked. "Feel like playing hooky with me?"

"It's a possibility," Ian said.

David gave him a sly grin. "Does that mean you're

waiting to see whether you get a better offer?"

"I haven't looked at tomorrow's schedule yet, but if it works out, I'll let you know."

Grace looked up as an attractive East Indian man approached the table. He wore a dark suit and appeared to be in his late forties.

David immediately jumped to his feet. "Ahmet, glad you could make it. I wanted you to meet Ian Callaway. Ian, this is Ahmet Mehati."

"Of course," Ian said, getting up to shake the other man's hand. "I was at your panel this morning; it was very informative. Would you like to sit down?"

"I can stay for a few moments." Ahmet took the chair next to Grace.

"This is Grace Donelan—sorry, O'Malley," Ian immediately corrected. "Ahmet Mehati. Ahmet is the owner of David's company, Vipercom."

"That sounds familiar," she said, shaking Ahmet's hand. "I think my father worked for you a long time ago."

"You are Seamus Donelan's daughter?"

"Yes."

Ahmet gave her a warm smile. "Seamus was one of my first associates and a great mentor. He has a brilliant mind. I was very sorry to hear about his accident."

"Thank you."

"I hope he'll make a full recovery."

"I hope so, too," she said. "What does your company do? It sounds a little frightening."

He grinned. "When I first started out, I had a young man's imagination and Vipercom sounded like a company that needed to be taken seriously. Now, at times, it feels a little like the name of one of the video games my son spends hours playing." He paused. "Our company specializes in security and spyware technology."

"Doesn't Draystar do the same thing?" she asked.

"Somewhat, but they focus more on drones, which is not where we concentrate our efforts."

She really had no idea what he was talking about. It all sounded very much like the video game he'd just mentioned. "Would you all excuse me? I'm going to use the restroom."

"It's in the back." David tipped his head toward the hall behind her.

"Thanks."

She made her way to the ladies' room. As she entered the room, she ran smack into the pretty blonde she'd seen with Ian earlier. "Sorry. I didn't see you."

The woman looked like she was going to dismiss her but then suddenly recognized her. "You came here with Ian," she said. "You're Donelan's daughter."

"Yes, Grace," she said. "And you are?"

"Brenna Pruitt. I used to date Ian."

"Oh, I didn't realize that."

"It was a long time ago—when we were in grad school. We were quite serious for a while. I regret that I let him go." Brenna paused, her gaze raking Grace's face as if she were assessing and analyzing every pore. "I told him that when we spoke in his room this morning, but I don't know that he felt the same way. Are you two together?"

She cleared her throat, thinking that was a pretty personal question for a stranger to ask. But Brenna didn't seem to have any boundaries. "I think Ian is a great guy, but I live here, and he lives somewhere else, so…"

"You're going to let geography get in the way? Take it from me, Grace—if you have a shot with him, don't let it slip through your fingers. Men like Ian Callaway don't come along very often. I know, trust me."

And with that parting shot, Brenna left the ladies' room.

Grace let out a breath, not sure why she felt so unsettled. Brenna hadn't warned her off Ian; in fact, she'd told her to go for it, but her words had seemed completely opposite to her demeanor.

Shaking her head, she used the restroom and then headed back to the table.

"You going to go for it with Grace?" David asked Ian, as Ahmet left the table to join another group at the bar.

He dragged his gaze back from the hallway leading to the restroom. "What?"

"You're into Grace. A blind man could see that."

He lifted his beer bottle to his lips, took a swig, and then said, "We don't need to talk about Grace."

"We don't, huh? Then she must be important in some way. Didn't the two of you just meet?"

"We did, which is why we're not talking about her." He wasn't going to tell David he'd been caught up in Grace since the first moment he'd seen her photo on Seamus Donelan's desk. "But we can talk about her father. Have you heard any rumors about who might have attacked him?"

"It's well known that he and Harry Ferguson had a falling out, but that was years ago."

"Anything else?"

"Well..." David looked around, then leaned forward, dropping his voice down a notch. "I did hear one other thing."

"What's that?"

"Donelan and Senator Barrows."

"What about them?"

"Word is they were having an affair. Her husband found out, and he didn't like it."

"How do you know that?"

"She made a bunch of trips to Ireland."

"So what?"

David shrugged. "You asked about rumors."

"You're suggesting that the senator's husband had Seamus attacked as revenge for sleeping with his wife?"

"It's the only other theory I've heard besides the Ferguson fight."

He sat back in his seat, truly surprised by that piece of news. Connie Barrows was an attractive woman in her late forties, but she'd often been an adversary to scientists, voting against important funding for political reasons. "When was this affair supposed to have happened?"

"As I said, Senator Barrows has been to Ireland several times in the past two years. And she was photographed with Seamus at a restaurant. Now, some might say she was just vacationing, and he was an old friend, but others might say differently. Oh, and one other thing. She was supposed to speak at the conference today, but she left early, claiming a personal family emergency."

"That could have nothing to do with Seamus."

"It was mentioned in context with the news about Seamus's attack. Now, if you could find out if she got on a plane to Ireland, that might be interesting."

He frowned. "I don't know. That sounds crazy."

"Yeah, it does," David admitted. "Probably just gossip. Look, I've got to run. I have to prep for my talk tomorrow morning. Let's touch base in the afternoon. Maybe we can hit the slopes."

"Sounds good."

As David got to his feet, Grace returned to the table. "You're leaving, David?" she asked.

"Unfortunately, yes, but I hope I see you again, Grace."

"You, too," she said with a smile.

"If you ever want some stories on this guy, I'm your man."

"I'll keep that in mind."

As David left, Grace slid back into her chair. "Did I miss anything?"

He looked into her beautiful green eyes and really didn't want to tell her what he'd heard about the senator and her father, because it would only remind her of her father's infidelity to her mother, his abandonment of her and her sister, and that's the last thing he wanted to do, especially since he doubted the theory David had floated had any merit. He'd research that one on his own time.

"No, not really."

She gave him a sharp look. "Are you sure?"

"We'll talk about it later. What did you get from Wesley?"

"He told me Harry and my dad fought over some piece of intellectual property, but that was years ago, and his father has never been willing to give him any details."

"Maybe you'll have to get that information from Harry."

"If he won't tell Westley, I doubt he'll tell me."

"Did Westley have anything else to say?"

She hesitated, then said, "He was really interested in why we were together, and he wasn't the only one. Your science friends are certainly interested in other peoples' relationships."

"What do you mean?" he asked in confusion. "Are you talking about David?"

"Actually, I was talking about Brenna. We met in the bathroom. She told me you were quite serious back in the day. You didn't mention you had a pretty blonde scientist ex-girlfriend here."

"Yeah, because that was a long time ago, like eight years ago."

"She said she regretted breaking up with you."

"That sounds a little like she's rewriting history," he murmured, wondering why Brenna had felt compelled to say anything to a woman she'd only seen from afar. He had told her that he'd brought Grace to the party because she wanted to talk to some of her father's friends, but he hadn't introduced them.

"Men and women don't always see relationships the same way. Maybe she was more into you than you were into her."

"She was more into herself, Grace. And to be fair, I was, too. We were both obsessed with our work, our dreams of ambitious achievements. The relationship came in last to everything else. It was a few months of our lives. She's been married since then."

"She didn't tell me that."

He frowned. "I don't know why she said anything at all to you. She must have been drinking."

Grace met his gaze. "She seemed quite sober. Who does she work for? Or does she have her own company?"

"She actually just joined Ferguson's company a few months ago."

"Really? It feels like this science world of yours is pretty small."

"Usually, everyone is spread out, but not this week."

"Is there anyone else here I should talk to?"

He looked around the room, then shook his head. "I don't see anyone. Do you want to get out of here?"

"Sure."

He led the way out of the bar, saying good night to a few people along the way. As they walked through the lobby, he realized how much he did not want to say good night to her. He'd been ready to get out of the bar, but not to leave her alone.

When they reached the bank of elevators, he stopped. "Do you want to come upstairs for a while?"

Indecision moved through her eyes. "I think that's a bad idea, Ian."

"Is it?" he countered. "We don't have to do anything, Grace. We can just talk."

"We've been talking. And when we're alone, we seem to have trouble not doing anything."

He smiled at her candor. "I can control myself. Can you?"

"Of course."

"Then let's go upstairs. We can compare notes on what we've learned, maybe do some research into your dad. It's only half-past nine, not that late." He didn't want to do any of what he'd just said, but if talking would persuade her to hang out for a while longer, then he'd go for that.

Grace gave him a doubtful look. "Half an hour," she agreed. "And then I really have to go."

He walked over and punched the elevator button before she could change her mind. They were joined on the elevator by several other people, so they didn't speak until they were walking down the hallway to his room.

"Do you have a lake view?" she asked, as he inserted his key card into the lock. "I've never stayed here, but I've heard some of the rooms have great views."

"No, I'm on the mountain side." He opened the door and flipped open the light, then stopped abruptly.

Grace ran into him, putting her hand on his back. "What's wrong?"

He drew her forward, putting his arm around her, as they both stared at his ransacked room. The mattress had been pulled apart, pillows and sheets on the floor, his closet door open. His suitcase was on its side, the lining slashed, his clothes dumped on the floor.

"Oh, my God," Grace breathed. "Who did this?"

"I don't know, but I'm going to find out," he said grimly.

Thirteen

Grace walked around the hotel room while Ian called security. When he got off the phone, he moved to his computer, which was sitting on the desk.

"I don't think you should touch anything," she told him.

"You're right." He pulled his hand back as anger ran through him, followed by resolve. He was going to get to the bottom of this. Whoever had done this had made the wrong move.

"It's weird they didn't take your computer, but it kind of makes me think that I wasn't imagining what happened at my house the other day, only that break-in was not this messy or this terrifying. Someone slashed the lining of your suitcase with a knife."

"I know," he said, pissed off at that thought.

"Do you think the events are related?"

"Absolutely."

She stared back at him, her green eyes wide with concern. "Why?"

"Because we've been together. Maybe when they didn't find what they were looking for at your house, they thought I might have it."

"How would anyone know this is your room? The hotel

wouldn't give out that information."

"No, but it's probably not that difficult to hack into the system, and right now this place is filled with people who could easily do that."

"I guess." She paused, a frown on her face. "Wait a second. When I ran into Brenna in the ladies' room, she said she'd had a conversation with you in your room this morning."

"Yes, that's right. She came up here before the conference. We had a brief chat, and then we walked out together."

"Then she knew where your room was."

"But she was with me in the bar," he said, his mind wrestling with the facts.

"Only for a short time. When was the last time you were in your room?"

"I stopped in right before I went to meet you at school—around two forty-five." He let out a breath. "Damn. They had hours to do this."

"What are they looking for? And why do they think we have it?" she asked, waving a hand in frustration.

"It has to be related to your father, Grace. It's the only thing that makes sense. It's what ties us together and connects the two break-ins. I told people I met you because your dad asked me to bring you something. Maybe that's how my room got targeted."

"But what my father sent me was just a puzzle box from my childhood. It isn't part of anything else."

"Maybe there's something inside. Where is the box now?"

"It's in my overnight bag in my car," she said. "I don't know why I've been carrying it around with me, but I took it to Tyler's last night, and I haven't been back to my house since then."

"We need to open that tonight."

As he finished speaking, a knock came at his door. Two men in business suits were in the hall. They introduced themselves as Ken Walker, hotel manager, and Roger Baxter from security. Both men were in their fifties. Walker seemed more unnerved by the scene than Baxter, who perused the room like an experienced detective.

He gave them a brief recap, without mentioning Grace's father or anything related to Seamus's assault. He had no idea if the information was related, and he didn't want to steer the investigation one way or another until they knew more. "I'm sure you have security footage of the hallway and elevators, correct?" he asked.

"Yes, of course," Roger Baxter replied.

"I'd like to see what the cameras caught," Ian said. "I'm attending the conference, and I know quite a few people. I might recognize someone who doesn't belong on this floor or near my door."

Baxter nodded. "I'll take a look at the footage first. I can't show you anything that might compromise someone else's privacy, but let me see if I can isolate activity around your door. That will take a few minutes."

"I've also contacted the police," the hotel manager said. "They should be here soon. I can assure you that we will do everything we can to catch whoever broke in here."

"Is anything missing?" Baxter asked.

"I don't think so," he said. "The laptop is here, and I have my phone. I didn't have much else with me but clothes."

"You mentioned you're part of the conference," Baxter said, giving him a speculative look. "Do you have any proprietary information that might be of interest to one of the other attendees?"

"I don't think it's about that, but no. I'm very careful about where I keep such information, and it would be most likely that someone would take my laptop if they were looking for that, wouldn't it?"

Baxter nodded. "True. I'll go downstairs to check the video footage. There's no sign of forced entry, so it appears someone used a key."

At Baxter's words, his mind went back to Brenna. Had he

left a spare key lying on the dresser? He couldn't remember now how many keys he'd had in the small envelope when he'd checked in. Could she have taken it?

But he couldn't imagine Brenna doing something like this. She was a respected scientist. She was smart as hell. She wouldn't let herself get used in any way. Still, he couldn't quite get rid of the niggling doubt. He'd definitely thought she'd had a hidden agenda for coming to his room. Now he had even more questions about her visit.

A moment later, a police officer arrived. He asked more questions, looked around, took some photographs and then accompanied Mr. Baxter down to security.

"The hotel will, of course, comp you another room," the hotel manager told him. "And we can send housekeeping in to help you clean up."

"I don't need housekeeping, but I will take another room," he said.

"If you'd like to come downstairs, I can get you a new room and a new set of keys."

"Sure," he said, as he and Grace followed the manager down to the front desk.

They'd just gotten a new set of keys when Roger Baxter came out of the back room. Judging by the grim set of his mouth, the videos had not revealed anything he wanted to see.

"The cameras in the elevator bank and your floor were off-line for two minutes around 4:05 and three minutes at 4:22," Baxter said. "At the time, we assumed it was a glitch. We've had some trouble from the weather in recent days."

"But it wasn't a glitch," he said. "Whoever broke into my room knew how to get into your camera system and hide their tracks."

"That would take a very skilled hacker," Baxter said.

"Or any number of people at this conference," he returned.

"Do you have any enemies? Anyone who would want to do you harm or just shake you up?"

"No, not that I'm aware of."

"We'll talk to housekeeping to see if they saw anyone near your room," Baxter said.

"You'll now be in one of our penthouse suites," the hotel manager added, handing him two new keys. "Room 3604. Do you need help moving your belongings?"

"No, I've got it."

"Please feel free to order room service or any other amenities that you need. It's on the house."

"We'll let you know if we find any other information," Baxter added.

He didn't have much hope of that happening, but he simply nodded. Then he and Grace went back upstairs to his room.

"It's kind of a coincidence that the security cameras in this hotel were disabled the way the ones were at the university where my dad was attacked," Grace commented.

"I had the same thought. We're not dealing with a random thug." He picked up his suitcase and put it on the bed. The lining was ripped out, but it would still hold his clothes. He started grabbing items off the floor and the bed and shoving them into the suitcase.

"Do you want help?" Grace asked.

"No. Luckily, I didn't bring much." Within minutes, he'd gathered his things together, and then they walked out of the room and took the elevator to the thirty-sixth floor.

"Wow," Grace said, as they walked into the penthouse suite which had a living room, kitchen, wet bar, and magnificent view of the lake. "This is amazing."

He couldn't really appreciate the luxury of the room, because his mind was still too caught up in what had happened.

Grace turned away from the window and came back to him. "I'm sorry, Ian."

"Why are you apologizing?"

"Because this has something to do with me and my father. You're unfortunately in the middle of it."

"That might be true, but it's not your fault, and I put

myself in the middle when I agreed to deliver your package."

"You were doing him a favor. Last time you'll probably make that mistake."

He could see she was trying to lighten the mood, and he appreciated her effort. He walked over to the kitchen and opened the refrigerator, happy to see it stocked with sodas, beer, and wine. "I could use a drink; how about you?"

"I wouldn't mind a glass of wine," she said, sliding onto a stool at the kitchen counter as he poured them each a glass. "I'm wondering what my house is going to look like when I go back."

"They were already at your house."

"We think they were; we don't know for sure."

He met her gaze. "You were sure when it happened, and I'm sure now."

"You're right. I'm really glad that I didn't stay at the house last night, just in case they did come back, and I'm even happier that Tyler is safe with his grandparents and away from whatever this is."

He nodded in agreement. "I feel the same way."

"We need to figure out what's going on, Ian."

"We can dig more into your father's past on my computer, but before we do that, you need to open the puzzle box." He set down his wine. "Give me your car keys. I'll go downstairs and get your bag."

"I can do it."

"Of course you can do it, but you're not going to."

She grabbed her keys out of her purse and tossed them to him. "It's on the backseat."

"Got it. Bolt the door behind me."

Her gaze narrowed as she followed him to the door. "You don't think we're in danger, do you?"

"Until we know what we're dealing with, I'm not ruling anything out."

After Ian left, Grace walked back to kitchen area, grabbed her glass of wine and then took it over to the window, looking out the floor-to-ceiling windows and wondering what secrets were hidden in the dark night. However, it probably wasn't the night that contained mysterious shadows; it was her father, it was his life, a life she barely knew about.

Who was Seamus Donelan?

In her childhood, he'd been her hero, her idol, the man who loved showing her new things. He had been her first teacher, and if she were completely honest with herself, he'd inspired her love of education. But by the time she reached her teen years, that man had vanished. He was never at home. When he was at home, he and her mother were fighting. Five years of that had led to a bitter, angry, painful split. And then he had truly become invisible.

She'd changed her name, the deepest link to him that she had. She'd put him completely out of her life. Ten years had passed with few to no thoughts about him, except when some unwanted letter or package showed up on her doorstep.

Now, he was consuming her thoughts with questions. She felt guilty that she didn't know her father as well as she should. But then she felt angry, because he'd been responsible for the distance between them. He'd kept himself away from her; it was his fault they were estranged. That's what her mother had always said.

What if her mother was wrong? What if she'd chosen her mom's side without really knowing the whole story, the complete truth? What if her father died before she ever had a chance to know him?

It could happen. She just really hoped it wouldn't. She sent up a silent prayer for his life.

Taking a sip of her wine, she walked over to the living room area and sat down on the couch. She took out her phone, surprised to see a message from Carrie. She was almost afraid to open it.

But the first few words soothed her soul.

Kevin is going to make it. Slow recovery. Could be months, but docs think he's stable now. Will call tomorrow. Mom says she's with Tyler. Thanks again, Grace. Love you!

She breathed out a breath of relief that Kevin would be all right, that he would one day make it home to be with his family, with his son. Tears pricked at her eyes, and she was still wiping them away when a knock came at the door.

She got up to answer it, checking the peephole to make sure it was Ian.

He gave her a sharp look as he entered. "What's happened? You're crying."

"Happy tears," she said with a sniff as she walked back to the couch and sat down. "Carrie just texted me. Kevin is stable. He's going to live."

Relief flooded Ian's eyes. He set her bag on the floor next to her and took a seat on the couch. "Looks like Tyler is going to get his Christmas wish. And he didn't even have to see Santa. Modern medicine wins again."

"It might not just be a win for science," she told him. "You don't know what made Kevin turn the corner."

"You're right. It could have been one of those miracles you love."

"It could have been," she echoed.

"Seriously, I'm glad it's good news. Maybe we're on a roll, and our luck is changing. Let's find out." He tipped his head toward her bag. "Time to open the box, Grace."

She groaned, then reached into the bag and pulled out the box with the Celtic knots on the top that had to be turned in just the right direction with the right sequence of moves.

She stared at it for a long moment. "I really don't know if I can remember how it goes."

"Just think for a minute. It will come back to you—if you let it."

"I know you think I'm being deliberately stubborn." She looked down at the box, then back at Ian. "Maybe I am. I wonder now why I sent everything back unopened. Why did I have to hate him so much? He didn't abuse me. He was a cheater and a liar, but he wasn't a monster. But I made him into one in my head."

"It sounds like your mother had a little something to do with that."

"She did. I think it was probably wrong, but it's hard to blame someone who's in a lot of pain."

"She has made a new life for herself, Grace. Maybe it's time for you to let some of the past go."

"I've been thinking that, too." She turned the box around in her hands. "You've made me think about a lot of things."

"Sometimes it takes an outsider to give you a new perspective."

She nodded and then put her fingers on the middle knot. It felt familiar, right...

"The last time I opened one of these, I was probably twelve," she said. "It was a hot summer night, and my father had just come back from one of his trips. My mom and sister were inside, but I was with him, because he and I liked to watch the stars. He'd tell me stories about the solar system. He seemed like the smartest man in the world."

"He is very smart."

"But his intelligence is not what I remember most about him—it's his humor, his smile, the way he looked at everything with a sense of wonder and curiosity. He'd ask me questions the way kids ask their parents, crazy things, like, 'Gracie, do you know why the sky is blue?'"

"I'd say it was blue, because God felt in a blue mood, and he'd laugh."

"That's not really what you thought, is it?" Ian asked.

"Of course not. He'd already told me a dozen times that molecules in the air scatter blue light from the sun." She smiled. "But he liked telling me again. That's why he'd ask me the questions, so he could give me the answers."

"You sound a little like you miss him," Ian said with a warm smile.

"I do, don't I? I don't really know why."

"Because the good memories are coming back, and that's

okay."

"Maybe." She moved from the center knot to the left. She turned the raised knob of the knot to the left, then moved onto the next knot, jumping across, back and forth, until each of the dozen knots had been manipulated. Then she pressed on the center knot again, and to her surprise and delight, the lid popped open. "I did it. I actually did it."

"I knew you could. What's inside?"

She looked at the necklace cradled in a cushion of velvet. It was a small heart with an engraved inscription that read *My Grace, My Heart*. More tears came to her eyes. "It's the necklace he gave me when I turned sixteen. I left it at the house when we moved out. I didn't want anything from him then." She picked up the chain, her fingers curling around the silver heart. It felt cold, and in an odd way that coolness sent a chill down her spine. *Would this be the last thing she ever got from her dad? Was it prophetic in a bad way?*

"Is that all that's there?" Ian asked.

She nodded. "No big mystery revelation, just an old necklace."

"I guess he wanted you to have it."

"He wanted me to think about him, too, and he got what he wanted." She set the necklace back in the box. "This doesn't have anything to do with the break-in at my house or your hotel room."

"It's possible that someone thinks he sent you something, but he didn't. I actually would have been more surprised if the box had held something he'd stolen—a mysterious key or a coded formula."

"Why would you have been surprised?"

"Because he wouldn't have sent you something that would put you in danger. He loved you, Grace. I don't know anything else for sure, but I know that."

His words brought more tears to her eyes, and she dabbed them away with her fingers. "I don't know why I'm so emotional tonight. First the news about Kevin made me cry, and then the stupid necklace brought more tears, and now you saying things I really didn't think I wanted to hear, but somehow I did."

He gave her a sympathetic smile. "It's been a long few days, Grace."

"It has." She set the box on the table. "But the puzzle box didn't have the answers we were looking for."

"No. But it was a potential clue we had to eliminate. So, are you going to keep the necklace or send it back?"

"I'm not going to decide tonight." She drank the rest of her wine and handed him the glass. "More, please."

He smiled. "Coming right up."

As Ian went to get the bottle, she took off her boots and kicked her feet up on the coffee table. She knew she should probably go home, but her house, while only a few miles away, felt like it was just a little too far at this moment.

"I found some snacks, too," Ian said, bringing a plate of salami, cheese, and crackers back with her wine.

"Great," she said. "Our Chinese food seems like days ago."

"A lot has happened since then." He sat down next to her and said, "I think you should sleep here tonight, Grace."

His words made her choke on her cracker.

As she finished coughing, he added, "Not with me, just here."

She cleared her throat. "I know what you meant. The cracker just went down the wrong way. I really think I'll be fine at home."

"Why take a chance? You can have the bed. I'll sleep out here. I don't mind the couch."

"If I stay here, I will take the couch."

"Why should you?"

"Because I'm smaller; I'll fit better."

"It's not going to happen, Grace. You get the bed. I want you to be comfortable. You have to work tomorrow. I'm just going to workshops and listening to speeches, some of which might give me another chance for a nap."

"What?" she asked in mock astonishment. "You're saying

some parts of science are boring?"

"More like the people giving the speeches need a shot of personality. There are a lot of unexciting people in my field."

"I'm shocked you would admit that."

"I don't usually see them all in one place."

As she settled back on the couch, she said, "Tell me about David. What's his story? Total party guy or is that a façade?"

"He does like to party, but he also has a serious side. In fact, the partying probably started as a cover-up and then became a habit. He's had some rough times."

"How so?"

"His father was a soldier. He served three tours and came back with a messed-up head when David was a freshman in college. David's mom ended up divorcing him. David tried to stay in touch with him, but he started gambling and whenever he got in touch with David, it was to ask for money. I met him a few times when David and I were living together, and I could see that he wasn't quite in his right mind."

"That's sad."

"It really was. But it got worse. Several years ago, David's dad committed suicide, and I'm sure David blamed himself."

"That's a terrible story. I had no idea."

"I know. David dove into work for a few months, but apparently that wasn't enough to make him feel better. So he quit his job, took his savings and started to travel. I've only exchanged a few texts with him over the last couple of years, usually to comment on some photo he'd sent me. I had no idea he was back at a full-time job until I saw him here at the conference. I felt guilty that I'd lost touch. I should have been a better friend."

"You can still do that."

"I'm going to try. He says things are good now. He's happy again."

"I'm glad. He seems nice."

"He is a good guy. Talks a little too much at times, and

he loves to gossip. I learned early on not to tell him anything I didn't want to get around."

"Hang on a second." She sat up straight, giving Ian a sharp look. "Earlier tonight when we were in the bar, you told me we'd talk about what David had to say later. So, it's later…"

He frowned. "It was just a rumor, Grace."

"What was just a rumor?"

"David said he heard that your father was sleeping with Senator Connie Barrows and that her husband found out about it and was very angry."

His words were not anything she'd expected him to say. "What? You're saying that the husband went after my dad because of an affair?"

"There's no proof, Grace. It's just talk. Apparently, Senator Barrows has spent a few vacations in Ireland the past few years and there was a photo with her and your father."

"What kind of photo?"

"They were just at dinner; they weren't in bed."

"At least not in the photo. We know my father isn't opposed to adultery," she said, feeling a taste of the old bitterness. Had she been giving her father too much credit today? Maybe he was exactly who her mother had always said he was.

"We can do some digging. I have a friend who works in DC. He might be able to tell me what he's heard."

"Why go to him? Senator Barrows is in Tahoe. We could just ask her."

"David said she left yesterday, bailed on her panel."

"Why would she do that?"

"I have no idea, but she's not here anymore."

"Then you have to call her. I saw her look at you with extreme interest the other day. She'll take your call."

"And I'm supposed to ask her if she's having an affair with your father?"

"Why not? At least we'll get an answer."

"And I'll make an enemy of a woman who controls a

great deal of the money the government gives to scientific research."

"So you don't want to jeopardize your job to help me. Great. I knew it was just a matter of time before your ambition would come before everything else." Anger ripped through her as she jumped to her feet. "We're done here."

"Hang on." He got up and grabbed her arm as she tried to move away from him. "I'm not your father, Grace. You have to stop trying to turn me into him, so you won't be disappointed."

"I'm not doing that. You are like him. You're choosing to protect your self-interests over finding out who tried to kill my father, your mentor, someone you revere. That's exactly the same choice my father would have made, so it's a little ironic."

"It's not ironic, and it's not the same," he snapped. "I will help you get to the truth, but it's not just my work I don't want to jeopardize; it's all the people around the world who will lose out if I can't get the government to help me distribute the clean water filters where they need to go, and Senator Barrows is a part of that process."

Logically, she got it, but emotionally it still ticked her off. "I'll do it myself then. I'll find a way to get to her on my own."

"Let me talk to my friend first. David could have been blowing smoke. There might not have been an affair. And even if there was, I doubt she would admit it to either one of us. She's too savvy of a politician to do that."

He had a point. The anger ran out of her like the air from a balloon, and all she felt was tired. "I need to go home."

"If you're going home, I'm coming with you."

"No, you're not."

"Yes, I am," he said, his fingers tightening on her arm as he forced her to look into his eyes. "You can hate me and be pissed off, Grace, but I'm not going to let you go home to an empty house when we don't know what's going on and how dangerous that could be."

"I am not your responsibility, Ian."

"No, but you're someone I care about, and I'm not going to let you get hurt."

She stared into his determined gaze and felt her emotions take a big right turn. She wasn't thinking about her father anymore or her past; she was thinking about the silver flickers of light in Ian's blue eyes, the flickers that shone more brightly right before he kissed her. And then there was his mouth—the firm, full lips that could take command so easily. Not to mention his strong jaw, his possessive hands, and his very, very appealing body.

She forced herself to say the words she needed to say, but it wasn't easy. "I can't stay with you."

"You don't have a choice. You're not going to be alone tonight. Wherever you go, I will be with you." He paused. "I know you're thinking that I'm going to make a move on you, but I won't. You can trust me. That's probably a difficult concept for you to grasp, because you clearly don't trust men, especially men of science, but I will not let you down."

Maybe he wouldn't let her down tonight. But what about tomorrow? Next week? She was falling for him. She knew that as clearly as she knew anything. She also knew that she was fighting a losing battle right now. Not with him—with herself.

"I know you won't make a move on me," she said. "But what are you going to do if I make a move on you?"

He started at her words, but the shining light in his eyes told her he found her statement as tempting as she did.

She felt like she was playing with fire, but she couldn't stop herself. She moved closer, sliding her free arm around his waist as she looked up at him. She didn't press her breasts against his chest, but she was close enough that the slightest movement would bring their bodies together in a very provocative way.

"You're confused. You're upset. You're looking for a way to stop thinking," he said, his voice edgy, rattled. "That's not the way to go into this. I don't want this to be about anger."

"I'm not actually mad at you. I was angry at myself and I took it out on you."

"Really?" he asked doubtfully. "You seemed pissed off at me."

"You've been beyond great, and I haven't been very appreciative." She slid her hand under his shirt, and he sucked in a breath. "I'm confused about a lot of things, but not this, not you, Ian. Maybe I do want to stop thinking. Is that so bad?"

"I don't want to take advantage of you."

"That's why I'm the one making the move."

"Grace."

"Ian," she said, leaning in so that her breath blew against his neck. "Do you really want to say no?"

"God, no," he said, his arms moving around her. "If this is what you want, then yes, yes, yes. I've wanted you since the first second I saw you."

She licked her lips. "It is exactly what I want."

He drew in another quick breath. "You know when you do that, it makes me a little crazy." The last word had barely left his mouth before he kissed her.

The way his lips moved on hers made her crazy. She opened her mouth, her tongue tangling with his, as the kiss went deeper. Ian kissed her like no one else ever had. He stirred her senses, and she inhaled him with every breath. It wasn't enough.

All the barriers for not getting together had vanished. There was no kid in the next room to worry about. There was no pretense that what was happening was just for tonight, because who knew what tomorrow would bring, and she was okay with that. Because all she wanted right now was him. No thinking, just feeling.

She broke away from the kiss to unbutton his shirt. She was surprised at how shaky and impatient her fingers were. She was filled with such a desperate need that she literally wanted to rip his shirt off him, because she just couldn't wait.

Finally, she got to the last button. She helped him off

with his shirt, then literally caught her breath at the spectacular male in front of her. His chest was broad, muscled, a smattering of dark- brown hair running down in a vee to his flat abs, disappearing into his pants. She swallowed hard. Ian might be a scientist, but right now he looked more like an athlete.

"My turn," he said with a teasing smile, as he grabbed the hem of her sweater and pulled it over her head.

She really wished she'd gone for sexier underwear, but she'd dressed for a day as a schoolteacher, not a night with this sexy guy.

"Beautiful," Ian said huskily as he ran his hands up her rib cage, his fingers playing with the front clasp of her bra as he leaned and kissed her neck.

Shivers ran down her spine as he unhooked her bra. She shrugged out of it, wanting no barrier between her body and his hands, his mouth.

He planted another kiss on her lips as he cupped her breasts with his hands, his fingers teasing her nipples as nerves shot through her body. She'd never felt so eager for a man as she did right now. As he slid his mouth down her neck, she ran her hands up and down his back, feeling the restrained power in his muscles. He felt so damn good. She wanted the moment to last forever.

When he lifted his head, words tumbled out of her mouth. "Don't stop."

He gave her a sensual smile. "No way is that happening, but I need to get something first." He moved away from her to grab his suitcase. He tossed it onto the couch, unzipped it and grabbed his shaving case, then a condom.

She'd been so caught up in him, she hadn't given protection a thought. Now, standing with her arms across her bare breasts, she felt a little cold and a tiny bit unsure. *She'd started this... was she insane? Would she get hurt? Would it be worth it?*

Her uncertainty fled as Ian came back to her, as he wrapped his arms around her, his mouth seeking hers. Heat flooded through her body. She wasn't going to worry about tomorrow. She wanted him tonight.

They slid out of the rest of their clothes, stumbling across the living room into the bedroom, where more floor-to-ceiling views and the city lights brightened up the shadowy room. They fell onto the huge king-sized bed together, the soft mattress embracing their bodies.

His hard, masculine power made her feel infinitely more feminine. She wanted him next to her, on top of her, everywhere he could be. Each touch, each taste, took her higher. She felt like she was flying, like earth was very far away. Her world was just her and Ian, and it was more than enough. She lost herself in him, and he lost himself in her.

The man who seemed to exercise so much control over his thoughts, his actions, was all physical now, his only focus on pleasing her, and she wanted to do the same.

It was moving so fast—the feelings, the nerves, the anticipation. She wanted it to last, but if it couldn't last, then she wanted it again, and again, and again. Happily, it appeared that Ian felt exactly the same way…

Fourteen

Grace felt deliciously weary and even a little sore as muscles she hadn't used in a while reminded her of the wonderful night she and Ian had shared. Rolling on to her side, she smiled as she saw the man beside her. The sun streaming through the windows lit up his handsome masculine face, the strong jaw, the long black lashes that framed his incredible eyes.

She had the rather incredulous feeling that she could stare at him forever. But as he rolled over onto his back, her gaze caught on the bedside clock. It was twenty past seven. Forever was coming to an abrupt end.

She sat up in bed, and her movement brought Ian awake.

He put a hand on her thigh as he shifted back onto his side. "Where are you going?" he asked in a sleepy voice.

"To take a shower. I have to go to work."

"Work? What's work?" he drawled, a smile curving his lips.

She smiled. "You—the intensely dedicated scientist—probably workaholic—are asking me that?"

He grinned back at her. "That's the old Ian. The new Ian thinks spending the next twelve hours in bed with you would be much more entertaining. I could make it worthwhile. You could call in sick."

She shivered a little at the intimate promise in his eyes. "I can't do that, Ian. I have a classroom full of kids to consider."

"Can't you get a sub?"

"I try not to do that very often, especially not for...*this*."

"*This* being incredible sex."

She flushed. "Yes. But we don't need to talk about that."

"We don't. It speaks for itself," he said with a grin. "Getting back to work..." He sat up and cupped the side of her face with his hand. "I know you have to go in. You're a dedicated teacher. I respect that."

"Thank you."

"There could be a child in your class who grows up and invents a drug to cure cancer or who runs for president or who stops a deadly epidemic. You're molding future generations, Grace. That's amazing."

She couldn't believe he really got how she felt about education. "That's exactly how I feel, Ian. Knowledge is power. And if I can plant a few seeds now, who knows where they'll sprout?"

He stroked her cheek with his fingers. "I like a woman who likes to work. So, we'll get you to school—after we take a shower."

She laughed at the gleam in his eyes. "I don't think I have time for a shower with you, Ian."

"Are you sure?"

"Positive." She paused. "But I do want to say that last night was amazing."

"Yes, it was." He leaned over and kissed her. "I want to see you later."

"I want to see you, too," she said, her heart racing at the look in his eyes, the promise of *later*.

"Good. I'll check out the conference while you're at school, and I'll see if I can get any more information on your father."

"That would be great. I have a staff meeting after school today, so I won't be free until five or five thirty."

"I'll meet you at school then."

"Sounds good." As she slid out of bed and walked to the bathroom, she was not only conscious of the very male stare following her but also the fact that this little interlude was going to end soon. Ian's conference would be over on Friday. *What then? Would he leave? Would she ever see him again? Would this all just be an amazing memory?*

As the questions entered her head, she stepped into the shower and told herself to stop looking too far down the road. He wasn't gone yet, and until he was, she was going to enjoy every minute.

While Grace showered, Ian got out of bed, put on his boxers and then grabbed his phone as it started to ring.

"Hello?"

"Hi, Ian. It's Emma. I hope I'm not calling too early."

"It's fine," he said, a little surprised to hear his cousin's voice. "What's up?"

"I'm in Ireland."

"Does this have something to do with Shannon?" he asked, hearing the excitement in her voice.

"Yes. I have some exciting news. There have been a flurry of conversations and meetings since we last spoke, and the end result is that Max and I are going to adopt Shannon. Her father is giving up his parental rights. Maeve has signed off on the adoption. We've talked to all the authorities, and while the official paperwork will take some time, she's going to be our daughter."

"That's amazing. And fast."

"I know. It's been a whirlwind, but you know me—once I make my mind up, there's no turning back, and I'm thrilled, Ian. I knew the first time I met Shannon that she was going to be important in my life. I had no idea exactly how that was going to work, but now I do."

"I'm really happy for you."

"I'm happy for me, too. I'm taking a month's leave of absence and Max is going to take two weeks off, then go back to the States until we're ready to bring Shannon home. We have a two-bedroom place, so we won't have to move, but there are a million other things to do. Our goal is to have her with us in San Francisco in January and get her enrolled in school." She paused for a quick breath. "Maeve's health is failing, and she's trying to hang on for the holidays, but she's told me that she'd like to say good-bye to Shannon before she gets much worse. She doesn't want Shannon to see her...well, you know. I don't want to think about the sad part of all this."

"You're making Maeve's last days comforting. She won't have to worry about Shannon anymore."

"I know. Maeve is such a sweetheart, Ian. And she's been telling me stories about Grandma that will make your toes curl."

He laughed. "I think I've already heard some of those."

"Our grandmother has definitely lived a full life. She's an inspiration."

"She is," he agreed.

"I can't believe I'm going to be a mother, Ian. It's not the way I expected. But it also feels perfect."

"Have you told Grandma yet?"

"Yes. She's very excited about it. I know she sent me to Ireland to meet Shannon. She won't admit it, but I'm convinced."

"I am, too."

"So, how are you? How's Tahoe? Did you meet that professor's daughter?"

"I did, and that's taken some interesting turns." As he spoke, an idea formulated in his head. *Emma and Max were in Ireland. Maybe he could get them to do him a favor.*

"What do you mean?" Emma asked.

"Professor Donelan was attacked in his university office in Waterford last week. He's in a coma at the local hospital, and the police don't have any suspects."

"What? That's terrible."

"I'm helping Grace try to piece together what happened to her father, but we have little information."

"I feel a favor coming on," she said.

"Would Max have any professional status with the police in Waterford? Any chance he could find out what they know about the investigation? Grace hasn't gotten a call back from anyone yet, and she's concerned about her dad."

"I can certainly ask him, Ian."

"I know it's a big favor."

"It's not that big. It's possible Max won't be able to get anywhere, but I'm sure he'll give it a shot for you. You're family."

Her words touched him in an unexpected way. Sometimes, he took family for granted, but seeing how messed up Grace's family was had made him appreciate his even more. Callaways were always there for one another. It was one thing in life he knew he could count on.

"So his name is Seamus Donelan?" Emma asked.

"Yes." He quickly related the other details he had. "Anything you can come up with would be helpful."

"I'll see what I can do."

"Thanks, Emma, and congratulations again."

"You're welcome. We'll talk soon."

As he set down the phone, Grace came back into the room, a towel around her lovely body. His mind immediately stripped that piece of white terry cloth away, envisioning the sweet, soft curves that he'd spent the night exploring.

"Don't," she warned, obviously reading his mind.

He laughed. "I used to think I had a good poker face."

She grinned. "Not when it comes to sex." She took a breath as she gathered up her clothes. "Who were you talking to?"

"My cousin Emma. She went to Ireland with me when I visited your father. We both have found ourselves on unexpected journeys since that trip."

"Are you calling me an unexpected journey?" she teased.

"Unexpected but also great."

"What was Emma's journey?"

"She's adopting a child we met there; the great-granddaughter of one of our grandmother's best friends. Emma has one of the biggest hearts of anyone I know. When I met the little girl in Ireland, I could see the bond between them already forming."

"Emma sounds like an amazing person."

"She's amazing enough to consider helping us, too."

"What do you mean? How could she help?"

"Emma's husband is a police detective in San Francisco. Since they're in Ireland right now and not too far from Waterford, I asked if her husband Max could find out from the local police what they know about your father's attack."

"That's a great idea, especially since the detective there hasn't called me back yet."

"He might do that today. But maybe Max can get more information than we can. Sometimes police officers will talk more freely to each other, but I don't know if that kind of relationship exists between police officers from different countries."

"It can't hurt. I'll try to call again during morning recess. And I'll check in with the hospital, too." She sighed. "There is a part of me that wishes I had called a sub for today."

"Don't worry," he said, getting to his feet. "You go to school. I'll do some digging around the conference, see if I can come up with any more theories and rumors or put some of them to bed."

"Okay." She walked over and kissed him on the mouth. "I don't know how to thank you for helping me through this, Ian."

He smiled. "I'm sure we could both come up with a few ideas."

She gave him a playful punch and then headed back into the bathroom to dress.

><

After he walked Grace to her car and kissed her good-bye, Ian went into the hotel restaurant and grabbed breakfast. Then he wandered into the conference area to see what was going on.

Harry Ferguson was standing alone at the coffee bar.

"Morning," he said as he reached for a coffee cup.

"Ian," Harry said with a nod. "Are you enjoying the conference?"

"I am. Your speech was very informative and entertaining."

"Thank you. Westley tells me that I missed seeing Grace Donelan last night in the bar."

"You did. She was hoping that someone might be able to tell her why her father was attacked last week."

Harry's lips tightened. "I've been asking similar questions, but everyone is quite stunned by what happened."

"But there's no love lost between you and Seamus."

"That's true, but there is a part of me that remembers a man who was once a friend," Harry said smoothly.

"What happened between you two?" he asked, deciding he didn't have time to beat around the bush. "Grace told me that you and her father had a falling out."

"We had a disagreement over some proprietary information that he took with him after he left my company."

"Did you take him to court?"

"No. It's a personal matter." Harry cocked his head to one side. "Why are you so interested? Do you believe I had something to do with the attack?"

Apparently, Harry had no problem with bluntness, either. "I have no idea. But Grace is looking for information on who would have a reason to dislike her father, and because of your earlier words to her, you did come up."

"I won't apologize for what I said to Grace, but I did not attack her father. Our problems go back over a decade. Believe me, if I had wanted to hurt him, I've had plenty of time to do that."

"Then what's your theory? You've known Seamus since

he was a young man. You've had mutual friends, a close relationship. Who do you think would hurt him now, so many years after he went back into academia?"

"I suspect it was someone who recently discovered that Seamus had betrayed him in some way. I always thought there was more to Seamus's renewed interest in academics than just a desire to bring more balance to his life. He worked on numerous government projects, some of which could be altered to have a negative impact rather than a positive one."

"You're talking about weaponry."

"And genetic mutations and many other things that Seamus dabbled in."

"You mentioned government projects. I've heard a rumor that Seamus was personally involved with Senator Barrows."

Harry nodded. "Yes, I've heard that, too. Connie is quite vague about their relationship, but she's definitely spent some time in Ireland in the past few years."

"I understand she left the conference rather abruptly, abandoning her panel."

"I heard it was a personal emergency."

"Any possibility she's rushing to Seamus's bedside?"

"Your guess is as good as mine," Harry replied. "I'm a little surprised you're so invested in this, Ian. I thought you just met Grace a few days ago."

"I did," he said, seeing the gleam in the other man's eyes.

"I can't quite see her settling down with a scientist, not after watching her parents' marriage disintegrate. Her mother couldn't stand all the time Seamus spent at work. She'd complain and complain and complain. A broken record, I used to say. I didn't blame her. I could see she was lonely, and she confided as much in my wife, who, of course, felt much the same way. It's not easy to keep a woman happy and bring innovative change to the world. You're a young man, Ian, with a bright future. I'd concentrate on that. When you reach for the stars, sometimes you have to leave someone behind. You have to let go of their hand, so they don't hold you back. I don't think Grace could take another man letting go of her, and I hope she doesn't have to."

He heard the underlying warning in Harry's voice. "You sound like you care about her."

"I do. Probably more than she could imagine. She and her sister were like daughters to me. I'm sorry I lost track of them after they left Seamus. Seeing her the other day brought back a lot of memories." He cleared his throat. "So, changing the subject, what's next for you, Ian? Your product will be heading into manufacturing soon; I would assume that would be someone else's focus, leaving you free to move on to something else."

"I have various options I'm considering."

"Why not consider Draystar? We could use a man with your vision."

"I have never worked in stealth technology."

"We're a multi-divisional company. We're involved in many other disciplines: robotics, artificial intelligence, space exploration...we're growing at a rapid rate, and we're going to be one of the leading companies moving forward. We could use a brilliant mind like yours. You could write your own ticket."

"I'm flattered."

"Don't be flattered; be interested. Give me a call next week. We can go into more depth about how we could each benefit from the other."

"I will think about it."

"Do that, but don't wait too long." Harry gave him a brief smile and then walked away.

He took a sip of his coffee, watching as Harry joined another group of men. While Harry had told him nothing about Seamus, some of his advice had resonated. Harry had said that when you reach for the stars, you have to leave someone behind; you have to let go of their hand...

He did want to reach for the stars. But he didn't want to let go of Grace. So where did that leave him?

But why did he have to make a choice? Why was he listening to two men who'd screwed up their marriages with ambition? That wasn't the way it had to go. He could have everything he wanted, couldn't he? For the first time in his life, he really wanted to believe that. But it was also the first time in his life he wasn't being at all logical. That wasn't a good sign.

———»»««———

Grace spent the school day veering between exhaustion due to a sleepless night and exhilaration at the thought of seeing Ian again. She would have loved to spend the day savoring the night they'd had together, but worries about her father and her students demanding her attention kept her too busy for that.

At morning recess, she called the hospital and was told her dad's condition was unchanged. She left another message at the police station in Waterford as well as with her mother, hoping that her mom had gotten an update from the police. It seemed odd that they wouldn't be talking to someone in the family.

As the day wore on, she forced herself to think about her work, but she had to admit that she didn't turn in her best performance as a teacher. She just couldn't seem to stay focused. Random thoughts kept derailing her attention.

Thankfully, her students didn't seem to notice. Tyler, in particular, was in a great mood, telling her all about his grandparents and their plans to pick out a Christmas tree after school. His comment reminded her that the holidays were quickly approaching. She needed to think about a tree and decorations as well as holiday projects for the students, but that wasn't going to happen today. She didn't want to look too far ahead. In fact, time was moving a little fast for her right now.

After school ended, she spent the next two hours in a staff meeting, then returned to her classroom to get her art project ready for the next day. She had just finished when she got a call back from her mother.

"Mom, thanks for calling me back."

"I'm sorry I missed your call, Grace. I had a luncheon. I was actually going to tell you I didn't have any more information, but the hospital just called me."

"And?" she asked impatiently.

"Your father woke up."

"Oh, my God!" She was shocked by the news. "He's going to be okay?"

"They're cautiously optimistic. They don't know if he's suffered any brain damage. They're taking it slow. They don't want to press his memories. They said they'll know more tomorrow, but it's certainly a positive sign."

"I'm so glad. This is great news."

"It is," her mom said in a rather lukewarm tone.

"Have you spoken to the police again? Do they have any leads on Dad's attacker?"

"No, I haven't spoken to them since the first time they called. They said they'd be in touch when they knew something, so I assume they don't know anything."

"Well, if Dad's awake, then he might be able to tell the police who attacked him."

"I'm sure that's the hope, but the nurse did say he's confused right now, so it may take a few more days before we get to the bottom of everything."

"I hope it clears up sooner than a few days. I really want whoever hurt him to be found." She didn't tell her mother about the break-in at her house or at Ian's hotel room, but both events still bothered her. Danger was lurking, and they needed to figure out where it was coming from.

"I have to go, Grace. I have a function tonight I have to get ready for."

She was a little disappointed in her mother's coolness, but she didn't want to get into a big discussion that would almost certainly lead to a reiteration of her father's faults and betrayals. "Thanks for letting me know."

"I told you I would. I hope you can stop worrying about him now. And certainly there's no need for you to rush to his side. Can we agree on that?"

"I suppose. I'll talk to you tomorrow." She set down her phone, feeling better about her dad's condition, but also worried that the police didn't have any leads. Hopefully, her dad would be able to tell them something that would help.

Her phone buzzed again—this time a text from Ian that he was heading over.

She texted back that she'd see him soon, a little thrill running down her spine at the thought.

She smiled to herself, thinking it had been a long time since she'd felt this giddy about a man.

She grabbed her computer and put it into her bag, then turned off the classroom lights, locked the door and headed outside. It was a little before six, but the sun had already set behind the tall mountains, leaving the parking lot and surrounding wooded area in dark shadows. The days were definitely getting shorter.

As she walked toward her car, she was suddenly aware of the fact that her vehicle was the only one left in the lot, and it was parked at the far end, by the patch of trees that stood between the school and the road. She'd been one of the last teachers to arrive this morning and now she was the last one to leave.

It was a very safe neighborhood she reminded herself; it was just the recent break-in at Ian's hotel room and her house that made her jittery.

She was a few feet from her car when she reached into her bag to get her keys. She heard the crack of a branch. Just an animal, she told herself. But her heart started to pound. Taking her keys out of her bag, she flipped the locks and hurried toward the vehicle, suddenly feeling like there was someone watching her, someone behind her.

She was almost to safety when an arm came crashing down on her shoulder and around her neck, stopping her in her tracks. She was hauled up against a solid male chest.

"Stop! Let me go!" she screamed.

His arm around her neck tightened, until she felt herself

struggling to breathe. He was dragging her backward...away from her car...toward the woods, and she couldn't seem to stop him.

Fifteen

Grace tried to dislodge the man's arm, to kick his feet out from under him, but she was off balance and couldn't find any traction. Her feet slipped on the dirt, and she knew she was only minutes away from being hidden in the trees and probably unable to escape. She used all the strength she had to jerk her body forward.

He stumbled slightly with the transference of her weight. She used an elbow to jab into his chest. He grunted but started dragging her again. She tried to yell, but her air was almost gone. She was starting to feel dizzy.

Lights suddenly blinded her eyes. *Was she losing consciousness?* She felt like she was slipping out of reality.

And then a horn blared.

It was a car turning into the lot. *Ian!*

She struggled again. The guy suddenly let go. She fell to the ground, gasping for breath.

Ian jumped out of the car, running toward her. She turned her head toward the woods, seeing the back end of a shadowy figure.

Ian dropped to his knees next to her. "My God, Grace! Are you all right?"

She nodded, unable to find her voice. She pointed to the

woods.

He nodded grimly, then took off into the trees. She suddenly wanted to call him back. *What if the guy had a gun or a knife? What if he attacked Ian?*

She had to call for help.

The sound of an engine revving drew her attention.

Had her assailant had a car on the road? She hoped Ian wasn't in it.

She stumbled to her feet. *Where was her phone?* She looked around the ground, then remembered she'd dropped her bag by the car. She was about to move when she saw a man coming back through the trees. Her heart caught in her chest until she realized it was Ian.

"I lost him," he said unhappily.

She ran into his arms, and he held her tight.

"I've got you," he said. "You're okay now."

She closed her eyes and drew in deep breaths, trying to calm her racing heart after the unthinkable had almost happened. It seemed surreal, like it couldn't possibly be true. She was a second-grade teacher. She lived a normal life—a small, boring life, some might say. But tonight, she had the terrible feeling she'd come very close to losing that life.

She pulled back slightly so she could look into Ian's eyes. "Did you see his face?"

"No. Did you?"

She shook her head. "He grabbed me from behind, and I couldn't turn around. He felt big. He was really strong. I tried to fight, Ian."

"I know you did. I saw you struggling when I turned into the parking lot." His lips tightened. "My heart stopped when I realized what was happening." His chest heaved as he let out a breath. "We need to call the police."

"My phone...my bag—it's by the car, I think. Or did he get it? I felt it come off my shoulder. I can't remember."

"Let's find it." He put an arm around her shoulders as they walked back to her car.

Her keys were on the ground, along with her shoulder

bag. She picked it up and looked inside. "My wallet is here."

"So we know this wasn't a typical mugging. They didn't want your money."

"No." She'd known that the second the guy had grabbed her.

"I'll call the police."

She zipped up her bag as he did that, feeling somewhat relieved that the man hadn't taken her wallet or her keys, although he could have taken her life, and that thought sent another wave of terror through her.

"Police are on their way," Ian said a moment later.

"Okay." She let out a breath. "I keep thinking I'm going to wake up, and this is just a bad dream."

"I wish that were true. But the important thing is that you're all right."

"He had a car waiting on the road, didn't he?"

"A dark SUV. I couldn't see the make. I think the license plate started with a 7, but that's not going to get us very far."

"Did he get in the passenger side or behind the wheel?"

Ian's gaze narrowed. "The passenger side. There was someone else driving."

"So there were two of them." Her stomach rolled at the thought of two men taking her God knows where.

"Don't think about it."

"I can't think about anything else. Why did they want to grab me?"

"I don't know. Maybe to get you to tell them where something is—whatever they're looking for."

"But I don't know what that is."

"They may not realize that. Where's the puzzle box your father sent you?"

She had to think for a second. "My overnight bag is still in the trunk. I haven't been home since I took Tyler to his house a few days ago." She walked over to her car and opened the trunk, and there was her bag. "It's still here, but we know there's nothing inside the box beyond my old necklace. I don't have what anyone is looking for."

"They're obviously not convinced," he said grimly.

A car turned in to the parking lot, its beams pinning them in light. She instinctively moved closer to Ian, even though she could see it was a police car.

A male officer got out of the car. He appeared to be in his mid-thirties with a stocky build and dark-brown hair.

"I'm Officer Stanford," he said. "Can you tell me what happened?"

"I'm a teacher here. My name is Grace O'Malley." It actually felt a little odd not to use Donelan at this moment. She shook that thought out of her head. "I came out to my car a few minutes ago, and as I was getting my keys out of my bag, a man grabbed me from behind. He was trying to drag me into the woods when my friend here drove into the lot. The man dropped me and took off through the trees."

"He had a car on the road," Ian continued. "It was a black SUV. I thought the first letter on the plate was 7, but that's all I got."

"And your name is?" Officer Stanford asked.

"Ian Callaway."

"Did you get a look at the guy?"

"I only saw him from the car when I drove into the lot, and he took off fast. He was dressed in black. I don't remember seeing his hair. He might have had a hat or a hood on."

The officer turned to Grace. "What about you? What did you see?"

"I never saw his face. He put his arm around my neck, and he was behind me. He felt big. He was taller than me by at least six or seven inches," she replied.

"Could you tell what he was wearing?"

"He had on a leather jacket. I could feel the material against my skin," she said, shaking as she relived that horrible memory. "I think he had on black jeans. That's all I remember."

"Can you show me where he took you?" Officer Stanford asked her.

As she retraced her steps, she felt a little sick, the shock turning to nausea, but she forced herself to work through it.

"Do you know anyone who would want to hurt you?" the officer asked. "Do you have a husband? A boyfriend? Have you gone through a divorce? A bad break-up? Has anyone befriended you online or been inappropriate at work?"

"No, no, to everything," she said. "I'm single. I'm a teacher. Everyone is great at the school. I don't have anyone in my life who doesn't like me or has threatened me in any way. But my father was attacked in his office last week."

"Where is that?"

"Thousands of miles from here. He lives in Ireland."

"Could the two events be related?" Officer Stanford asked.

"I think so. My father is a well-known scientist, and there's a science convention in town. A lot of people he has worked with over the years are here."

"Tell him about your house, Grace," Ian put in.

"Right." She looked into the officer's inquiring eyes. "I felt like someone broke into my house a few days ago, but I wasn't sure. The front door was ajar, but nothing was taken, so I thought I might have left the door open. But then Ian's hotel room was trashed yesterday, and we've been together all week, so we started to think that someone is looking for something they think I have."

"What is the relationship between the two of you?" the officer asked, giving them a speculative look.

"We're..." She wasn't quite sure how to describe Ian. "Friends," she said. "Ian brought me a gift from my father; that's how we met."

"What was the gift?"

"A necklace from my youth."

"Do you live here in Tahoe?" Officer Stanford asked, turning to Ian.

"No, I live in San Francisco. I'm here for the conference. Her father, Professor Seamus Donelan, asked me to drop off the gift on my way into town, which is what I did."

"You said your hotel room was vandalized," the officer continued. "Where are you staying?"

"At Silverstone's. We spoke to the hotel manager and head of security about it. Unfortunately, there was no video footage of my floor or the elevators closest to my room for several minutes around the time of the break-in."

Officer Stanford looked surprised at that piece of information. "You're saying someone tampered with the hotel security system? That hotel was just finished a few months ago. It has state-of-the-art equipment."

"Yes, but still hackable by any number of people at the conference."

"Would any of those people be holding a grudge against you or Ms. O'Malley?" he asked.

"Not us, but her father is a different story. There seem to be a few rumors going around about some of his business dealings."

"Okay. It sounds like this may be a complicated situation. What I'd like to do is bring in one of our detectives—Gary Johnson. He'll interview you both in more detail. He can also touch base with the police in Ireland to find out what they know about your father's assault as well as the hotel in regards to the missing security footage."

"That sounds good," she said, relieved to have more help.

"Are you hurt in any way, Ms. O'Malley? Do you need to go to the ER?"

"No, I'm fine. He didn't have a chance to hurt me."

"I would suggest that you don't go anywhere alone until we know what you're dealing with," the officer advised her.

"Trust me, I do not want to be alone right now."

"Give me your number and address," the officer said. "I'll have Detective Johnson contact you tonight."

"Thank you," she said, then relayed her personal information.

As the patrol officer got into his car, Ian gave her a sharp look. "Can you drive, Grace?"

"I'm okay now. I don't feel as shaky as I did."

"Still, I'd feel better if you just came with me. We can leave your car here."

"I don't want to leave it here. I don't think it's a good idea. I'll drive home. You can follow me."

"All right. But we're staying very close together."

"I'm counting on that."

She got into her car and locked the doors, then started the engine. Ian was true to his word, staying close to the back of her car all the way home. She parked in her driveway, not wanting to open the garage yet. For some reason, she felt like she might need a quick getaway, which was ridiculous, because Ian's car was parked behind hers.

They walked up to the front of the house together, and when she saw the front door not just ajar but wide open, her heart sank.

"I should have expected this," she muttered.

"I should have, too," Ian said somberly. "I'll check it out."

"Not alone. We're sticking together, remember? Should we call Officer Stanford?"

"Let's take a look first. I don't think anyone is still here," he said, glancing around the yard and the street. "Then we'll call the police."

She put her hand on his back as he entered the house and flipped on the lights. The same ransacked mess she'd seen inside Ian's hotel room was visible here: cushions ripped off the couches, drawers open and dumped on the floors in every room, clothes pulled off hangers and pockets turned inside out.

She felt nauseous again. Her personal space had been completely violated, and she shivered at the thought of someone trashing her things, slashing cushions with a knife. Had the man who'd grabbed her had that same knife? Would he have used it on her?

She started to sway, her legs weak, her head spinning.

Ian grabbed her and pulled her back up against him. "You're all right, Grace. Breathe."

"I—I can't."

"You can. You're strong."

She struggled to move her chest, to suck in the air she needed. She could not collapse now. There was work to be done. She needed to find out who had done this, who had threatened her, who had almost killed her father. That wasn't going to happen if she gave in to her emotions.

She straightened and pulled away. "You're right. I am strong. Let's check out the rest of the house."

They made their way through the rooms in silence. Every new view was incredibly painful, especially her bedroom. And the kitchen was a disaster. Even the flour and sugar canisters had been dumped out on the sink.

"I don't get it," she muttered. "What are they looking for?"

"Something small enough to fit into those containers," Ian replied.

"That doesn't tell me much."

"I know, but that's all I have at the moment. I do feel like someone is getting impatient, frustrated, as if time is running out."

"Because the conference is almost over?"

"Or because whatever it is has to be found or used before something else can happen," he replied. "It might not have anything to do with the conference."

"But someone there is probably involved, don't you think?"

"We don't have any evidence, Grace. It's possible that someone followed the package Seamus sent to me and then followed me to you."

She considered his words and then realized she hadn't told Ian about her dad. "My father," she said abruptly. "I didn't get a chance to tell you. My dad is awake."

"What?" he asked in surprise. "When did you find that out?"

"My mother called right before I left school tonight. My dad woke up. He's confused, and his memory is apparently still blurry, but they're optimistic about his long-term prognosis. I should have told the police officer that. I wasn't thinking."

"You were shaken up. Has your father spoken to the police in Waterford?"

"I don't know."

"That's great, Grace." Excitement lit up his eyes.

She wanted to feel just as excited as she had when she'd first heard the news, but now she had another worry. "I hope someone is watching over him there. He could be in danger."

"I'm sure the police are keeping their eye on him."

"We need to make certain." She paused. "What about your cousin—did she come up with anything?"

"Emma hasn't gotten back to me yet, but I will call her. We need to get everyone working together: the police here, the detective in Waterford, and the security people at Silverstone's. If that isn't enough, I'll call my sister Kate. She's with the FBI. She'll want to help."

She liked his plan of attack, but she also felt a little overwhelmed. "How did I go from being a teacher to being involved in an international problem like this?"

He gave her a sympathetic smile. "I think that was me— doing your dad a favor."

She sighed. "I'll call Officer Stanford back and see if he can get Detective Johnson to speak to us sooner rather than later."

"While you're doing that, I'll see if I can reach Kate." He finished his statement off with a reassuring kiss. "We're going to figure this out, Grace."

"We have to, and we better do it quick, because I don't think anyone has given up."

As Grace called the police from the kitchen, Ian moved into the living room to call Kate. He didn't trust the local guys to be able to deal with something that was looking to be of international significance.

"Ian?" Kate said in surprise. "What's wrong?"

"Your FBI instincts are good."

"Actually, that's my sisterly instincts. You never call me just to chat. Is it the family?"

He heard the alarm in her voice. "No. Everyone is fine. I just have a problem that I might need your help on. Is this a good time?"

"Sure. Let me just turn off the stove."

"You're cooking?" he asked in astonishment. "My kickass FBI agent sister is cooking dinner?"

"Don't get all worked up," she said dryly. "It's after nine in DC. I was just about to make some scrambled eggs as I got off work late and Devin is working even later, so I'm on my own."

"Got it. Scrambled eggs are good."

"So what's the problem?"

"Remember that package I got on Thanksgiving?"

"Yes. The one you seemed surprised to receive on a holiday."

He'd forgotten about that. He had wondered how the man had gotten into his building and why he'd come on Thanksgiving, but that could have just been random. Someone rang him in. Some services delivered on holidays. Whatever. He couldn't worry about that now. "That was odd, but things have gotten stranger since then. Inside my large box was a small package that Professor Donelan asked me to deliver to his daughter Grace when I went to the conference in Tahoe. That's where I am now. To make a long story short, since I've been here and gotten to know Grace, we've become targets."

"What do you mean?"

"Someone broke into my hotel room and trashed it. Same thing happened at Grace's house with violent slashing of pillow cushions, suitcase linings, and mattresses."

"So more of a search than a robbery?"

"Yes. But tonight the stakes went up. Grace was leaving

the elementary school where she works when she was grabbed from behind. She was being dragged into the woods. When I showed up in my car, the guy dropped her and ran into the trees. I followed but I couldn't catch him, nor could I see him. I just got one letter from the license plate."

"I don't like the sound of this, Ian," she said with concern. "What are you involved in?"

"That's the problem; I don't know. Oh, and I left out what might be the most important piece of information. Grace's father, Professor Donelan, was attacked last week in Waterford, Ireland, at the university where he teaches. I didn't hear about it until I got here and one of my old college buddies told me about it. Seamus has been in a coma since the assault, but this afternoon he apparently woke up. We don't have any other information. We're talking to the police here. Grace's mom has spoken to the police in Ireland, but I think this is big, Kate. I think this has something to do with Donelan's work."

"What kind of work?"

"It could be anything. Before he was a professor, he worked for a number of companies involved in cutting-edge technology, some of which is of great value to our government and others. I wish I could pin it down, but I don't have enough information. I don't know what you can do, but I thought I should get your advice."

"I'm glad you called. And it's about time you realized your little sister might actually be able to help you."

"You're going to hold this over me, aren't you?"

"Definitely. Let me start by finding out what I can about Professor Donelan's condition and the investigation in Ireland."

"That would be great. Emma is actually in Ireland right now. She and Max were going to try to help me out, too, with the police there, but I haven't heard back from them."

"What's Emma doing in Ireland so soon after the last trip?"

"She and Max are adopting a kid we met there, the great-granddaughter of our grandmother's best friend."

"Are you serious? She said something about trying to find that girl's father. Now she's adopting her? I feel like I've missed a big chunk of that story."

"It's all happening very fast. The end result is we're getting another Callaway."

"Well, that's great. Emma will be a fantastic mom. Okay, so, I'll see if I can reach Emma, although with the time change, it's probably the middle of the night there, so it may be tomorrow before I can reach anyone. In the meantime, I'm worried about you, Ian. I think you need to get out of Tahoe."

"I'm not going to leave Grace," he said flatly.

"Really? You're not going to leave a woman you met a few days ago?"

He knew it sounded crazy, but it was the truth. "That's right."

"Is she becoming important to you?" Kate asked, a curious note in her voice.

"I brought danger to her. I feel an obligation," he said, not sure why he had to rationalize his feelings about Grace, because she was important to him. He just wasn't quite ready to share that with his sister.

"I'll make some calls," Kate said. "I'll get back to you."

"Thanks." As he got off the phone, the police were at the door.

For the next half hour, he and Grace spoke to Officer Stanford and Detective Gary Johnson, rehashing everything they knew, which didn't amount to much. They had a lot of theories and speculation but no hard evidence. Their best bet would be for Seamus to be able to tell the police what he knew, but who knew when that would happen?

When the interview was completed, he followed the officers to the door. After watching them drive away, he returned to the living room to see Grace wandering aimlessly around.

"I don't know what to do first," she said, helpless frustration in her eyes. "Should we stay here? Should we go back to Silverstone's? I don't know if we'll be safe anywhere."

"The hotel would probably be the best bet. There is security there."

"Not that it did us much good."

"It's a little more protected than here. Fewer ways to get in and out, and we do have the penthouse, don't forget." His words did little to ease her tension. In fact, he wasn't sure she'd heard him. He couldn't blame her. It had been a hellish few hours, and he couldn't begin to imagine the fear that had run through her when that guy had grabbed her from behind. *If he'd been one minute later...* Damn. He felt sick at the thought.

"Look, Grace, wherever you want to go, we'll go. I'm not leaving you. If I have to go to school and be your assistant teacher tomorrow, I'll do that."

She gave him a faint smile. "I suppose you'd want to teach science."

He smiled back at her. "It is my specialty."

"I don't know if I'm up for school. I don't want to bring danger to the kids. Maybe the odds are against that, but we don't know for sure."

"We don't know," he agreed. "Can I throw out another idea?"

"Please."

"We could leave Tahoe. We could drive to San Francisco. You could stay at your mother's house."

"I wouldn't want to bring her and her husband danger, either."

"Then you'll stay with me."

"You're a target, too."

"Still, I think we need to get out of town, Grace. We can't keep reacting—we have to start taking back control. We have to make moves that whoever is after us isn't going to expect."

She stared back at him, clearly considering his suggestion. "You're right. We do need to go on offense, but I don't want to go to San Francisco. I want to go to Ireland. I want to see my father. He's the only person who can tell me what's going on."

"Ireland, huh?" He was surprised, but the idea actually made sense. "Okay. Let's do that."

"You don't have to go with me."

"Of course I do."

"This isn't your problem, Ian. You have your work, your life—"

"This is my problem. Where you go, I go, and if that's Ireland, then let's make some plane reservations."

Sixteen

After her impulsive idea to go to Ireland, Grace quickly learned that there were no flights from any of the surrounding airports until tomorrow morning at eleven through Sacramento, which was a two-hour drive from Lake Tahoe. She was itching to get on a plane immediately, but they agreed to book tickets on that flight and then figure out where to spend the night.

"It feels odd to be here with this mess all around me," Grace told Ian as they sat at her kitchen table. "Should I do some cleanup before we go? What about the broken window at the back of the house where they came in? Do I just leave it open? Or cover it up?" She paused, her mind spinning with questions and random thoughts. "Maybe going to Ireland is a bad idea. Am I running away? Or am I running to something? Why don't I know?"

His smile was both patient and sympathetic, something she was coming to count on from him.

"You're looking for answers, Grace, and this all started with your dad, so I don't think going to Ireland is a bad idea."

"Yes, but..."

He arched an eyebrow. "But?"

"I haven't seen him in ten years. I changed my last name.

I disowned him. I've sent every package back but this last one. How can I just show up now? And what about my mother?" she continued, not waiting for an answer. "She does not want me to go to Ireland."

"Surely she'll understand your motivation."

"She won't. She hates him. She hates what he did to her life—our lives. She cut off all contact and she asked us to do the same. Going there means I'm choosing to ignore her. That won't sit well, and she has been a good mother to me, Ian."

"Look, I don't know her, and I'm really not trying to judge."

"But you're going to judge." She could see it in his eyes.

"I don't think anyone should ever have to choose between their parents. You can love your mother and still want to see your dad."

"I know you're right. Logically, I get that. But emotionally, I feel guilty already, and I haven't even left."

"That's something you're going to have to figure out, Grace. But if going to see your father can protect you, then I don't think you have a choice. Tonight..." His lips tightened. "I don't think I've ever experienced fear the way I did when I saw that man trying to take you away. I don't know what I would have done if I'd arrived in that parking lot and you were gone, and all I could find was your bag on the ground."

His blue eyes filled with shadows, and she reached across the table to put her hand on his arm. "I'm okay, Ian."

"I want to make sure you stay that way."

"Me, too. I was terrified. I felt so powerless, and I don't want to feel like that again." She paused. "There's something I don't understand. They break in here and your hotel. That makes sense if they're looking for something, but why go after me? What was the plan?"

"I think that someone else found out your father was awake and decided you would make a good bargaining chip."

She stared at him in shock. It was so clear now. Of course, his sharp mind would get there before hers. "You're right. That has to be it. They can't find whatever is missing, so they want to force my father to tell them. My sister and mom could be in danger, too."

"You could definitely warn them, but I think right now you're the target."

"Because you think someone here in Tahoe is the problem."

"I can't imagine anyone who we've talked to grabbing you tonight, but I wouldn't put it beyond any of their capabilities to hire someone."

"You're talking about Harry or Westley."

"They stand out to me."

"Your ex-girlfriend stands out to me, too," she couldn't help putting in. "She was very odd to me, and she was in your room, so she knew your room number. Plus, she works for Draystar now."

"And there's still Senator Barrows," he reminded her. "An affair could hurt her career, not to mention her marriage. If she or her husband thought that your dad sent you incriminating photos, that could provide motivation."

"I don't know. That almost seems too easy."

"Some things aren't as complicated as we make them." He paused, pushing back his chair and standing up. "Do you have any wood that I could use to cover the broken window?"

"There's some plywood in the garage."

"Great. I'll take care of that now. Why don't you pack a bag, then we'll figure out our next step?"

"Okay," she said, slowly getting to her feet. She still felt a little shocked, so it was good to have someone telling her what to do.

Over the next half hour, she packed and straightened up her room a little, but she just didn't have the energy or the will to put everything back together. It felt too overwhelming, and every slashed piece of fabric reminded her of the violence and terror she'd experienced earlier. She couldn't get rid of the goose bumps on her arms or the prickling feeling at the back of her neck. If Ian hadn't been in the house with her, she probably couldn't have stayed there for this long.

She took her suitcase out to the front, then called the school and put in a request for an sub. After that, she went into the kitchen and found Ian packing a cooler. "I thought you might get hungry later," he told her.

"I can't imagine feeling hungry again. Right now I just feel numb."

"That will wear off. The window is covered. The house should be safe for now, and I don't think anyone will come back for another search."

"All right. I'm ready to go; I just don't know where we're going."

"I was thinking we might as well head out of town tonight. We can get a motel in Sacramento by the airport. I think we'll both feel better the more distance we put between Tahoe and ourselves."

"I like that idea," she said in agreement. "Ian?"

He gave her an inquiring look.

"I don't know what I'd do without you."

His smile warmed her all the way through. "You're not going to have to find out, Grace. Let's go. And we'll take my car. We'll leave yours in the driveway, make it look like you're here in the house."

"You're always one step ahead of me."

"But not who's after us, and that's where we need to get to."

After leaving her house, they went to the hotel so Ian could grab his suitcase. She was happy to see the penthouse intact when they arrived, but she still wanted to be on her way, and Ian seemed to feel the same. When they got back to the lobby, they ran into a group of people who asked Ian if he was leaving the conference early. He told them he had a family party to get to and that shut down any further questions.

Grace felt on edge during the brief conversation,

wondering if every question had some hidden meaning, if there were people watching them that she couldn't see. She felt like there were shadows around every corner. She knew her imagination was running out of control, and her nerves were on edge, but there was nothing she could tell herself that made her relax. She wouldn't feel like she was truly away from the madness until she got on the plane for Ireland. Although, why she'd feel safe in the country where her father had been attacked was another question. Maybe she'd never feel safe, not until she knew who had hurt her father and who had tried to hurt her.

Finally, they were back in Ian's car and headed toward the mountains.

They didn't talk for the first twenty minutes. She kept checking her side view mirror while Ian's gaze moved between the road ahead of them and the rearview mirror.

"Do you see anyone?" she asked.

"I don't think so. There are cars behind us, but none that have been there since we left the hotel."

She let out a breath and glanced at her watch. It was after nine. She didn't know where the hours had gone. It seemed like both a minute and a year since she'd left school. "I'm glad Tyler is safe with his grandparents tonight. If they hadn't come back, I could have put him in danger without even knowing it."

"He's safe, Grace. Have you spoken to his mother again?"

"Carrie texted me earlier today and said Kevin's condition is still improving."

"That's good news."

"It is." She stared out the window at the dark night and the looming shadowy mountains that they were about to weave through for the next hour. "It's been a long time since I've made this drive. I haven't been back to the Bay Area in over a year. My mom and Jillian have come up to visit me, but I haven't gone back."

"Is there a reason for that?"

"I didn't really know where to go, for one thing. Jillian has a studio apartment in Sonoma, and my mom has a husband and a house that I've never lived in. She has a guest room, but I haven't really wanted to stay there. She wants me to come home for Christmas. I guess I'll try it out then."

"You don't sound very enthusiastic. Do you like your mother's second husband?"

"He's fine. He's a nice, solid, good guy. But I don't feel close to him. They have their relationship, and he's very pleasant to me on the few occasions that I've seen him, but he's little more than a stranger to me."

"I can't imagine my parents with other people," he murmured. "That would be weird."

"It is weird. You're lucky, Ian."

As she finished speaking, Ian's cell phone rang. He put it on speaker.

"Hi, Kate. You've caught me in the car. I'm with Grace. Have you found out anything?" he asked.

"Only a little, but I thought you'd like to know." She paused. "Hi, Grace, it's nice to sort of meet you."

"You, too," she muttered.

"I just got a hold of Emma," Kate continued. "You know she gets up with the dawn. She saw my text and called me right away. She said she was about to call you to give you an update. Anyway, Max spoke to the detective in Waterford last night, who informed him that Professor Donelan is awake, but he has not been able to identify his attacker. The professor doesn't appear at the moment to have any short-term memory. The last thing he remembered was having breakfast at a café a few days before the attack."

Grace's heart sank at that piece of information. "Do the doctors think he'll get his memory back?" she interjected.

"Max hadn't spoken to the doctors, but the police said they're hopeful that he will remember more as he recovers," Kate answered.

"What about protection? Does he have someone watching over him?" Ian asked.

"Yes, they've posted a guard at his hospital room. Apparently, he's somewhat of a celebrity in his town, so everyone is very concerned about his condition and his safety. Oh, and Max told the police that Donelan sent you a package. It was the first they'd heard about that. They called the professor's assistant, who told them that she'd seen the box in Donelan's office before she left that night, and he mentioned he was going to send it down to the mailroom before he left. She didn't think anything more about it. Apparently, he'd had it open on his table for weeks, so it wasn't something new or that stood out to her. It was good that you had Max contact the local police. Now they have some information they didn't have," Kate finished.

"Not that we know what to do with that information," he muttered.

"I'm going to keep researching Donelan and his business dealings; that's going to take some time. I've asked Devin to help as well. He's a great investigator. Between the two of us, we should be able to get to the truth."

"I hope so. Thanks, Kate. I appreciate it."

"Hey, it's not often you let me into your life, even if it's just to do you a favor." She paused. "And Grace, I hope we meet some day."

"Me, too," she said.

Ian disconnected the call and flung her a questioning glance. "What do you think?"

"That I'm glad you have a sister in the FBI. I feel like the more people we have looking into this, the faster we'll get some answers. I'm a little concerned about my father's lack of memory."

"Maybe he'll remember more when he sees you."

"Or else I'll shock him into having a heart attack," she said.

"I suppose that's a possibility."

"I was really hoping he'd be able to tell the police who was after him. What if he doesn't ever remember?"

"Even if he doesn't recall the attack, he should be able to

tell you if he has something that someone else wants. Knowing that you were almost kidnapped for whatever that is should jog his memory."

"True." She shifted in her seat. "What did your sister mean when she said you never let her into your life?"

"I have no idea."

"Come on, Ian. I don't believe that for a second."

"I tend to like my privacy," he murmured.

"Is that really all it is?" she pressed, sensing there was something beneath the surface of his answer.

He hesitated, then said, "Growing up in my family was great but also…let's just say I was the odd man out."

"Because you're so smart?"

"And when I was a kid, I liked school, and I didn't want to be a fireman. My brothers were entranced by the firehouse and the fire engine from the time they could walk. They went there whenever they could. I never wanted to go."

"Okay, I get that. But your sisters aren't firefighters."

"No, but the family business isn't as impressed upon the girls in the Callaway family as it is the boys."

"So you felt pressure from your dad?"

"And my Uncle Jack and some of my cousins. But I don't want to give you the wrong idea. No one said I had to be a firefighter. No one hated me when I went in a different direction. I just felt left out of a lot of conversations, and it wasn't just the lack of interest in firefighting that was responsible for that. I liked to talk about science. I didn't just do my homework; I always did extra-credit. I crushed my siblings' dreams of tooth fairy visits. I messed up my mother's kitchen more times than I can count with experiments that went awry."

She smiled at that. "I'm sure she was willing to put up with a little mess for a budding genius."

He laughed. "I'm not sure she saw it that way." He paused for a moment. "When I met with your dad in Ireland, he mentioned to me how isolating it was to be the smartest person in the room. You don't want to always show it, so sometimes you say nothing just so you can fit in with the normal people."

"The normal people?" she echoed. "I'm not sure anyone is really normal. But I get it. I can see how you might have felt isolated, how keeping your thoughts to yourself created a distance between you and your family and friends." She turned in her seat so she could face him. "But you haven't been that way with me. Why?"

"Maybe because you stated up front you hate scientists; I didn't have to worry about disappointing you with my high IQ. You were disappointed as soon as you heard what I did for a living."

He had a point. "I know I was a little rude to you when we first met. I've had a big chip on my shoulder when it comes to scientists. But you reminded me that men of science can also be kind, funny, and generous as well as smart. I'd forgotten that." She licked her dry lips. "I'm not saying I forgive my father for all his sins, but you did make me remember some of the good times I had with him. We're all flawed; I know that. But I couldn't see past my father's flaws. There was a wall there. It's coming down. I don't know if that would have happened if his gift to me hadn't created a ripple effect of danger and kidnapping, but here we are."

"Here we are," he echoed. "I can't believe I'm going back to Ireland."

"Me, either."

"Are you going to tell your family?"

"Not until I get there. I don't want anyone to talk me out of it." She let out a sigh. "Let's talk about something else, something not science or danger or family related."

"That's narrowing the topics, Grace."

"Do you like to go to the movies?"

"Not really."

"Because you're a workaholic?"

"I prefer books to acting. Words feel more real when they're written down."

"That's interesting. Movies can bring words to life."

"Because of the actors, not always the words. But I do make an exception for science fiction or futuristic films."

"Got it. Are you one of those *Star Trek, Star Wars* kind of guys?"

"Not since I was fourteen," he said with a laugh. "What about you? Let me guess—you like romance movies with sappy endings?"

"Happy endings," she corrected. "And, yes, I like romance and comedy, but I also love a good spy thriller. I never thought I'd be living one, though. I can't imagine working for the FBI. Your sister must have a lot of guts."

"Some might say more guts than brains."

"I hope you didn't say that in front of her."

"I might have. We Callaways tend to tell it like it is. We don't pull our punches."

"You are very candid and honest; I like that. The men I've dated in the past few years have been sorely lacking in those areas. There's a lot of game playing, and I often feel like they're just wasting my time."

"I'm not big on games, especially when it comes to dating." He paused. "But I am big on you, Grace. Last night was something else."

"It was," she admitted, meeting his gaze, sharing a moment of remembered intimacy. "It feels like a long time ago now."

"And yet I haven't forgotten a second."

Her heart twisted at his words. "For a man who claims not to like sappy romances, you can come up with some pretty good lines."

"Again, I was just speaking the truth."

"Well, I like your brand of truth."

Ian turned his attention back to the road as it became a twist-and-turn two-lane highway. Several minutes later, he stiffened, his gaze moving to the rearview mirror every two seconds.

"What's going on?" She'd just been starting to relax.

"There's a car behind me. It comes closer, then drops

back. It didn't pass on the last passing lane, yet it seems to want to go faster than I do."

"You think someone is following us?" She was suddenly very aware of the fact that they hadn't passed a car coming in the opposite direction for several minutes, and there was only one vehicle behind them, the car that concerned Ian.

He sped up and went around a curve. The car behind them drew closer. She strained to see who was driving, but the lights in the mirror were blinding.

"He has his brights on," she said.

"Yeah," Ian said grimly. "Hang on, Grace."

"What are you going to do?"

"Try to lose him."

"There's nowhere to go," she said, feeling panicked and terrified again. "If we turn off the highway, we'll be a sitting duck."

"Not if we can find the right turnoff and get far enough ahead of him so he doesn't see us make the turn."

"Now, who's acting like he believes in miracles?" she retorted.

"Don't give up on me now, Grace. You always believe. I need you to do that now."

She looked into his eyes and nodded. "I believe in miracles, but mostly I believe in you."

"And I believe in this Mustang my brother lent me. The one good thing about cars from the 70s—they were built for speed."

He pushed the gas pedal to the floor, and the car flew down the straight away. He took the next turn on what felt like two wheels. She didn't know if they were going to lose the car behind them or die in the process.

Two more turns; another straight away. Up ahead she saw a few houses in the trees by the river, a road leading down to them. The car behind them hadn't come around the last bend. They had one chance.

"Turn there," she shouted, pointing to the road across the highway.

Ian shot across the pavement with the quickest reflexes she'd ever imagined. Then he did something more terrifying—he turned off the lights.

Seventeen

Grace tensed for impact, sure that the many trees flying by her window would somehow end up crushing them. She knew that Ian didn't want to hit the brakes for fear the lights would give them away, but there was a solid chance that this move might kill them.

Branches cracked against her window as the car bounced off rocks and brush. They were slowing down but not fast enough. Suddenly they were off the road, going down a slippery slope, and then they slammed into something hard. She let out a scream as she was thrown forward. The car came to a crashing halt as the airbag hit her in the chest, and her neck snapped back and forth on her shoulders.

She didn't know if she passed out for a second, but suddenly she was very aware of the dark silence. "Ian, Ian," she said, finding her voice as she pushed at the airbag so she could see him. "Are you all right?"

It was dark in the car, only slivers of light peeking through the trees that surrounded them.

Ian moved his head, blinked. "Grace?"

Her heart flooded with relief. "Are you okay?"

"No idea," he muttered. "You?"

Nothing felt incredibly painful, and she seemed to be

able to move her fingers and toes. "I think so." She looked out the window. "We hit a tree."

"One? It felt like a dozen."

She looked through the shattered windshield. The front of the car was smashed in, folded up like an accordion. Thank God the structure of the car had held up enough to save their lives.

She unfastened her seat belt and turned to look behind her. She saw an incline rising up behind them, but the highway was nowhere in view. That was probably a good thing.

She reached out her hand to Ian.

His fingers curled around hers.

"Do you think we lost them?" she asked.

"I hope so."

They didn't speak for two more minutes. In fact, she was pretty sure she was holding her breath for most of that time.

At any moment, she expected to see lights, a car coming off the highway, someone with a flashlight peering down the hill. Then what would they do?

They waited another few moments. She wanted to get out of the car. She wanted to get to safety. She wanted to try to find her phone, but she felt like any movement, any flash of light could give their position away.

Ian was also still, waiting, watching, barely breathing.

"I think we're good," he said finally. "We need to get out of the car."

"And go where?"

"Wherever this road goes. I don't think the car is drivable, even if we could get back up the hill. But we can't stay here. It's starting to snow."

He was right. She hadn't registered the shimmery flakes of snow until just now. "But we can't just wander around the forest."

"I saw some houses before we turned. We'll look for help."

"If whoever was following us doesn't see us on the

highway, they might circle back, try to figure out where we turned off."

"Hopefully, the snow will cover our tracks."

"Then I'm going to start wishing for a blizzard."

"Don't make that wish until we get somewhere dry. I don't want freezing to death to be one of our alternatives."

"Good point."

"Let's see if we can find some shelter. Can you get out?"

She tried her door, but it wouldn't budge past the tree next to her. "Not on my side."

He managed to open his door after a few attempts and got out of the car. "I can take a walk, Grace, and then come back and get you."

"No way. I am not staying here alone. We're sticking together, remember?"

"Can you climb across the console?"

"Yes." It took her some awkward and clumsy maneuvering, but she managed to get herself and her handbag out of the car. As her feet hit the ground, she looked around. They'd gone off the road they'd been on and were about thirty feet down a hill. She could hear the sound of water in the distance, which meant they weren't too far from the river.

She pulled out her phone and checked the bars. "No signal."

"Mine, either," he said with a frown, slipping the phone back into his pocket. "Maybe if we get to higher ground, we'll have more success."

Ian led the way up the slippery, rocky hillside. It took them about ten minutes to get to the top and by the time they reached the road, her hair was wet from the drizzling snow and her fingers were very, very cold. Looking down the road, she was happy to see that the highway was still not visible. If the person following them had seen them make the turn, they would have been here by now, which made her feel marginally better.

"Let's see what's up ahead," Ian said, taking her hand as they walked through the trees.

It was cold and dark, with blustery gusts of wind and snow. Slivers of light went in and out of the clouds. It was during one of those brief moments that she saw three houses set along the river. All of them were dark. They climbed up the steps to the first house. It was completely boarded up.

They moved on, finding the same situation at the other two houses. The third house was tucked back even farther into the hillside and behind another row of trees. There were a few boards over the front window, but around the back they found a window near ground level that was uncovered. After a few tries, Ian was able to jimmy the lock and raise the window up high enough for them to climb inside.

Ian went first, then pulled her in after him. They landed in a bedroom. There was a double bed covered with a plaid quilt and a tall dresser, but no other furniture in the room. Ian used the flashlight on his phone to move through the rest of the house, which was basically only three rooms: a combination living room-kitchenette and a small bathroom along with the bedroom. The furnishings in every room were sparse. It was definitely a rustic cabin and felt masculine. There were fishing pictures on the walls, a brown leather couch in the living room, and a worn recliner in front of a television that had to be at least twenty years old.

But it was shelter, so she wasn't going to complain.

"This will work," Ian said, as he looked around. He took out his phone. "Still no signal, though. What about you?"

She checked her phone and shook her head. "Nope. Maybe we should go back out toward the highway. We can call Officer Stanford. He'll send someone to come and get us."

"We'd be taking a huge chance if the person following us circles back and sees us."

"But we're going to need assistance to get out of here."

"And we'll get it. But we have to be smart about it."

"You're not the only one with a brain, Ian," she snapped, mostly because she was tired and scared and feeling completely overwhelmed. She wanted to yell at someone, and he was there.

"Grace."

"What?" she demanded.

He walked over to her and put his arms around her.

She resisted for a moment, but his warmth was too appealing to resist. The stiffness of her body went out of her as she slid her arms around his waist, and they held each other for a long minute. It was really exactly what she'd needed.

"Damn you," she said, but there was a lightness in her voice now.

"For what?" he asked warily.

"For being right. For knowing what I needed."

A slow smile curved his mouth. "I hardly think that's worth a *damn you*."

"I want to be mad at you, because I'm really angry, and I don't know where to put the emotion."

"You can put it on me. I can take it."

"But you don't deserve it. I'm sorry. I'm scared."

"Don't apologize, Grace. I was silently cursing you a little while ago."

"Really? Why?"

"Because I wanted to be mad at you, too, for upending my life—the life I keep really good control over. But none of this is your fault. If anything, it's mine for trying to be a bridge between you and your dad."

"He's the one we should both be mad at," she said.

"We'll tell him when we see him."

"If we can get there. That's not looking too good right now."

"Things will be clearer in the light. We can hike up to wherever we can get a signal and call for help. If we have to get a police escort to the airport, then I'll find a way to make that happen."

Judging by the steel in his voice, she had a feeling he would do that. "Okay." She stepped away from him. "So I guess we're staying here tonight." She walked over to the lamp and tried to turn it on. "There's no electricity."

"Just as well. We don't want to turn on any lights. Let's see if there are some candles."

"I'll look for blankets," she said, heading to the closet. "It's going to get colder, but this will be better than the car."

She found stacks of blankets in the hall closet, for which she was eternally grateful. She took them out to the couch and sat down. Ian had found a pack of candles in the kitchen as well as matches. He lit one of the candles and put it on the coffee table.

"Do you think it's too much light?" she asked.

"I'll take a look from the outside. I want to go back to the car and get the cooler."

As much as she wanted water and some snacks, she didn't care to be left alone. "I'll go with you."

"You're freezing already."

"So are you. Don't argue. I'm your shadow tonight, remember?"

"You are a stubborn woman," he muttered.

She smiled. "And you're a stubborn man. Let's go."

They left the small candle burning as they went out the front door. Checking it from the outside, they couldn't see any light behind the boards. The back might be a different story, but at least from here the house appeared unoccupied.

They went back down the road. As they neared the incline where they had gone over the side, Ian paused. They waited in silence for a few minutes to make sure no one was around, then they scrambled down the hillside. Seeing the car again made her realize how closely they'd come to a more fatal outcome. Tonight had certainly been a night of near misses. She just hoped that bad things didn't really come in threes, because the first two events had almost killed her.

Ian grabbed the cooler out of the back seat, then opened the trunk. "Do you want your overnight bag?"

"No, I'm good with these clothes, and it will be too hard to get it up the hill."

"Can you carry this?" he asked, putting a box into her

hands.

"Yes, but what's inside?"

"My great-grandfather's journals. This is the box your father sent me. It's been in my trunk all week. I kept meaning to get it out and look through it, but there never seemed to be time."

"And there's time now?"

"I'm going to make time. The only places that were never searched were our cars, and that's where you had your puzzle box and where this box has been. I should have looked through it before. I don't think it's important, but you never know." He paused. "Before we go..." He pulled some heavy branches off the ground and across the roof of the car.

She quickly realized he was trying to hide the vehicle. She set down the box so she could help. They couldn't completely cover it, but unless someone looked very closely, they wouldn't see it from the road. Then she grabbed the box while Ian swung the cooler strap over his shoulder and they made their way up the hill.

The snow was coming down harder when they reached the road, and she was happy to see an inch of the white flakes covering the road they'd driven down earlier. Hopefully, no one would ever realize where they'd made their turn.

When they got back to the cabin, Ian locked the front door and then went into the attached garage to find some blocks of wood, which he hammered up against the window they'd climbed through earlier.

While he was doing that, she grabbed a bottle of water and some cheese and crackers from the cooler and then rummaged in the kitchen for a knife and a couple of plates. By the time Ian returned to the living room, she had snacks ready to go.

"It's not much," she said, "but if you're hungry..."

"I am."

He sat down on the couch next to her as they ate, and finally, she started to relax.

"My heart rate is going back to normal," she told him,

settling back against the couch. "I'm sure yours recovered within five minutes. You're a very calm person."

"Tonight it was more like fifteen minutes," he said with a wry smile. "But I try to think through the fear."

"I wish I could get better at that."

"Or we could just get rid of the scary situations," he returned.

"Or we could do that," she agreed. "I just don't know how. I feel like every minute gets worse, and I don't know why. We're racing a clock, but we don't know how much time we have left."

He frowned. "Okay, that kind of talk is not going to be good for your racing heart."

She smiled and blew out a breath. "You're right—again. I need to think about something else."

"You do."

"Okay. What do you think your brother is going to say when you tell him you smashed his car?"

"A lot of bad words. But Dylan is the one who insisted I take it. I had to have some repairs done on my car, and he said take the Mustang, have some fun for once in your life."

"I wish you could say you were having fun when you crashed it. I think the car is beyond repair."

"I'm sure of it. But I'm grateful we were in it. We needed that horsepower to make our turn. I'll have to pay Dylan back. But I will say that out of everyone in the family, he'd probably appreciate the move I made on the highway more than anyone. He loves fast cars. At one time, I thought he'd be a race car driver instead of a firefighter."

"He's a thrill seeker?"

"Actually, I'd call my brother Hunter the thrill seeker. Dylan is more restrained, but he loves speed. The only place he lets loose is on the racetrack. I think it's his outlet for stress. But we don't talk about it."

"Why not?"

"Because we don't talk about our feelings, Grace."

"Not macho enough?" she teased.

He took a swig of water. "My dad always said actions speak louder than words. Don't talk about what you want to do; do it. We all took that to heart in some way."

"That's a good philosophy." She leaned over to brush a strand of hair away from his bruised forehead. "You have a bump." She gently ran her fingers over it. "I hope you don't have a concussion."

"I'm fine. I've hit my head harder than this."

"On what? A physics problem?"

He laughed. "You're feeling better."

"I am. I'm starting to appreciate the fact that I'm alive. I just hope there isn't a third strike."

"I think we're safe here for the moment, Grace. If they'd seen us come down the road, they'd have been here already. With the storm picking up, they'll probably have to get off the road until morning."

"That would be good." She licked her lips, still feeling the adrenaline rushing through her body, and she thought she had a good idea on how to burn it off. She leaned forward and kissed him.

His surprise didn't last more than a second as he put his hands on her head, taking the kiss deeper. She fell back against the couch cushions, and he went with her. She loved the feel of his hard body on hers, and as she ran her hands up under his sweater, his skin heated up with her touch.

Ian lifted his head for a second, his gaze searching. "Grace? Are you sure?"

"Didn't you just tell me actions speak louder than words? Don't talk about what you want, just do it. I want us— together, the way we were last night. I want that more than anything."

"That's the perfect answer."

She laughed. "I'm not as smart as you, but I get some questions right. Now show me what you want."

"Oh, I will show you," he promised as he kissed her mouth and started a fire that would burn all night.

Eighteen

Ian woke up as dawn was starting to break. He wanted to get up and out on the road early, but as he glanced at Grace curled up against him on the couch where they'd spent the night, he felt like she could use a few more minutes of happy sleep before she had to deal with reality. He carefully slid away from her.

She muttered something sleepily as he got up, but then she just rolled onto her side and fell back asleep. He fixed the blanket around her bare body before heading to the bathroom to change. Once he was dressed, he returned to the living room and sat down on the recliner. The box he'd been lugging around since he'd left San Francisco was sitting on the floor next to the chair.

He opened the box and picked up the journal on top. The leather-bound book was very old, the cover scratched, the pages faded. He could hardly believe the year printed on the first page, 1918, almost a hundred years ago. His great-grandfather had been a teenager at the time, and throughout the journal, he'd jotted down experiments, ideas, sketching out things he wanted to do.

In between those pages of science, he talked about his hopes and his dreams. He kept changing his mind on what kind of science he wanted to do, but Ian could feel his energy, his desire to learn, his obsession with invention and change in every page.

As he read through each journal, he grew more and more impressed. Donald Rafferty had certainly been prolific, filling page after page with his thoughts. There were certainly some interesting ideas in there, too. A few gave him pause as he realized that his great-grandfather had actually been ahead of his time, dreaming of things that would be invented fifty years later.

He wished he could tell his great-grandfather what had happened after his death, answer the questions he'd written up in his notes. It made him think about the questions he had now and how they might be answered one day in the future. Science was always evolving...mostly for the better, but sometimes for the worse.

"What are you doing?" Grace asked, interrupting his thoughts. She sat up on the couch, wrapping the blanket around her body as she gave him a sleepy smile.

"Looking through my great-grandfather's journals."

"What's in them?"

"His passion for science and learning, his vision for the future, for his life."

"I take it you never met him?"

"No, he passed away before I was born, and I don't think he ever left Ireland. He taught school there. He was one of your father's teachers."

"That's right. Your grandmother sent you to see my dad. It's funny the connections that linked us together. You might almost call it a little fateful."

He saw the tease in her eyes. "I wouldn't go that far."

She laughed. "Really? Even you have to admit, a lot of things had to come together to get you and me here at this moment."

"I'll admit that, but I won't call it destiny."

She sighed. "Of course not. That would be a little too magical. So did you learn anything from the journals?"

"He did some interesting experiments. I'll have to read some of them again more closely." He paused. "It's weird, but I kind of feel like I could have written these pages."

"Because you're interested in the same things?"

"That, but mostly because I can feel who he is in his excitement to explore and to learn. Even when the experiments fail, he wants to try another one. And he talks about feeling isolated from his family. His brothers want him to party on the weekends, but all he wants to do is get back to his next experiment."

"That's why you relate to him. He's you, just a bunch of decades earlier."

Grace was getting to know him a little too well. "I always wondered where I'd gotten my love of learning from. Not that my parents didn't like school or value learning. They're both educated people, but I'm the only one who had the unquenchable thirst for knowledge. I know that genetically it didn't have to come from anywhere—"

"But it feels kind of good that it did," she finished.

He nodded. "It does."

Her gaze moved toward the window, where light was filtering through the cracks in the plywood covering. "It's getting light."

"We should get outside soon," he agreed. "See if we can find a phone signal or someone who can help us get out of here."

"I'll get dressed."

She got up, collected her clothes and went into the bathroom. He flipped through the rest of the journals, putting each one on the coffee table as he finished. He was about to close the last book when an odd page jumped out at him. The ink was different, brighter, newer. Chemical formulas played across the page followed up by a sketch. It looked like a bug of some sort. His gaze narrowed. *What was it?*

He flipped the page, seeing more computations, but there was something unusual about them. They weren't in his great-grandfather's handwriting for one.

His pulse sped up. *Had Seamus sent him a message in the journal? Was that what someone was looking for? He'd thought the package he'd sent to Grace was the clue, but what if it wasn't? What if Seamus had hidden something in his great-grandfather's journals?*

When Grace came out of the bathroom, he said, "I think I found something." He held up the book. "The pages in the back of this journal stand out. They're in fresher ink. I think Seamus might have written down a formula for something. He hid it in the pages of these old science notes."

"What would the formula be used for?" she asked, a sparkle in her eyes as she came forward.

"I don't know. It would take me some time to figure out, but I think we might finally have a clue. I should have looked in the box before now. I need to figure this out."

"You will," she said confidently. "But it will have to be later. We need to get some help."

"You're right."

As Grace put their snacks and empty water bottles in the cooler, he glanced back in the box. It was empty now, but there was something off about the bottom. He blinked, feeling like he was seeing something that wasn't there. He put his hand on the cardboard, shocked when his fingers curled around something hard. It felt like it was about the size of a pebble, but he couldn't really see it.

He pulled his hand out, his heart thudding against his chest as he considered the implications. "Grace."

"What?"

He opened his palm. "What do you see?"

"Nothing. Why are you showing me your empty hand?"

"It's not empty. I'm holding something that's invisible."

She gave him a look that suggested he'd lost his mind. "Maybe that bump on your head is worse than you thought, Ian."

"Open your hand."

She walked over to him and put out her hand. He put the object on her palm.

She started. "Oh, my God, I can feel something, but I can't see it. How is that possible?"

He pulled out his phone and focused the light on her palm and then he could see the tiniest bit of color. He picked at the one spot with his fingernail and revealed more color.

"What is it?" she asked.

As it became more visible, he took it out of her hand and scraped away what seemed to be paint. In the end, the object looked like a very small wasp. "It's a bee."

"I don't understand," she said in confusion. "How could we not see it?"

"Invisible paint."

"There's such a thing as invisible paint?"

He nodded. "There is. And I have a feeling the chemical formula in the book is what makes this paint."

"But why would someone paint something that looks like a bee?"

"It's not a bee, Grace; it's a drone," he said, turning the object around in his hand.

"Are you serious? That's a drone? I thought they were much bigger than that."

"They usually are, but several companies are experimenting with almost microscopic drones." His mind played with the possibilities. "There's been research into weaponizing drones. The fact that this is a bee leads me to believe that there might be a stinger."

Grace stared back at him with uncertainty. "Seriously? You're saying that little thing is going to sting someone with what? Poison?"

"Yes." His heart sped up at the thought. "You could assassinate someone from thousands of miles away with something that looks like a bee. How could anyone defend against that?"

"The Fergusons work with drones, don't they?" Grace asked.

He met her gaze. "And Harry claims your father stole something from him that he didn't want to talk about or take him to court over. Maybe it was this bee."

"But I can't believe Harry or Westley would try to hurt me. They're family friends. I knew them when I was a child," she said in disbelief.

"Maybe they didn't want to hurt you. First they just wanted to find this. Then, when they couldn't, they figured they could use you to get your father to talk."

"That makes sense. But this bee—is it that special? Couldn't they just build this again?"

"There must be something about it that they don't have, a formula to create one part of it. If it is a stinger, then it has to be activated in some way. The invisibility shield obviously could be picked away, as we did. It could be that parts of this are still experimental."

"But my father left Draystar years ago, right? Why now? Why is all this happening now?"

"Harry never said when your dad stole from him. Maybe it wasn't when he left; perhaps it was more recent." He thought for a moment. "Seamus said something to me about how science sometimes skates along a fine line between good and evil. You create something for one purpose, and it's used for another. That could be what happened here."

"But weapons are always used for killing. That seems obvious."

"Sometimes they're for defense. I'm speculating, but maybe the target turned out to be someone or some group that Seamus didn't see as an enemy. When weapons fall into the wrong hands—"

"The wrong people die," she finished, her green eyes wide. "This could be huge, Ian."

"It could be. I don't have the feeling this bee is usable right now. I think there's something missing to make it reach its potential."

"So you're suggesting that it's not the bee but the formula in the journal that's important?"

"Or both. I need time to figure it out."

"I'm confident you could, because I'm pretty sure you can

do anything right about now, but we don't have that time. We need to get out of here. We need to get to Ireland. We need to put all the pieces together."

As much as he wanted to argue that deciphering the formula made more sense, he couldn't. Grace's logic couldn't be disputed. "You're right." He ripped out the pages from the journal, then put the other books back into the box. Then he got up and went into the kitchen where he found a baggie to put the prototype drone into. He slipped both into his pocket. If anyone wanted the items, they would have to go through him.

Grace's frown told him she'd come to the same conclusion. "Maybe we should stash those somewhere. I feel like you just put a bullseye on yourself, Ian."

"It was already there. I don't want to take a chance that we'll lose these things."

"Your pocket isn't exactly Fort Knox."

He smiled. "Better than your purse or this box here. Ready to go?"

"Why don't you give me one of the pieces? That way they'll need both of us to get what they want."

He looked into her eyes and saw her worry, and it touched him deeply. "No, but thanks for being concerned."

"I can be your partner, Ian. You don't have to protect me."

"But I want to protect you, Grace. And that's just the way it is." He held her gaze for a long moment, then added, "Besides, you've been the target more than me. This will change the game."

She let out a breath. "All right. Since we're sticking together anyway, it probably doesn't matter which one of us is carrying the items."

He would let her think that, but if there was a choice between sticking together and getting her to safety, he knew what decision would be made.

"What should we take with us?" she asked.

"Nothing," he said, a vision of them standing on the

highway like sitting ducks was not looking too good. "Let's go find a signal; we'll call for help, then come back here to wait."

"Really?" she asked doubtfully. "I don't know that it would take much for a few guys with guns to break down the doors, even if we barricaded ourselves in here with what little furniture we have."

"I don't think we should wait inside the house. We'll set up somewhere outside where we can see the road and this cabin. If the bad guys get here before the good guys, they'll head to the house."

Her green eyes sparked. "That's an excellent plan, although should I remind you that it's cold outside?"

"We'll keep each other warm."

She smiled. "And maybe we'll take some blankets, too."

"First things first—let's find a signal. Then we'll figure out our hideout."

"Yes," she agreed, following him out the door. "I'll feel better knowing help is on the way."

———⋙⋘———

Despite her words, Grace knew she wasn't going to feel better until they'd turned the device over to the cops and the people who were chasing them had been caught. She'd thought getting to Ireland would be an escape, but maybe the danger would follow them there. The drone they'd discovered was obviously of great value. No one was just going to give up, no matter how many planes they got on.

"I really hope my dad has protection," she said to Ian as they made their way down the road.

"I'm sure he does," he said. "And hopefully, he's told the detective there exactly who's after him."

"Maybe he can't tell the police that. I've been thinking about how and why he kept this drone a secret and hidden away in the box. It must not belong to him. He must have felt it would put his life in danger if anyone knew he had it. But he put your life in danger when he sent it to you."

"That might have been a moment of desperation. We won't know for sure until we ask him. But right now, we need to stay focused on ourselves."

She checked her phone, seeing one bar. "I have one bar. You?"

"Nothing yet."

She tried to contact the police, but the call didn't connect. They kept walking, staying on the edge of the road, so as not to leave visible footprints. Ian really did think of everything. When they got to where they'd gone off the road, they looked down at the car. It was still covered exactly as they'd left it, which made her feel good.

They walked another twenty feet and around a bend. She could see the highway a quarter of a mile away. An occasional car passed by, but not a steady stream. It was only seven a.m.

Ian stopped. "I've got a signal."

"Me, too. I'll call the Tahoe police. I have Detective Johnson's number in my phone."

"I'll call Kate and tell her what's going on."

Her call to the detective went to voice mail. "He's not in yet," she told Ian. "Should I call 9-1-1? But I don't know where to tell them we are. We'll have to get closer to the highway to see the sign."

"Hang on," he said, putting his phone on speaker. "Kate?"

"Ian. What's going on?"

"We're in trouble. We were trying to leave Tahoe last night but we were followed down Highway 50. We holed up in a cabin last night, but we need help getting out. I totaled Dylan's car."

"Are you all right?" she asked worriedly.

"Yeah, I'm fine. So is Grace. But I discovered a piece of technology in the box Seamus sent me."

"I thought it was just old journals."

"So did I, but there was a microscopic drone, about the

size of a bee. It looks like a weaponized drone that was covered with an invisible paint."

"Oh, my God, Ian. What have you stumbled onto?"

"Something dangerous," he said. "Can you help?"

"Yes. I'll call the field office and the local sheriff to get someone out to help you. Do you know your exact location?"

"Let me walk farther down the road. I'll see if there's a sign."

"You should have called last night."

"It was dark, and I couldn't find a signal," he said as they moved closer to the highway. "Plus, I didn't know if someone was coming after us." He paused. "The sign says Hammeker Road. We're probably halfway between Tahoe and Placerville."

"I'll get someone out there right away. In the meantime, stay out of sight."

"Will do. After you send us help, I need you to look into Draystar. I'm pretty sure Seamus's old company is the one who created this drone. It looks like it has a stinger capable of injecting poison."

"I've heard of that."

"The invisibility cloak is an added advantage, but my guess is that Seamus found out Draystar was interested in selling the weapon outside of the US and that's why he took the prototype."

"Got it. By the way, your friend in Ireland hasn't remembered anything, or if he has remembered, he's not saying."

"Is there still a guard on his room, Kate? I think Seamus could be in danger, too."

"They've assured me he's being protected. You need to turn off your phone, Ian, or put it somewhere far from you until the police get there. I don't want anyone to be able to ping your location through your phone."

"Shit!" he swore. "I didn't think of that."

"Stay safe, Ian."

As Kate said good-bye, Ian turned off his phone. Grace

was already ahead of him, doing the same with hers.

"I should have thought about our phones," he said, new tension in his face.

"We had to call for help, Ian."

"Yeah, but we should have turned them off last night." His lips drew together in a taut line. "Nothing we can do about it now. Let's go back to the cabin. We need to get ready for whoever comes next."

"I hope that will be the police."

"I'm sure it will be."

He might have said the right words, but she wasn't sure he believed them. She had to almost jog to keep up with him as they returned to the cabin.

"So, what do you want to do?" she asked, as they moved into the house.

"Grab blankets, water, and anything we can use as a weapon," he said briskly, as he went into the kitchen. He came back with a couple of kitchen knives. "These aren't worth much, but they're something."

"I don't see anything else in here that will beat someone with a gun."

"There has to be something." His gaze scanned the room. "Let's look in the garage."

She followed him into the attached garage. He handed her a snow shovel. "We can use this."

"Okay."

He walked over to the tool bench, where she saw screwdrivers and twine, screws and bolts, and a couple of pieces of wood. On the ground were several paint cans and a can of gasoline.

"Now we're in business," he said.

She raised an eyebrow. "Really? What are you seeing that I'm not?"

"The makings of a trap, of course."

"We're going to try to catch them now?" she asked in astonishment.

"Better than them catching us. But if they get into the

house, we can take them down."

"How so?"

"We have matches, flammable liquid, and fuel."

Her stomach turned over. "You're talking about setting this house on fire? We can't do that, Ian. What about the owners?"

"Grace, I appreciate your sense of ethics. But we could be fighting for our lives. If we have to replace the cabin, we will."

"You have that kind of money?"

"I'm thinking whoever is responsible for this could be made to pay. But even if we had to rebuild the cabin, it's not much more than a shack; I could cover it. Look, if the police get here in time, nothing will happen. But until we're safe, I'm going to protect us. Help me take this stuff into the house."

Watching Ian set traps to the front and back door of the cabin was both upsetting and mind-boggling. Within minutes, he'd created a scenario in which the front or back door opening would turn a lit candle into an open can of paint or bowl of gasoline that would set off an explosion, maybe take at least one or two people out, or at least slow them down. She was more than a little impressed and also happy to watch him finish off the trap from the safety of the back yard.

Ian managed to get out of the house without setting off the trap, and then they took the blankets, shovel and knives with them as they walked through the trees. They were about a hundred yards away when Ian pointed to a group of large boulders about twenty-five yards up a steep hill. She liked the idea of a higher vantage point.

With some considerable effort, they made their way through the newly fallen snow to the rocks and ducked down so that they wouldn't be seen, but through the cracks between the boulders they had a good view of the road and the cabin.

"Now, we wait," Ian said. He glanced down at his watch. "It's been about twenty-five minutes since I called Kate. Someone should be here soon."

"The right someone," she said, feeling incredibly

nervous. They didn't speak for a couple of minutes, and the silence made her more tense. "I still can't believe the Fergusons are behind this. Harry is an old guy and Westley seems too clean-cut to be involved in this kind of thuggish behavior."

"But Westley would have no problem hiring someone to do his dirty work."

"I guess."

"If it makes you feel better, I'm not completely sold on the Fergusons."

"Why not?"

"Because it feels almost too easy."

"Easy?" she asked incredulously. "None of this has been easy."

"We're going to be okay, Grace."

"I really like it when you tell me that," she admitted. "Even though I'm not sure it's true."

"Hey, I never lie, remember?"

"I know you want it to be true." She let out a breath. "I'm keeping the faith." She'd no sooner finished speaking then she heard the sound of an engine. "Someone is coming." She held her breath, wondering if she'd see a police car...or the dark SUV...

Nineteen

—⟫⟪—

It was the SUV. "It's them," she whispered, terror racing through her as she put her hand on Ian's arm.

He gave her a tense look. "We're out of sight. Just don't move."

She really hoped they were out of view. As the car stopped a few yards from the house, she could see doors open, and boots hit the ground, but she couldn't see exactly who got out. "How many?"

"Looks like three to me."

"Do you recognize anyone?" she whispered.

"Can't see their faces."

As they watched, one of the men came around the back of the house. He was dressed in black jeans and a black leather jacket, and she was quite sure it was the same man who had grabbed her. He had a black beanie on his head, and she couldn't really see his face, but she doubted he was anyone she'd met before.

The man peered through one of the windows that wasn't boarded up. He could probably see the candlelight inside.

Her grip tightened on Ian's arm.

The man stepped back then kicked at the door. She could see more movement at the front of the house. They were going inside.

When the door didn't immediately bust open, the man pulled out a gun and shot out the lock.

She jumped at the shocking sound, and Ian had to pull her back down.

The next kick sent the door flying open, and the man ran inside, his gun drawn.

For a second, she thought the trap wouldn't work, and then an explosion lit the air, followed immediately by another. Flames shot out of the doors and windows. The man came running back outside, caught up in flames. He was screaming, rolling around on the ground, trying to put out the fire.

The sound of distant sirens followed the intense crackling of the fire. Help was on its way.

"We're going to be okay," she said excitedly. "It worked." The traps Ian had made had set the house on fire and sparks were leaping into the nearby trees, turning the branches into flames. The police would know where they were now, and there was no way out for the guys in the van. The one who had been caught up in flames had stopped rolling around on the ground. The fire on his clothes was out, but he seemed to be barely conscious. "Do you think he's dead?"

"Don't know," Ian said tersely.

"Well, at least the others are trapped now. They can't get away."

She'd no sooner finished speaking when she saw a man running from the front of the house, into the woods and away from the property.

"No way," Ian said, anger in his voice. "Stay here."

"What?" she asked in shock as he jumped up. "Ian, no."

"Stay here until the police come. I'm not letting him get away."

As Ian ran after the man, she debated what to do. The sirens were coming closer, but no one had come down the road yet. *What if the man Ian was chasing had a gun? What the hell was he going to do then? By the time help arrived, it might be too late.*

She grabbed the shovel and ran after him.

———➤➤◄◄——

Ian jumped over rocks and branches as he ran through the trees. He was not going to let this man escape. If he did, who knew if he would ever be found? He needed this to be over. He needed Grace to be safe. And he needed to find whoever had hurt Seamus. Even if it wasn't this guy, he knew something—maybe everything.

The man was fast, agile, moving too quickly for him to see who he was. He wore dark jeans and a black jacket, like the other man they'd seen. Those clothes might have been good at night, but in the daylight, against the snow, there was no place for him to hide.

As he got deeper into the woods, the sounds of the sirens weren't as loud.

For a split second, he hoped he'd made the right decision. *What if the third man got to Grace before the police arrived? He had no idea whether he was alive or not.*

It was too late to turn back. Grace was hidden away. She wouldn't show herself until the police were there. But he felt a renewed sense of urgency to be done with the danger. He pushed harder, running so fast he was almost flying. The guy in front of him was getting closer...and closer...

One last burst of adrenaline sent him airborne as he tackled the man to the ground.

He landed on top of him, but was immediately thrown off the guy's back, as the man lurched to his feet.

He jumped up, grabbing one of the man's arms as he tried to get away. The man yanked free and whirled around, his fist coming at Ian's face.

He ducked and hit back, striking the guy right in the middle of his nose.

The man stumbled backward with a yell, blood pouring

from his nose.

Ian stared in shock as he finally saw exactly who he was fighting with. "You?" he asked in shock. "No. It can't be you."

His old friend David gazed back at him, a mix of anger, regret, and fear in his eyes. "I didn't have a choice, Ian."

"You broke into my room, into Grace's house? You tried to kidnap her?" he asked, his voice rising in stunned amazement.

"I had to."

"No, you didn't."

"Yes, I did. You have no idea what this is about."

"It's about a bee-sized drone with a poisonous stinger."

David stared back at him, wiping more blood from his nose. "You found it."

"What the hell is going on? Is this about money?"

"No, it's about saving the world. You think you know what's right and what's wrong, but you don't. I went around the world. I met the people we're using our weapons against. They don't deserve the annihilation we want to rain down on them."

He couldn't believe the words that were spouting from David's bitter lips. "You're going to sell the drone to a terrorist group, aren't you?"

"They're not the terrorists—we are. I've seen what we do to poor people."

He shook his head. "You're wrong. You're messed up, David. Is that why you went to work for Ahmet, for Vipercom?"

"Yes. I thought he had what I needed. But then I heard about the bee-stinger and the prototype Donelan made years ago. There were samples at Vipercom but none with the cloak of invisibility that Donelan had created, none with the stinger set up exactly the right way. I went to Donelan and asked him if he knew where it was. He told me it was at Vipercom, but I knew he was lying."

"So you broke into his office and almost killed him?"

"That wasn't me."

"But you ordered it, didn't you? And what about the man who tried to kidnap Grace earlier?"

"We weren't going to hurt her."

He didn't believe David for a second.

"And this whole thing was Donelan's fault anyway," David rationalized. "He sent her the drone. I wasn't sure she had it. But when we couldn't find it in Donelan's office or his home, we knew he'd sent it somewhere. Since I was coming to Tahoe, I figured I'd start with her. We did a quick search of her place first. I didn't think there was anything there until you told me about the package you delivered to her, I knew we had to go back."

"That package was a puzzle box. Seamus didn't send the drone to Grace; he sent it to me. I just didn't know I had it until yesterday. That's why you couldn't find it in her house or my hotel room. It was in my car."

"Where is it now?" David asked.

"Somewhere safe." He paused. "It's not too late to make this right, David."

"Yes it is. You always wanted to believe the best in me, Ian. But you were wrong about me before, and you're wrong about me now. You can't save me. And I'm afraid to say— you can't save yourself, either."

David pulled out a gun, aiming it straight at his chest.

Damn! He should have expected that. "You're not getting away; the police are here. There's nowhere to go."

"There are plenty of ways for me to disappear in these mountains. No one else knows it's me."

"What about the men you were with? One of them will talk."

"They're both probably dead by now after the explosions you set. I should have figured you'd outsmart me," he said. "You always had the bigger brain. I didn't intend for you to get hurt, but the stakes are too high to let you go. You'll tell everyone."

His old friend knew him too well. There was no point in

pretending. "It doesn't have to end this way."

David lifted his gun. "I'm afraid it does. I really am sorry, but it's you or me, Ian, and you know I always pick myself."

Ian saw a movement out of the corner of his eye and knew he had to keep David focused on him. "What changed you, David?"

"You know what happened. My dad killed himself after he gave his life to this country of ours, a country that later turned its back on him."

"You want revenge?"

"I want everything. Give me the drone. There's no way you came out here without it."

"You don't know that."

"I know you. It would have been too dangerous to give it to Grace."

"I won't give it to you."

"Then I'll take it after you're dead."

"The gunshot will be heard. You'll be found."

David wavered slightly. "No, I'll get away." As he took aim, a figure rushed out from behind the trees and swung a shovel at David's head.

As David went down, he fired off a shot, but Ian jumped out of the way. He stared in amazement as Grace looked back at him, the unconscious David lying on the ground between them.

He walked forward and picked up David's gun. Then he looked back at Grace, whose face was as white as the snow, her green eyes huge but determined and now a little triumphant. "I told you to stay where you were, Grace."

"I thought you might need my help, and you did." She looked down at David, then back at him. "I can't believe it was David. God, Ian, your friend?" She shook her head in bewilderment. "I never suspected it was him."

"Me, either," he said grimly. "He said we were on the wrong side. His mind was twisted. I guess it started when his dad died. And then it got worse when he traveled around the world, when he met people who fed into his anger against our country. He took the job at Vipercom to get access to weaponry, to sell it to his new friends." He shook his head, still in disbelief at the realization that David had been behind everything.

"Are you all right?"

"I am now."

Grace dropped the shovel on the ground and ran over to him. They hugged out the fear for a good long minute.

"Thanks for saving my life, Grace."

"You're welcome." Her bottom lip trembled, but she drew in a deep breath and kept her chin up. "I'm not going to cry—not yet anyway."

He gave her a loving smile. "You are so amazing, Grace. I can't believe how strong you are."

"Well, you told me the shovel might come in handy. Turns out you were right—again."

They both jumped as they heard people in the woods. He put his arm around Grace and kept the gun handy just in case, but it was Detective Johnson and two FBI agents who came through the trees.

"Everyone okay?" the detective asked, his gun drawn.

"We're fine. He's the one who set everything up." Ian tipped his head to his unconscious and former friend. "His name is David Pennington. He was after a weaponized drone that I didn't realize I had. It's quite small." He pulled the baggie from his pocket and showed it to the detective. "It was covered with an invisible paint, and it's set up so that the stinger will inject poison into the target."

"Just like a bee sting," the detective said in amazement. "It's so small. Does it actually work?"

"No idea. Apparently this is a prototype. I also have formulas that are part of how it works." He handed Detective Johnson the papers he'd ripped from the journal.

"We're going to need to take a look at all of that," the FBI agent told the detective.

"We'll get it worked out," the detective said.

"What happened to the guys who broke into the house?"

Grace asked.

"One of them is dead from the fire. The other has suffered serious burns." The detective gave Ian a side look. "That your handiwork?"

"Wasn't sure you'd find us before they did," he replied. "So I set a trap."

"Genius idea. But you almost set the whole mountain on fire."

"Sorry about that," Ian muttered. "I'll pay for the damage to the cabin."

"We'll sort that out later," the detective said, as two medics came through the woods with a stretcher. "You think this is the head guy?"

"I do."

"We'll need you both to make a statement."

"Of course," Ian said, figuring they'd be making statements to both the local police and the FBI. "I'm also going to need a tow truck to get my car out of the ravine."

"There's one on the way. You two were lucky. What were you doing out here?"

"Trying to get out of danger," Grace put in. "We were headed to Sacramento, but they followed us. We had to make a quick turn to lose them."

"We tried to call you last night," Ian said, as they started walking back toward the cabin. "But we couldn't get a signal and we didn't want to get too close to the road to find one."

"I spoke to your sister on my way out here," the detective said. "She's hell on wheels. Within minutes, she had every FBI agent within twenty miles out looking for you."

"That's Kate," he said with a smile. "When she wants to get something done, she does it."

When they reached the row of cabins, he saw that not only the one they'd stayed in had been demolished but the one next to it had also been damaged and firefighters were still firing a spray of water at trees going up the mountain.

"Oh, no," Grace said suddenly. "I just realized we left your great-grandfather's journals in the house."

He felt a wave of loss for those old books, but maybe they'd already served their purpose. They'd saved his life and Grace's, too. "It's all right," he said. "I read through them. I got what I needed."

"I wish we'd taken them with us."

"Don't worry about it. Those journals gave your dad an opportunity to ask me for a favor, and that favor led me to you."

"And a whole hell of a lot of trouble."

"That's true. But it hasn't been all bad."

She smiled back at him, as she slid her hand into his. "No, it hasn't. So did David tell you how my father got the prototype?"

"He had it all along. He's the one who developed the invisible paint formula. He must have realized that what he'd invented could be used in the wrong way. So he took the main prototype from the company, leaving behind the ones that wouldn't work, buying time until someone else figured out how to make the shield."

Grace stared back at him with thoughtful eyes. "I guess when it comes to science, my dad has a heightened sense of right and wrong. Too bad it didn't work that way in the rest of his life. But," she added, as he started to interrupt. "I know I made him all bad in my head, and he's more complicated than that."

"He is, Grace."

"It's kind of weird that he came up with a paint that could make things invisible, because that's what I did to him. I made it like he never existed. I wouldn't even let myself see him in my dreams."

"You did that for your mother."

"And for myself, too. It would be wrong to blame her for everything."

"Do you still want to go to Ireland?"

She let out a breath. "Well, not today. But I'll think about it. Right now, I really just want to go home and do something normal."

"Like what?"

"I don't know…make some pancakes?"

He smiled. "I can do that for you."

"I was hoping you'd say that, because I'm really good at burning pancakes."

"You got it, Grace."

Unfortunately, his promise to make pancakes for her had to wait awhile.

They got a ride back to Tahoe with Detective Johnson but then spent the next three hours talking to him and the FBI agents before they were finally dropped off at Grace's house a little past noon.

As they walked into the house, Grace paused in the entry and said, "Well, it still looks the same. But now it just feels messy and not scary."

"We'll get it cleaned up—after we eat. I know it's more like lunchtime, but are we still on for pancakes?"

"We definitely are," she said, leading the way into the kitchen. She pulled a box of pancake mix from the cabinet. "I've got this. Will it work?"

"Well, it won't allow me to show off all my skills, but since we're both starving, it will do."

"Ian." She put her hand on his arm. "I just want to say again that I couldn't have gotten through this without you."

"Right back at you, Grace. Now, why don't you go take a shower, and I'll make us breakfast?"

"We could shower together."

"You know what? I like that idea better."

She laughed. "I had a feeling you would."

Before he could move, his phone rang, and Dylan's name flashed across the screen. He inwardly groaned. "This is my brother." He'd left Dylan a vague message earlier about a problem with his car.

"You better get that," she said. "And I don't think I'll wait for you in the shower. You have some explaining to do."

"Yes, I do." He answered the call as Grace left the room. "Hello, Dylan."

"What the hell happened to my car, Ian? I didn't understand your message at all."

"I had an accident."

"Are you all right?"

"I'm fine, but your car isn't."

"Is it scratched? Dented? What's the bad news?"

He winced, knowing he had to tell the truth. "It's totaled."

"Totaled? What did you hit—a bus?"

"A couple of trees, some pretty big boulders, and I ended up in a ravine."

"Shit! Do you know how expensive that car is to fix?"

"You won't be able to fix it."

"Are you serious?"

"I'm sorry. I'll get you another car."

"You can't get me the same car. It's a classic."

"I know. If it makes you feel better, it saved my life. It had great power when I needed it."

"I guess I should be happy about that," Dylan said, some of the anger fading out of his tone. "You're sure you're all right? It sounds like a bad accident."

"It could have been a lot worse. It's a long story. I'll fill you in later. And I will find a way to pay you back."

"I know you will. Did you at least have some fun in it before you crashed it?"

"I did," he admitted. "More than I expected."

"Are you still in Tahoe? When are you coming back? Do you need a ride home?"

"I'll figure something out. I'll be here a few more days."

"I thought your conference was ending today."

"I have some other things I'm working on."

"Really? Sounds like you met someone. But wait—you don't mix business with pleasure, so I must be wrong."

"I did this time," he admitted.

"So, what's she like?"

He thought for a moment. Normally, he'd give Dylan some glib answer, just enough to get his brother to back off. "She's—amazing."

"Well, I've never heard that before. I think we should meet her."

"Maybe someday," he said. "Again, I'm sorry about the car."

"I have to say, Ian, I never would have expected you to be the one to crash it. Hunter—yes, you, no."

"Sorry to ruin my reputation after all these years."

"I have a feeling you were due for a crash. Sometimes that's what it takes to set you on the right path."

There was something in his brother's voice that told him Dylan was no longer talking about him. "Is something going on with you, Dylan?"

"Me? No. Business as usual. I'll see you when you get back."

"Sure." He ended the call, thinking there was definitely something up with his brother, but the Callaway men, like himself, never talked before they were ready.

As he set down the phone, he thought about joining Grace in the shower, but she was probably done, and he was starving, so he decided to make the pancakes instead.

In between flipping the flapjacks, he also scrambled eggs and cut up some oranges. He was more than ready to dig into the meal until Grace walked into the kitchen, wearing leggings and a clingy knit top, her red hair damp, her green eyes bright, her body so sweet and sexy at the same time that all he wanted to do was make love to her.

"It smells good in here," she said.

He dropped everything he was doing to put his arms around her. He went in for a kiss inhaling the sweet scent that was Grace. "You smell good, too."

"But not good enough to eat," she teased.

"I don't know about that," he said with a grin.

She gave him a playful slap on the arm. "As flattered as I am, I've been dreaming about those pancakes." She ducked out from under his arms and grabbed one of the plates he'd just dished up. "And you made eggs, too. I'm in heaven. You are so good, Ian. I will thank you later."

"I will make sure of that," he said, joining her at the table.

They devoured the food in record time. As they were finishing, he heard a car pull up outside. As he glanced out the window, he was surprised to see a cab in front of the house.

"Who's that?" Grace asked, her tone suddenly wary again.

He started to say he had no idea until the pretty blonde got out of the taxi.

"That's not Brenna, is it?" Grace asked with a frown.

"I'm afraid so."

"What do you think she wants?"

"I have no idea."

"Should I get the snow shovel out of the garage? Do I need to take down another one of your old friends?"

"I know you're joking, but..." His voice drifted away as he got up to answer the door.

Twenty

"Ian. You're here," Brenna said, relief in her voice.

"I am. The question is—what are you doing here?"

"Looking for you."

"How did you know where to find me?"

"You've been hanging out with Grace. It wasn't that difficult to find her address." She looked over her shoulder, as if she were worried someone was watching them. "Can I come in?"

"What do you want?" he asked, not inviting her inside. After David's recent betrayal, he didn't know who to trust anymore.

"I can't have this conversation out here," she said tightly.

"Well, too bad. This isn't my house."

"It's okay," Grace said from behind him. "Let her in. I want to hear what she has to say."

"Hand me your purse," he said shortly.

Brenna gave him an astonished look. "Why?"

"Why? Because David just tried to shoot me, and I want to make sure you didn't come to finish the job."

Her jaw dropped. "You can't possibly be serious."

He grabbed the bag out of her hand and opened it. There was nothing but cosmetics and a wallet inside. He handed it back to her and waved her inside.

"What do you mean David just tried to shoot you?" she asked.

"You haven't heard?"

She shook her head. "But I have been worrying about David. We had a strange conversation yesterday. That's why I came here to talk to you. I kept trying your room, but you didn't answer."

"You went to my room, but you didn't text me?" he asked. "Doesn't sound like you were trying that hard to get in touch with me."

She licked her lips. "I wanted to see you in person. I didn't want to put anything in writing."

"Why don't we sit down?" Grace said, waving them into the living room.

Brenna stopped short when she saw the mess. "Oh, my God! What happened in here?"

"Someone searched my house," Grace replied. "As you can see, they were very thorough."

"What were they looking for?" Brenna asked.

"You tell me," Ian said, as he put the cushions back on the couch so Brenna and Grace could sit down. He took the chair next to them. "What about this strange conversation with David?"

"He asked me if I had done any work with invisible paint. I said I'd heard about it, but so far I didn't think anyone had come up with anything that worked or lasted long enough to be effective." She paused. "He told me he was on to something that could change the world, and maybe I could help him. He said he could pay me a quarter of a million dollars. I was shocked and suspicious, but he wouldn't say what he was into. He also said that if I told anyone I'd be very sorry." She shook her head. "I never thought David would threaten me, but I could tell he wasn't joking."

"I'm sure he wasn't," Ian said heavily.

"After we finished our conversation, David got a text. The phone was on the table between us. I saw your name and

Grace's name pop up; I thought it was odd, especially after the threat he'd just laid on me. I worried about it all night. I knew I needed to talk to you. So when I couldn't find you at the hotel, I decided to come here. What happened, Ian?"

"David and several colleagues tried to kidnap Grace yesterday. When that didn't work, they tried again this morning. But we turned the tables, and David is now being interrogated by the local police and the FBI."

"Oh, my God. I had a feeling he was into something bad. He hasn't really been the same since his dad killed himself."

"No," he agreed, wondering if David had had some sort of breakdown. "The sad thing is he seemed completely sane when he told me he was going to kill me to get what he needed."

"He wouldn't have killed you," she said in disbelief.

"I think he would have."

"What did you have that he wanted?"

"I can't tell you, Brenna. It's a classified piece of technology. All I can say is that it's in safe hands now, and whatever plan David had is over."

She didn't look particularly happy with that answer. "All right. You really can't tell me more?"

"I really can't."

"Well, I'm glad you're okay. I've always cared about you, Ian. I wish I'd done things differently a long time ago."

"There's no need to apologize for anything."

"I guess not. So, are the two of you together?"

Silence followed her question. He didn't know why he hesitated to say yes, and he could see that his hesitation put a frown on Grace's face. They had a lot of things to talk about, but none of that could happen in front of Brenna.

"I'll walk you out," he told her, getting to his feet.

Brenna had no choice but to follow. "I'm glad you're all right, Grace," she said.

"Thanks," Grace muttered, following them to the door.

As Brenna went down the steps, another car pulled up out front, a silver sedan this time. And another pretty blonde got out from behind the wheel.

"Seriously, Ian?" Grace asked, an edge to her voice. "How many blonde ex-girlfriends do you have?"

"That's not an ex-girlfriend," he said with a sigh. "That's my sister Kate."

Grace perked up. "Now her I want to meet."

And he had a feeling Kate wanted to meet Grace, too.

—»»«—

Grace hadn't liked Brenna at all, but Kate was another story. Kate, with sparkling blue eyes that were a lighter version of Ian's, a warm, friendly smile, as well as the big bear hug she forced her brother into, was endearing.

"I'm Kate," she said, turning her gaze on Grace after she finally let Ian go.

"Grace," she returned. "Thanks for all your help."

"No problem. Ian is usually the last sibling to ask me to save his ass. Now I have something to hold over him," she said with a laugh.

"And I'm sure you will," Ian said, as they went back into the living room and sat down.

"Oh, wow," Kate said, looking around. "I guess you haven't had time to clean up yet."

"Been a little busy running for our lives," Ian said dryly. "Now, tell me how you are here and not in DC where you're supposed to be."

"I jumped on a plane the second after I called the police. I wanted to make sure everything that needed to be done was being done."

"How did your bosses like that?" Ian asked.

"They know there's no stopping me when it comes to family," she said with a shrug. "I spoke to our field agents. They filled me in. It sounds like things got a little exciting and very personal. Was it really David Pennington who was behind all this? I thought he was such a nice guy. I had a big crush on him when you were guys were roommates."

"He's changed—a lot. I didn't even recognize the guy who pulled a gun on me. He was a stranger."

"What made him change?"

"I don't think it was exactly one thing. His dad's mental health after leaving the Army and his subsequent suicide certainly affected David more deeply than I or probably anyone realized. I thought David was getting his head together as he traveled around the world, but actually he was in a very vulnerable frame of mind. He met people who saw that they could use that vulnerability, make him question his patriotism, and then they turned him into a player for their side." He paused. "I think the only reason David took the job at Vipercom was to find a way to bring the latest weapons technology to whatever militant groups he was involved with. I don't know who his partners are. I suspect you'll find that out before I will."

Kate nodded, her gaze a little sad. "I'm sure it will all come out. David is already talking to the agents and negotiating his position in return for information."

"Of course he is," Ian said with a heavy sigh.

Grace's heart went out to Ian. She could see the pain in his eyes, the sense of betrayal. She couldn't imagine what he'd gone through when he'd realized his good friend was willing to kill him to get away. And this pain wasn't going to go away fast. He would need time to process, to work through it in his head. Ian might claim to be a man who lived only by facts and not by emotion, but she knew that wasn't true at all. He cared deeply about his family, his friends…maybe even her.

Although, his hesitation when Brenna had questioned their relationship had reminded her how fast everything had been moving and how many obstacles there still were between them. They might have eliminated the danger threatening their lives, but what about everything else?

"Grace?" Kate said.

"Sorry," she said, realizing that both Ian and Kate were giving her a questioning look. "What did you ask?"

"It doesn't matter," Ian said quickly. "You're exhausted,

Grace. If you want to take a nap..."

"No, I'm fine." She turned to Kate. "What's going to happen to my father? Is he in any sort of trouble for taking the prototype from Vipercom all those years ago?"

"I don't know; I don't think so," Kate replied. "It will take some time to work everything out, especially since we're dealing with police and investigators in two countries. But a case could be made that your father is a hero."

"Well, that's something," she murmured. "I just hope he's going to be all right. Do you know anything more about his condition?"

"Only that he's improving." With a frown, she added, "Professor Donelan really shouldn't have sent something so dangerous to you, Ian. I don't know what he was thinking."

"Probably that I wouldn't find it or wouldn't realize what it was. He wanted to get it far away from him, and it was hidden for a while. What tripped everything up was the box he asked me to deliver to Grace. Everyone suddenly thought that that's where the device was being kept."

"It's always the little things," Kate murmured. "So, what's your plan, Ian? Are you staying here for a few more days? I'm going to head down to San Francisco today. I'll stop in to see Mom and Dad before I take a plane back to DC tomorrow. I hear you totaled Dylan's car, so if you need a ride..."

"No, I'm good. I'll rent a car when I'm ready to leave."

"Are you sure?"

"Positive."

"Did you tell Dylan about his car yet?" she asked with interest. "I wish I could have heard that conversation."

"He took it reasonably well."

"No way he did that," Kate said in disbelief. "He loves his cars more than he loves anything. I was shocked he even let you borrow it. He certainly never lets me drive his cars."

"Because you drive too fast, Kate."

"So does Dylan. Apparently, so do you."

"To save my life, yes."

"So when are you leaving?" Kate asked.

"I don't know yet," he returned.

Grace licked her lips, thinking that she really didn't want to think about Ian's imminent departure. She got to her feet. "I think I will lie down. Kate, it was really great to meet you. And thanks again for saving us. Detective Johnson said you called out the cavalry, and I appreciate that more than I can say."

"Happy to help," Kate said with a smile. "Any friend of Ian's is a friend of mine. Although, he rarely introduces me to any of his friends, especially his female friends."

"Because you are rarely around," Ian protested.

"And you are super private," she returned. "It's like you think I'm going to embarrass you or something."

"I have reason for that," he said. "Remember the Halloween incident?"

She laughed. "You never forget anything. I was twelve."

Grace smiled as they bickered about some embarrassing Halloween costume. There was clearly a tremendous amount of love between them even though they were obviously very different people. If she hadn't suddenly felt so exhausted, she would have liked getting to know Kate better. *But what was the point?* Getting more entrenched in Ian's family was not going to make saying good-bye any easier.

She got to her feet, murmured good-bye to Kate, and then headed down the hall to her bedroom. She knew a mess awaited her, but all she cared about right now was a soft mattress under her body and a pillow for her head.

Ian's gaze followed Grace down the hall. When he turned back to his sister, he saw a knowing gleam in her eyes and had a feeling the personal interrogation was about to begin.

"Grace is beautiful," Kate said.

"She is," he agreed.

"And that's all you're going to say? Come on, Ian. You like her, don't you? Isn't that why you've been hanging around her? Isn't that why you don't know when you're going to leave?"

"There's been a lot going on." He didn't really need to be so guarded with Kate, but he'd always kept his feelings to himself; it was a hard habit to break. Besides that, there was a lot of turmoil going on in his gut right now. He didn't know when he was going to leave, because he couldn't quite imagine actually leaving Grace. He decided to change the subject. "I do appreciate all your help, Kate. I knew I could count on you to act with very little information."

"I trusted your instincts. You wouldn't have called me if you weren't in real trouble. Although, Detective Johnson said you rigged up booby traps and brought down the bad guys all on your own. Not bad for a science geek."

He laughed. "Thanks. But the arrival of the police helped. David ran because he heard the sirens. But he was blocked in. He couldn't escape by car, and he wasn't going to get far in the snowy mountains."

"Don't be modest," she said with a grin. "Your brain has always gotten you out of trouble."

"Today it took some brawn, too. I think I broke David's nose," he added, feeling some satisfaction at that thought.

"You must have been stunned when you realized it was him. There was a time when you were like brothers."

"There was, but there's a part of me now that realizes there was always a little disconnect between us. But we were in school, living together, growing up together. We shared a common goal at that time. It was easier to see the similarities than the differences."

"It's good that you can be so analytical about it. But I'm kind of glad you broke his nose. You can thank Dylan for that. He made sure you and Hunter knew how to fight."

He'd almost forgotten that. "You're right. I owe him for more than the car."

"I'm sure he'll collect." She stood up. "I'm going to take off. I hope I'll see Grace again."

"We'll see."

"Always so noncommittal," she said with a sigh.

He walked her to the door. "Have a safe drive back. And don't say too much to Mom and Dad."

"I won't, but they'll still be hounding you with questions, so be prepared. Even when you don't tell them what's going on, Mom has this uncanny sense of knowing when one of her kids is in trouble."

"I'm not in trouble anymore, and I'll call them later," he promised.

"Ian, can I give you a little advice?"

"Have I ever been able to stop you?"

She ignored that. "You've always been better at acting than at talking, but sometimes a woman needs words. If you have feelings for Grace, don't assume she knows—tell her." With that, she gave him a hug and walked out to her car.

As he closed the door behind her, he thought about her words. He wanted to tell Grace how he felt; he just hadn't had a second...until now.

When he got to her bedroom, she was lying on her side on top of the covers, and her eyes were closed. He could see the purple shadows of weariness under her eyes and thought maybe his words needed to wait after all.

Then her eyes opened, her amazingly beautiful green eyes, and his breath caught in his chest.

"I'm not asleep," she said.

"You should be."

She patted the bed, and he stretched out next to her, turning on his side so he could face her. He wanted to kiss her, to touch her, but as Kate had said, this was probably more the time for words than for actions.

"How are you feeling?" he asked.

"Exhausted but wired. You?"

"Pretty much the same. But it's over, Grace. You're safe now. You can go back to your life."

"And you can go back to yours," she said, meeting his gaze. "That's the plan, isn't it?"

"It *was* the plan."

She raised an eyebrow. "What changed?"

"You. Us."

She let out a sigh. "Is there an *us*? It's been great, but my life is here, and yours is not."

"That's true," he admitted. "But are we really going to let where we live determine whether or not we're together?"

Her gaze narrowed. "Do you want to be together, Ian?"

"Yes, I do. I've wanted to say that for a while, but I've never been really good with words that aren't science related."

She smiled. "I think you're better than you think."

"Then let me give you a few more important words. I'm falling in love with you, Grace."

She sucked in a quick breath. "Really?"

"I'm hoping I'm not alone."

She put her hand on his arm. "You're not alone, Ian. I feel the same way. I didn't want to at first. You seemed to be absolutely the wrong person for me, until I realized how right we were together. I know I tried to pretend you were just like my dad, but the truth is I knew from the beginning that you were your own man, a man I could really care about—a man I *do* care about. I've dreaded the thought of you leaving; not seeing you again would break my heart. But I don't know how to ask you to stay when you need to be where you can be brilliant."

He smiled at her earnest and loving honesty. "You don't think I can be brilliant in Tahoe?"

"It's a small town in the mountains. You have the kind of intelligence and dreams that could change the world. You can't tell me that it wouldn't be better for you to be in a big city."

"It would be better," he admitted. "What about you? Any chance you could teach somewhere else? There are a lot of schools in San Francisco."

"I do like it here," she said slowly. "But I could compromise."

"So could I. The bottom line is that I'm not willing to let you go, Grace. If you need to be in Tahoe, then I'll work from here."

Her eyes sparkled. "You would really move to Tahoe for me?"

"I'd move to the moon for you."

"Everything is happening so fast. Should we slow things down? You could go back to the city. I could stay here. We could get together on weekends, take turns making the drive."

She was being logical and practical, two traits he usually admired greatly, but not tonight. "That sounds awful, Grace. I don't want to see you on the weekends; I want to see you every day and every night."

Her eyes blurred with moisture and her lips trembled. "You're being amazing."

"Just trying to keep up with your awesomeness," he teased. "We make a good team. I've never felt like this about anyone, Grace. I am not going to let you go. And I'm confident we can make *us* work."

"I do like your confidence. School gets out in two weeks, then I have a break. We could go to San Francisco, spend some time there, figure things out."

"That's a good plan, but I have another idea for where we should go when school gets out."

She looked into his eyes. "Really? Ireland?"

"It's where it all began. The first time I saw your photo in your dad's office, I couldn't take my eyes off you. And that's exactly how I feel right now. But it isn't just about that. You need to see your dad."

"I don't just need it; I want it," she admitted. "I want to end the anger and the bitterness. I can't change the past, but knowing how close I came to never speaking another word to him has made me realize how much I want to see him again."

"Then we'll go." He leaned over and gave her a long, tender kiss that he wished could go on forever. *Maybe it could...*

But as he lifted his head, he saw those shadows under her eyes again and despite the pink of her lips and the spark of desire, he knew what she really needed. "Sleep, Grace."

"Really? But we were just starting something…"

He laughed. "We can find our place again, but you're exhausted, and so am I." He flopped onto his back and pulled her close enough for her head to rest on his shoulder. "This is good," he murmured, finally feeling relaxed enough to completely let down his guard. He had Grace in his arms, in his life, in his future; that's all he needed.

———❖———

When Grace woke up, it was dark, with moonlight streaming through the curtains of her bedroom. She was happy to realize she was home. For a moment, she'd been reliving the night before: the cabin, the fear of someone coming after them at any second, the terrifying run through the woods, seeing Ian about to get shot…

Her heart beat faster at the memories.

But they were safe. All was well. She looked over at Ian and felt an enormous swell of love for him. She loved his face, his body, his intelligence, his humor, his drive…so many things. He was the complete package, and he wanted her. She almost couldn't quite believe it.

But she didn't want to let doubt into her head. She'd spent too long hating on the bitter part of love—the abandonment, the betrayal. But she was finally beginning to see that her parents' relationship was not hers, and she never should have been put in the middle.

She couldn't blame her mother; she loved her too much for that. However, she could make some changes going forward, and she would. Because she'd been reminded in bold terms that the life she took for granted could be fleeting, and she didn't want to waste a second of it.

She slowly got out of the bed, trying not to wake Ian. A glance at the bedside clock told her it was eight o'clock at night. They'd slept for six hours.

Walking over to the window, she looked out at the night. A full moon shined brightly in the sky next to bunches of twinkling stars. It was a beautiful landscape with the snow still on the ground and the tall trees surrounding her property.

She heard the mattress creak as Ian got up and walked over to her. "What are you doing?" he asked.

"Just looking outside. It's a beautiful night. The storm is gone. It's peaceful."

"It is nice," he agreed, putting his arms around her waist.

She leaned back against him, her head coming under his chin. They stayed that way for a long moment. She was just about to suggest going downstairs to make some dinner when she saw shadows in the sky.

"Oh, my God, Ian," she said in amazement. "Look! Am I crazy, or does that look like Santa and his reindeers?"

"No," he said immediately, but she could feel his doubt as they watched the shadows cross the moon.

"I think it's Santa."

"That's impossible," he muttered. "It's just the shadows from the trees."

"Is it?" she asked, turning in his arms to give him a loving smile. "Or did we just get our miracle?"

He gazed down at her with his heart in his eyes. "We did get a miracle, Grace—we got each other."

"Sometimes impossible things are possible if you try hard enough, if you love well enough. That's what my grandmother used to tell me."

"Then you better get ready for a lifetime of love, babe, because I intend to love you better than anyone could."

"And I'm going to do the same." Her lips curved upward again. "My dad finally sent me something I don't want to send back."

"I hope I'm better than a puzzle box."

"You have a lot of potential, and I think I'm going to enjoy finding out your secrets."

"I don't have any, Grace. What you see is what you get."

"I think that's what I like the most about you."

"And here I thought it was the way I make you sigh and say my name with that sexy little catch in your voice, when I slide my lips along your neck like this."

She flushed as the heat of his mouth started the fire again. "I like that, too. Do it again."

He laughed. "Oh, I intend to," he said, claiming her mouth this time. "Every night for the rest of your life."

"That sounds just about long enough."

Epilogue

Two weeks later

"We have to make one stop on the way to the airport, so I'm driving," Ian told Grace as he picked up her suitcase and carried it out to her car. Since Grace had just finished teaching for the semester, they were finally going to make the trip to Ireland, but there was something he wanted her to see first.

"Where's that?" she asked curiously.

"It's a surprise."

"I thought you didn't like surprises."

"When I'm the one in charge, I'm good with them," he said with a laugh. "Trust me, you're going to like this one."

"I do trust you, Ian."

The serious note in her voice touched his heart. "I feel the same way about you, Grace." The last two weeks they'd spent together had been amazing. He'd never imagined he could love someone as much as he loved her, and they were only at the beginning. They had the rest of their lives ahead of them, and he couldn't wait. He wanted everything with her—marriage, kids, and years of loving each other.

But he also wanted to tie up some loose ends from the

past, so they could really move forward.

"It's cold," she said, as she got into her car, rubbing her already gloved hands together. They'd only been outside a few minutes, but her cheeks were pink from the Tahoe wind.

"Better get used to it. I don't think Ireland will be any warmer."

"There's a part of me that's still wondering if I'm making the right move."

"I don't think you'll get rid of that doubt until we see your dad. Then you'll finally know whether it was right or not."

"That's not exactly reassuring," she murmured.

"Whatever happens, we'll be together. And aside from your father, I'm eager to see Ireland through your eyes."

"It will be interesting to go back. But again, I'm not sure I'm ready."

"You are," he said confidently. "You're ready for anything. If I've learned anything about you the past few weeks, it's that."

She smiled. "So where are we going now?"

"Haven't you guessed yet?"

"Tyler's house," she said, as he pulled up in front of the little boy's home. "I already gave Tyler his present."

"I know, but there's something else you need to see." He parked and turned off the engine. "No more questions."

"Fine," she said, following him out of the car and into the house.

Tyler's grandmother opened the door with a warm smile and welcomed them inside as if she'd been expecting them.

"Grace," Tyler said, running out of the living room to greet her with a hug. "We just finished decorating the tree."

"I can see that," she said, as Tyler grabbed her hand and took her into the room for a closer look.

Ian smiled as she admired Tyler's tree. The scene in front of him was almost perfect: the fire in the fireplace, the grandparents helping their grandson decorate the tree, Christmas carols playing in the background. It was the kind of scene he'd experienced many times while he was growing up, but he hadn't really appreciated it until now. Now, he wanted to recreate it for himself. In his head, he could see Grace and a child of their own in a different house with a different tree, but just as special.

Grace looked over at him, giving him a questioning look. "Is there something else?"

"Be patient," he said.

He'd no sooner finished speaking when the front door opened, followed by a female voice. "Hello, anybody home?"

"Carrie?" Grace said, as everyone turned toward the entryway.

Carrie appeared, a happy smile across her face.

"Mommy!" Tyler squealed. "You made it home for Christmas." He ran into his mom's arms.

"I told you I would," Carrie said.

Grace came over to his side. "You wanted to give me a chance to see Carrie before we left for the holidays. That was thoughtful, Ian."

"Not just Carrie," he said. "Watch."

"I have an early present for you," Carrie told Tyler, her eyes suddenly very bright.

"What is it?" Tyler asked, a breathless, hopeful note in his voice.

"It's me, son." A man appeared behind Carrie. He was on crutches, his left wrist in a cast, and healing scars across his face.

"Dad?" Tyler looked like he couldn't believe what he was seeing.

Kevin put the crutches against the wall and opened his arms.

Tyler moved into his father's embrace, and then Carrie wrapped her arms around both of them.

Ian looked down at Grace, who wiped a tear from her eye.

"How did you know?" she asked.

"I spoke to Tyler's grandmother at the science fair last week. I told her to call me when she knew for sure Kevin would be coming home. I knew you'd want to see Tyler get his Christmas miracle."

She slid her arm around his waist and gazed up at him with an emotional, teary gaze. "Thank you, Ian."

Carrie broke apart from her husband and son and came over to them, as she dabbed at the tears on her cheeks. "Grace," she said, as the two friends hugged it out. "Can you believe it?"

"I had faith," Grace told Carrie.

"Kevin isn't just home for Christmas," Carrie continued. "He's home for good. We'll be ringing in a new life on the new year."

"I'm so glad."

Carrie turned to Ian. "You must be the man who stole my best friend's heart and turned my son into a budding scientist."

He laughed. "Guilty on both counts. It's nice to finally meet you."

She shook his hand. "And you. I can't wait until we can get better acquainted."

"Me, either. But that will have to wait. We need to go if we want to get to the airport on time."

"Okay. Love you, Grace," Carrie said. "Thanks again for your help."

"I was happy to do it," Grace said.

They said their good-byes to Tyler and everyone else and then walked back to the car.

As Grace fastened her seat belt, she said, "That was the perfect Christmas present, Ian."

"It was good, but it's not the only thing you're getting."

"Really? What else?"

He laughed at her impatience. "You're going to have to wait. First things first…"

"I know. Ready or not—Ireland, here we come."

—⊷⊶—

They arrived in Ireland just before four o'clock on a Wednesday afternoon after almost twenty hours of traveling.

"How does it feel to be back?" Ian asked, glancing over at her, as the taxi took them back to the place where she was born.

"It feels right...and wrong. I'm happy but also sad. I remember the good times, but the bad images follow those up. The day we left my dad will be forever imprinted on my brain, and we didn't even see him that day. The last time I actually spoke to him was twenty-four hours before that. Now it's been more than ten years. Where did the time go?"

He took her hand in his. "I'm glad you're doing this, Grace."

Ian had been a big supporter of her journey home. Her mother and sister had not been nearly as enthusiastic, but in the end they'd both wished her well.

"I don't think I made your mom into a fan of mine, though," Ian said, giving her a rueful look. "She blames me for your renewed interest in your father."

"Maybe a little," she admitted. "But she'll get over it. She's always had to blame someone; I don't think I realized that about her until recently. But she is a good person. She loves me, and she's going to love you, too, because she wants me to be happy. And you make me happy."

"I always want to make you happy, Grace."

"I want to make you happy, too."

"We're off to a good start, and this is only the beginning, babe."

As she looked out the windows at the familiar streets, retail shops, bakeries, cafés and pubs, she was assailed with nostalgic longing. Maybe she could go home again. Maybe this wouldn't be a total disaster.

When they arrived at her father's apartment building, her sentimental feelings fled, replaced by tension and uncertainty.

Ian held her hand all the way up the stairs, releasing her only when she had to knock.

A moment later, her father opened the door. She froze as

their gazes locked. He'd definitely aged since she'd last seen him. There was more gray in his dark-red hair now. His brown eyes held a weariness that she didn't remember, and his tall frame was leaner, more fragile. But his beard and glasses were oh so familiar. Her heart squeezed with a painful love that almost was hard to bear. But she'd come this far; she couldn't turn and run.

"Grace," he murmured, finally getting out a word. "You're beautiful."

"Thanks."

"Come in."

As she moved into the apartment, her father gave Ian a pat on the shoulder. "It's good to see you Ian. I can't believe you brought my girl home."

"She brought herself here," Ian returned.

She was once again grateful and appreciative of Ian's support, his respect for her decisions. He might have encouraged her, but she'd made the final call.

"Well, however it came to be, I'm happy." Her dad motioned them toward the loveseat in the living room and the small armchair next to it. "Please sit down. Can I get you some tea? Something to eat?"

"We're fine." Grace sat down on the couch, happy to have Ian next to her. "How are you feeling?"

"Much better than I was a few weeks ago." He paused. "Shall we get right into it? That's why you came, isn't it? To hear my side of the story?"

"Not completely," she said, her words bringing surprise to his eyes. "But we do want to hear the story before we talk about anything else. We know bits and pieces of it, but I want to hear what you have to say."

"I developed that stinging drone when I was working at Vipercom with Ahmet. It was ahead of its time then, and it didn't work as I envisioned. There were a lot of problems. The stinger didn't always sting. We couldn't figure out how to keep the injectable in its most dangerous form until needed and then how to cloak it was another challenge. I spent long,

long hours developing the prototype."

"This was ten years ago?" she asked.

"Yes, Grace, it's the project I was working on for the months right before you all left. I was obsessed with that bee. I knew it could be huge, not just as a spy camera but as a weapon." He paused. "After your mom took you to the States, I realized what I'd given up for that little bee—everything that mattered to me. I couldn't bring myself to keep working on it, so I put it aside. A year later, I quit the company and I took the bee with me. It wasn't just because it was my invention; it was because I'd begun to see how it could be used against the wrong enemy. I told the people at Vipercom that it didn't work, that it had a fatal flaw, and at the time they believed me. They didn't realize that I'd taken some of the critical pieces of information with me. Until someone started to put it together last year."

"David Pennington," Ian said.

"Yes. I had a visit from David a few months ago. He asked a lot of questions about the drone and wondered where it had gone. After that, I started to feel like someone was watching me, following me. I knew I had to get rid of the drone and the information I had to make it invisible. The box I was sending you was sitting on my coffee table for weeks, Ian. I decided to write down the formula for the invisible paint in one of the journals. I doubted anyone would go through all of them to find it. Then, when I saw someone trying to get into my locked office, I put the drone in the box, too. I wasn't sure you'd see it, but if you did, I thought I could trust you with it. I know your views of science. You have unbreakable integrity. I knew that from our first meeting." He paused. "But then I was attacked. I never imagined that the package I was sending to Grace would become the target. They were separate in my mind, but when you took Grace the puzzle box, it was all the same to Pennington and his colleagues." He turned to her. "I am so sorry, Grace. I never ever meant to put you in danger."

"I know," she said. "I'm glad you took the prototype

away from the people who wanted to use it against us."

He let out a sigh. "I don't know if it will matter. Someone else will figure it out one day. But that day won't be today."

"There's something else I'm curious about," Ian interrupted. "Grace and I ran into the Fergusons in Tahoe. They said you stole something from them. They wouldn't tell us what it was."

"Oh." Seamus smiled. "Is Harry still talking about that? He thinks I stole credit for a paper I published, a theory he took ownership of, but it wasn't true. He was always competitive. He couldn't stand when I beat him, and I always beat him."

A touch of her father's arrogance reminded her that he would probably never completely change. Maybe that was all right. He was who he was, flaws and all.

"We thought Harry and Westley were after us for a while," she put in. "We never imagined it was David, Ian's old college roommate."

"I didn't realize the two of you were connected in that way," Seamus said. "Not until the police told me. But I wasn't completely surprised. There are so many unexpected connections in the universe." He took a breath as he turned back to her. "Is there anything else you want to ask me, Grace?"

"I have a lot of questions," she said. "But here's the big one." She was almost afraid to ask it, but it had been burning in her heart for over a decade. "Why did you cheat on Mom?"

Seamus tensed and then blew out a breath. "Because I was selfish, Grace. We were fighting all the time. I thought she wanted me to choose between science and her, and I couldn't do that."

"But you didn't choose science; you chose another woman. You had another kid, another family. You deserted us. We—I—loved you." Her voice cracked, and she wished it hadn't, because she didn't want him to see her pain, but she just couldn't hide it.

"It was wrong, Grace. I can't excuse what I did. Back then, I was on the ultimate ego trip. I thought I could have everything, that I was entitled, but I wasn't. I betrayed your mother and you and Jillian. I deserved what I got. I deserved losing you. I didn't realize it until it was too late. I am sorry. I wish I could change it. But I can't. I regret my actions every single day of my life."

There was nothing but sincerity in his voice, in his eyes. "I want to forgive you," she said slowly. "But I think I inherited some of your selfishness, because I want it more for me than for you. I don't want to be burdened by anger, resentment, and bitterness."

"I don't want that for you, either. If never forgiving me, never seeing me again, would relieve that burden, I would urge you to make that choice."

She thought for a moment. "I changed my name to punish you, but that decision was influenced by Mom. I felt like I had to take her side."

"Of course you did. I understood. And your mother had every right to tell you whatever she needed to say."

"But our relationship—yours and mine—should have been separate. It took me a long time to see that. I don't know where we go from here. I'm not ready to be your daughter again. But..."

"But?" he echoed, a hopeful gleam in his eyes.

"I won't send your packages back anymore. If you want to write or email me, I might write back. Or I might not," she warned. "Saying you're sorry doesn't make everything right again."

"I understand. I just want you to know that I tried to reach out to you and your sister, but I couldn't get past your mother, and then I couldn't get past the two of you. I don't want to rehash the past, but I care about you and I hope that you'll have a happy and long life filled with everything your heart desires."

His words brought tears to her eyes. They were words he used to say to her every night after she said her prayers. "I want that, too—Dad," she whispered.

Now Seamus looked like he was about to cry, but he cleared his throat and gave a tight nod. "Good."

She got to her feet. "I have to go now."

He rose. "I hope one day we'll see each other again."

"We will," she said. "One day."

"You have always had a big and kind heart, Gracie."

"Thanks." She walked to the door, then paused, taking Ian's hand. "You did one thing right, Dad. You sent me Ian."

He nodded approvingly. "I had a feeling you two would get along. When we met last summer, he couldn't take his eyes off your picture."

"You didn't see that," Ian protested.

Seamus grinned. "Of course I did. Why do you think I asked you to take her the box? It wasn't just for me; it was for you, too. Because I know what happens to a man when work consumes his soul. It's too late for me, but not for you."

"It's not too late for you, either," Ian said. "Good-bye, Seamus."

"Good-bye," Seamus returned. He stood at the door until they hailed a taxi.

Grace let out a breath as she got into the cab and looked over at Ian. "Was I too hard on him?"

"You said what was in your heart. That's all that matters."

She nodded. "Now that that's out of the way, let's go meet Emma." Ian's cousin and her husband were still in Ireland, and she was more than a little curious to meet another one of the Callaway clan.

* * *

Snow was starting to fall as they walked toward the café on Caldwell Street. Ian held open the door for Grace as they entered. He was immediately hit by the warmth of the room, the fire blazing in the grate, the dark wood, the melodious hum of conversation and laughter. And across the room, at a table by the fireplace, was his cousin Emma, her husband Max, and an adorable freckle-faced, seven-year-old girl.

Emma jumped to her feet, a happy light in her blue eyes, as she came over to hug him. "Ian, I can't quite believe we're back in Ireland together."

"It does seem surreal," he admitted. "Max, how are you?" He shook Emma's husband's hand.

The police detective with the brown hair and green eyes gave him a smile. "I'm a father now; that's how I am."

"So I hear. Congratulations. I want you to meet Grace."

"I feel like I already know you," Emma told Grace. "I heard about you long before Ian ever met you."

Grace gave him a questioning look.

"I might have mentioned your beautiful photo to my cousin," he said sheepishly.

"Mentioned it?" Emma teased. "He talked about it on our eleven-hour flight home."

"I can't believe my picture stuck with you that much," Grace told him.

"I couldn't forget you," he said, giving her a warm smile.

"Now, sit, sit," Emma said. She put her arm around her little girl as they all sat down at the table. "Shannon, do you remember my cousin Ian? You met him in the summer."

Shannon gave a vigorous nod and a toothless smile. "Hi, Ian."

"I see you lost another tooth," he said.

She grinned again, then went back to her coloring.

"We ordered Guinness and appetizers all around," Max said.

"Perfect," Ian replied. "We wanted to thank you for trying to help us out with Grace's father."

"We honestly didn't do much. Kate was the one who pulled her FBI strings to get more information," Emma said.

"Still, you made the effort, and I appreciate it."

"We both do," Grace added.

Ian sat back as the waiter set down their drinks.

"How long are you going to stay in Ireland?" Emma

asked.

"Until the day after Christmas," he replied. "Grace and I are going to have an Irish Christmas. Care to join us?"

"We're actually headed to the airport tomorrow," Emma said. "We finally got the paperwork straightened out, and I can't wait to introduce Shannon to the family."

"She's going to be a great addition," he said, thinking how happy Emma looked compared to when they'd last been in Ireland. Then she'd been worrying about a recent series of miscarriages and wondering if she'd ever have a child. "What does Grandma think about all this?"

"She's over the moon," Emma replied. "She won't admit it, but I know she sent Max and me here so that we could meet Shannon. This little girl was our destiny."

"Well, I'm glad it all worked out."

Emma made a face at him, then turned to Grace. "Ian is one of the most cynical and pragmatic of all my cousins. He doesn't believe in fate. Can you imagine?"

"No," Grace said with a laugh. "I keep telling him destiny brought us together."

"And I finally believe it," Ian put in, surprising both of them with his words.

Max groaned. "Not you, too, Ian. I thought I could count on you to stay logical."

"Hard to do when you fall in love with a picture and then meet the actual woman and realize she's even better than you ever imagined," he said dryly.

"So you're in love?" Emma asked, wide-eyed. "Really? That sounds serious."

He took Grace's hand. "It's absolutely serious. And tonight feels like a new beginning."

"It is," Grace agreed. "The past is behind me. No more looking back."

"Only looking forward." He picked up his beer glass. "Let's have a toast. To a new family—Emma, Max, and Shannon. And to the love of my life—Grace O'Malley."

"Grace O'Malley Donelan," she said, clinking her glass

with his. "And you're the love of my life, too, Ian. I might not have fallen in love with your picture, but I definitely fell in love with you."

He leaned over and gave her a quick kiss. Then he took a sip of his beer. That's when he noticed that Emma had toasted with water instead of Guinness. "Wait a second," he said sharply. "You're not drinking, Emma. Is something else going on?"

"Well, since you asked..." Emma gave her husband a quick look. "I can't hold back."

"Then don't," Max said with an encouraging smile.

"I'm pregnant," Emma said, the words coming out in a happy rush. "I'm going to have Shannon and a baby. Of course, things could still go wrong, but I'm thinking positively. It's a second miracle. Can you believe it?"

He actually could. It seemed to be the season for miracles. "I'm so happy for you, Em."

"Me, too," Grace put in. "Congratulations."

"Thanks. It's been a struggle to carry a child. Now I feel so blessed."

"I do, too," he said, looking back at Grace. "Can you handle one more surprise? I was going to wait until Christmas Eve, but now I don't want to."

"Okay," she said warily.

He pulled out a black velvet box and flipped open the lid to reveal a diamond set on a gold band of Celtic knots.

"Oh, my God," Grace murmured. "It's so beautiful."

"Will you marry me, Grace? Will you let me love you for the rest of my life?"

Her eyes blurred with tears. "Yes, yes—a million times yes."

Emma clapped her hands. "This is amazing. I never imagined you were going to propose, Ian."

"I didn't, either," Grace said with a teary laugh as he slipped the ring on her finger.

"I couldn't wait." He looked deep into her eyes. "I need you to be mine as soon as possible."

"Oh, Ian," she said, cupping his face with her hands. "I already am yours. I love you, and I can't wait to be your wife. We're going to be so happy."

"We already are," he said, repeating her words before he kissed her again.

THE END

If you love romantic suspense, don't miss out on Barbara's new *Lightning Strikes Trilogy*:

Beautiful Storm (#1)
Lightning Lingers (#2)
Summer Rain (#3)

About The Author

Barbara Freethy is a #1 New York Times Bestselling Author of 52 novels ranging from contemporary romance to romantic suspense and women's fiction. Traditionally published for many years, Barbara opened her own publishing company in 2011 and has since sold over 6.5 million books! Twenty of her titles have appeared on the New York Times and USA Today Bestseller Lists.

Known for her emotional and compelling stories of love, family, mystery and romance, Barbara enjoys writing about ordinary people caught up in extraordinary adventures. Barbara's books have won numerous awards. She is a six-time finalist for the RITA for best contemporary romance from Romance Writers of America and a two-time winner for DANIEL'S GIFT and THE WAY BACK HOME.

Barbara has lived all over the state of California and currently resides in Northern California where she draws much of her inspiration from the beautiful bay area.

For a complete listing of books, as well as excerpts and contests, and to connect with Barbara:

Visit Barbara's Website:
www.barbarafreethy.com

Join Barbara on Facebook:
www.facebook.com/barbarafreethybooks

Follow Barbara on Twitter:
www.twitter.com/barbarafreethy

CPSIA information can be obtained
at www.ICGtesting.com
Printed in the USA
LVOW11*1430220217

525090LV00006B/68/P